THE ENDS OF
THE EARTH

THE ENDS OF
THE EARTH

John Fraser

AESOP Modern Fiction
Oxford

AESOP Modern Fiction
An imprint of AESOP Publications
Martin Noble Editorial / AESOP
28 Abberbury Road, Oxford OX4 4ES, UK
www.aesopbooks.com

First edition published by AESOP Publications
Copyright (c) 2020 John Fraser

www.johnfraserfiction.com

The right of John Fraser to be identified as the author of this work
has been asserted in accordance with sections 77 and 78
of the copyright designs and Patents Act 1988.

A catalogue record of this book is
available from the British Library.

First paperback edition 2020

ISBN: 978-1-910301-62-3

CONTENTS

RAIN

Achille, gruff in his sheepskin, says –

'We shan't have great wealth. Be assured: never. They bring amounts, on show. As though it made them ours, somehow. Jewels, as if we'd used our axes to break down the sultan's doors and steal. Frescoes scraped off – as if we'd prayed in caves for comfort when the caravan was lost. And painted saints.... The good – they look like demons – you need them to fight the others, the bad demons. The good smooth blues against the scaly greens.

'Riches, faith, despair – all goes in a glass case, like Sleeping Beauty – we kiss the crystal but she doesn't wake.

'My – our – father hadn't been a miner – "here's your snap", my mother used to say, giving a sandwich. She must have thought a miner would be eager for her, more used to digging and to tunnels. Then he left. The mine was closed. Neither ever spoke about their work, so it was as if they did nothing, just had to leave the house all day and come back tired.

'You can't complain – besides, it makes no difference, the complaining, and the situation. I knew I was a tragic figure – I didn't realise that everyone is, except the stupid who don't know what's coming for them. Not all of us have moral dilemmas, but we all wait for fate, Osud, judgment, to have its say and invent our crimes.

'On the vast empty moors – there, I felt – not free, not solitary, but overwhelmed. It's very hot, where once were sheep, there's dunes, as if there's sea receded, returning one day with

7

tidal waves that would raise up ordinary things, dumping them high, grotesque.'

'You and your brother,' says Zenia, dressed in red, in case it snows and she is lost. 'If I'd known how you planned turning out...! Would I have chosen either? Two puzzles, having anniversaries, moving so rhythmically on to somewhere. Yves and you could be twins – except he's more immersed in himself – both struggling to break out of the carapace. Your eggs.'

'Of course we see things in a similar way,' Achille says. 'We all do. Otherwise each would see things as differently as they pleased, or as something pleased. It would be crazy. Very interesting, but unclassifiable, livable but chance. Total fluidity and happenstance. No social, to each their uncertain personal universe.'

*

Yves, city-suited, says:

'This village was nearly deserted. I thought I'd restore the houses, have music in them, in the square – all turning back like last century, except we'd wear modern clothes, such as they are, and I'd be the engineer, smooth down ascents, stop floods and droughts. Now you see: people were smart: they died, they went away, there's only monsters left. Once, long ago, they were shepherds, barmen – now their faces have caved in, eyes yellow under aspic, teeth a cemetery, the noses spiked swollen teasels... Dirty wool all round. Food in a credence. Bread, an onion, and a can of beans.

'Dusk brings them out, they scurry, then it's dark – what do they do all night? They sleep, the bed's a pasture full of sheep. Smell the kerosene!'

*

Zenia sees a vinyl disc – 'The brass junkies' – it's famous, horns in a row, aping to the snapper. 'I model myself on the drummer, Ginger,' Achille says: 'Talent and fortitude. I'm sure I've talent, but it's latent. I know I have the power. Don't exaggerate when you see clues, Zenia: it's my hidden side – we all have one – mostly the sculptor doesn't bother to smooth it down – it's rough and knobbly, invisible when you're on your plinth.'

Zenia can't decide who's more interesting, Yves or Achille. People who try impossible things – they always have a following, though it's perverse. Both brothers look quite nondescript – human beauty is a myth – if I were a panther, Zenia thinks, I'd laugh at them! Except the men have machines to make up for their lack of skills.

'Our father,' says Yves, bending down from height to seem more interested in shorter people, 'started in a clan. In Albania, the family chooses who's to go to jail for what is done. He fled, instead. He went on, we suppose, for ever, fleeing the good, the bad, the dutiful, and the rebellious.'

'Our mother,' Achille says, 'came from an Africa. Everybody's mother did, they say. Was it the Maghreb? Or Senegal? Congo? She knew each song, and so, maybe, wasn't trusted, came from nowhere. That chimes. Professionally, I'm an expert in Nothing. "Everything"'s been done. There's an enormity of Nothing, and you can work on it from anywhere – a moving tank; from space – or from a shepherd's hut. A *baita*. This was a luxury – *tufo* walls. There'd have been a thousand baas, at night a rustling, never quiet.

'Nowheres seem to fit in Nothing. Families come from one, and that's our destination. Where we've tried to live right here.'

He laughs, stands tall – he's still quite short, a useful travel size.

'He'll do for me,' thinks Zenia.

*

The brothers pick up, drop, loose clothes, stuff books into a bag
– *Nomades et caravanes d'Orient*.... *Morality and Criminality*,
Tongues in Trees, *Minima Moralia* – 'Throw them out!' shouts
Yves. 'We've lived it all. You don't read, Achille, you *think*:
don't burden us with snobbery....'

'Where do we go?' asks Zenia. 'We've little time, then we
must evacuate. Maybe they only need our space, there's fresh
people coming in. Or else they've dropped, spilled something –
or an attack.... Marauders? The young? The old?'

'Oh,' says Yves, 'just wild weather, I expect. It happens
everywhere – for some, leaving is for ever – no water, winter or
summer all the time. It seems quite urgent – but it never is.
There's ample time for fear, dread, and hope.'

'We have to walk,' Achille says. 'They only bus those who
say they may return.'

The stones of the little house are firm – it's the roof, the floor,
the rest, that's finished.

'It could all be fixed,' says Yves. 'I'd do it – but the
landscapes shift, and we shift with them. There's seep and sand
and crack. Best not trust what's underfoot, walk light and wear a
mask.'

'No trains, if there's a poison,' says Achille. 'A crash. No
road if it's a flood. We'll have to walk to Zenia's.'

'Oh, well,' says Zenia. 'The trouble is – I'm between houses.
Between most things. Work and money too.'

'Yves and me – we didn't live by happenstance, expedients,
or finding empty shells and creeping in, like crabs,' Achille
says. 'We had a plan. Now there is none. We've nowhere left to
go.'

'It's clear,' says Yves. 'In all I did, there was a progression –
a seed that sometimes sprouted, and on you went, and it might
be grass, or palms. You were long gone – you'd never know.
The palm – that might become an arm, *l'homme armé*,' and he
laughs. 'Or an odd seed, big as a bobbin, that might become a

tree. Tales – a strophe that becomes a Ramayana. How we went to Africa, what we did there. What use we made of Siberia, the expanse. How we recovered from a war. Kosova – someone remembers that, and who stayed, who left. How they suffered, every one.... Each happening becomes strange, muddy and ethereal. Anyway – time fools us all: it seems there is progression. One thing after another, big grey clouds each holding the tail of one in front – it seems there is a story, plot, a logic.... And yet – people see events, history, quite differently. A sequence without meaning, without reflection. People act "as if" it's like that, as if events don't have an eye, or even hundreds, set in a circle ... watching everything. So, are they right?'

'I imagine – yes, a thousand eyes set in one brain, that all at once – they weep,' says Zenia, trying to make up for her inhospitality, or indigence. 'If I knew more about your life, Yves, I'd see there was growth in it, I'm sure.'

'No,' says Achille. 'Yves and I discard all the precedents, and expect to find another route. Not force, not violence – they're venomous, they disappoint, they vitiate. Another way, there had to be, that's not the state, nor the unrestricted will. Not soviet and not kibbutz. But – it's too late. It's gone beyond us. There is no return, it's coda time, recapitulation, climax.... You can see – it's what we live, right now.'

'It sounds grand,' says Zenia. 'So big I don't understand a thing. It's true, that people who can't find a way ahead – they always say that it's too late. No doubt it is....'

'Ahead?' asks Achille. 'It's not a march, Zenia.'

'I constructed,' Yves says. 'Achille found the sites. All hypothetical. All left behind, all trace and record – left back there, the *baita*.'

'Thought experiments – they're done in empires,' Zenia says.

'The earth now,' says Achille, 'is Austro-Hungary. The rich and educated – they're the Austrians.'

'*Assez vu, assez connu.* That's where we're at,' says Yves. 'Look at the mist. I'll go down, see if there is anyone.....' and off he goes. It's cold and silent.

He goes invisible – the mist is motionless, covers the valley.

They never see Yves again.

They daren't go in the mist. It kills everything: a test, or a mistake?

'There's nothing left for him to build,' says Achille.

He and Zenia – they are suspects. It seems improbable: sex? The suspicion lasts.

'They never say if they have poisoned you,' Achille says. 'A question? Is it worth it, an inquiry, that will last out your life?'

They don't know how to respond, and Achille presses on. 'You may have thought – our project sounds like "model villages, potato soup". It isn't so, but leave it there.'

*

Bodies should function like machines. Certainly, they stop when we feel fine. Our brains, that is, would go on for much more time.

Achille and Zenia – together, the bodies do not work. Too bad. No pleasure there.

'I love to show my body,' Zenia says. 'Being painted – irrelevant if it doesn't look like me, it never does, often not human either – that's my fun. Roller-skating, movies, being picked up: freaks are genius, don't you think, Achille?'

'My body,' Achille says, resisting her whirl, 'is a heap. I stuff it in a sack – brown clothes every day. We don't make music together, Zenia – it's empty cauldrons toppling down cellar steps.'

'Anything,' she says, 'so long as it's not decorative. Gristle and bones, Achille – don't spit them out. They build you up....'

So, they think of Yves. Building a bunker, deep, like a tomb; dismantling a tower. His spirit undoing somewhere what he'd done in life.

'Your world, Zenia, is full of people, and each one does a dance for you,' Achille says. 'Mine is shadows.'

'Yes,' she says. 'That's it.'

Later, she says, 'It's a scene – things that look like precious scrawls, painted with a single hair, or heaps of earth – it's all the same to me. Serious colours laid out and freaks with opinions walking round – that's living. I love it, it loves me.'

'Oh no,' Achille thinks. 'A connoisseur!'

They keep close together, notwithstanding, because of Yves. They're what he built.

'What I need, Zenia,' says Achille, 'is a keel. My ship – it yaws, it turns about without one.'

'What you need, Achille,' says Zenia, 'is cash. As for your ship – you need someone who knows about the sailing art. A dredger doesn't need a keel. Hugo will instruct you. He's done philosophy – read about it when it changed, and fell into its bits. He knows about Vienna. He filled his mind with bags of sand, floated it aloft. He throws down a bag whenever he starts to fall, to crash.'

'And when the sand runs out?' asks Achille, not much attracted.

'The right sand's much in demand,' says Zenia, 'for cement. But throwing-out-the-basket kind – that sand, you find it everywhere.'

*

'"Nothings"?' says Hugo. 'The Nazi? That old fox again? Caught and eaten long ago. Gassed in his hole. Forget it – only death is nothing. Move on, Achille!'

'Oh, I have,' says Achille. 'I don't want philosophy. It all depends where you start from, and that's always wrong. I don't see well, I blabber, I've no dilemmas, moral or of any other kind. Black holes? We're in them, them in us. Wet, dry, with flags and drums, dolmens and thornbushes. Everyone has resources enough for ten. It's sadness, the sadness with the world that ties us down. I want a set of bricks, that's all.'

'To make a wall?' Hugo asks, 'or to throw?'

'Oh Hugo,' says Achille, 'I've been so silly! I thought – when I've the power, I must be delicate, not use my force.... I'd spoil the fragility, the design.... Now, I see. It isn't mine, ours, to avoid. It's theirs! The violence comes from them. Poor Yves....'

'Well,' Hugo says. 'Now you know. You don't need lessons. Let's have a good unusual time. It's much too late for other things.'

'It sounds like pointless fun,' says Achille, trying to please and still be sceptical. 'You've given up, then, Hugo – science, language, all that stuff.'

'Oh absolutely,' Hugo says. 'What were they, we, looking for? What's real, where is it anyway? What weight's in what I feel, or what I say? They laughed at us, Achille, the white coats. They made the gas, and did for us. They made the airships that would shoot us off, and leave the earth their weapons and their gadgetry had spoiled..... They laugh, they play a round of golf, they're paid on time – nothing to do with us, my friend. They're in another world: we are their savages, our books are fluttering rags, our music is a foolish frolic in the glade.... They scribble, there's applause: they use the backs of envelopes and hear the music of the spheres....'

'You didn't get paid on time, then, Hugo....?' Achille asks.

'Oh, that was just the start of it,' Hugo says.

'They'll say....' Achille starts –

'Yes,' Hugo says. 'They say, "you eat exotic food, bunches of it, we cure your clap and fuel your motor". But – your brother's gassed. Good and bad. You said it, Achille. Now, no anti-modern stuff, my friend. You're here. Suffer, enjoy, go on the moors and sing, be sure there's no one hears you, and make it excellent – put in the Maghreb, Senegal, the Congos.... The drummers – they'll be listening. They know if you're stoned... You're from everywhere, doesn't mean you belong somewhere. You're on the road!'

*

Zenia tells Hugo, 'I collected Achille. I won't trade him. He fits. I went to see him on the mountain, him and Yves. My regret – there were no sheep, not even the sound. In the wind, there is the sound of everything that's gone – but they had nothing. No animals. The brothers, they were leaving, even before the poisoning.'

'I don't collect,' says Hugo. 'Not like you, Zenia. I teach. The Circle. The Secession. That says it all – first you bind, then you hive off – it's like you wind your arm, and then you throw.'

'Hugo's like a brother, Zenia,' says Achille. 'But there are contradictions....'

'It's the philosophy,' says Zenia. 'Anomalies exist to be smoothed out. There's shades of shades. He brags, but when he thinks, he separates the shadow from the shadow. So what. Bear with him. You know quite well what living is. You like things tidy – that can be cured. You want things in their place. Perhaps everything has a place – it's not up to you to put it there.'

'Why me?' asks Achille. 'Leave me alone. Stop sculpting me.'

'Your innocence: the tragedy. Quite irresistible,' she says. 'Your ignorance, stupidity – the nothings straight from Heidegger. You touch the untouchable, Achille, you bathe in it. All around you there are *fachos*, millions of them. You roll upon their dirt and think it's Mother Earth. You take the risk, unknowing, and then fly away.'

'You're right,' Achille says. 'I hadn't thought, or known.'

'Forget that,' Zenia says. 'Think. Emptiness, not nothingness. Emptiness is where it starts.'

'What?' asks Achille.

'Everything a person can invent, create with,' Zenia says. 'It may look like nothing, but it's not – it's what you need to mix with something else; that makes the grand design, knocks it all down and starts it off again.'

'This is ridiculous,' Achille says, exasperated. 'I had in mind black holes. They're "No-things-in-themselves". Besides, Sartre exploded nothingness. Sartre's the antidote to Heidegger, the antidote to any poison gas. Through him, I am in the clear. Names are enough, no one bothers what they thought. You wonder – what if after me, there isn't anything. I'd only found a place to think: a hut, no sheep. The thinking hadn't started then.'

'You must do a manifesto,' Hugo says. 'Making your stand, avoiding calumnies.'

'It's all too late,' Achille says. 'The first guys – they are always right, they foretell, they prophesy, and when catastrophe's announced – it's on you. It's too late....'

'You haven't understood,' says Hugo. 'It's your reputation we care about, not the world's end. You're more important.'

'It was all politics,' says Zenia. '"They" knew and they prevaricated. The point of no return – ignored. Now – it's too late. Kupka saw it all – it's him, I think, who speaks to me through space. As a species, we are doomed. Conditions extreme – we shan't survive. We weren't designed for that. Stagger through one crisis – there's another. Greater. That is why – Hugo and I, we want to turn you, Achille. Forget the Nothing, join us, in Being!'

'I was never otherwise,' says Achille. 'You got me wrong, you two.... Knowing about the universe, and how you explore what you have guessed – it doesn't solve a thing for us. You do it, though; you persist, there's nothing else you or anyone is capable of....'

*

The three meet regularly, talking of Yves; of Sartre, Carnap and the rest; of concept art, of multiples.... Golden ages, turned to brass. Achille dreads the hours spent in joshing on, of quips and puns ... and they always eat the same, Breton oysters, Knokke mussels, and he always draws the dodgy one, suffers for days, the poison from the waves rolling in on banks of grey-green chemistry ... hates Hugo with his jutty russet beard, talking of new currencies, new ideas, put together, conjuring big bucks.... He quite dislikes dear Zenia, dressed like a bright bird, her waxy dolly face full of sharp opinions – a marzipan apple, constellated with cloves....

To evade a ritual, you need a stronger one. A pilgrimage.

'I may leave the country,' Achille says.

'Why? You've done nothing wrong,' says Zenia, astonished.

'And you may never do,' says Hugo. 'If it's us – just turn away, and it's done. Finished. "I love you" but – go away and nevermore. That's that, and we're a nuisance. Don't punish yourself for what you are.'

'No, no, nothing of that,' says Achille. 'Not enough desire, I think, not enough to stay put.'

'*Ennui*,' says Zenia. 'That's terrible. On top of all your talent, too. You'd find all countries end like that – dull. Or you're surrounded by excited people you don't know, can't understand.'

'We know your trouble, Achille,' Hugo says.

They have him brought – a silver-looking dish, on it, a silver fish. It lies, still, one-eyed, one sided. As if it's dead. After this –

all others, they might be extinct. If you think about it – you could cry.

'There!' Hugo says. 'That will sit well in your gut, and cure your ennui too.'

'Oh, the pity,' Achille thinks. 'It's perfect, untouched, just suffocated.'

'Listen,' Zenia says. 'We are your friends, and this is what friends do. We push you on. We're tolerant, enlightened, that is what we are. It may not avail – and Achille, don't eat the fish. It won't forgive. Totemise it. And see – you're sinking. We have you by the foot, the rest is under, drowning.... Shout: "Save me, save me!"'

'It's the loss,' Achille says. 'Of what there is and was, and what will be.'

'There's no more countries,' Hugo says. 'It's all been beaten into one, that has everything. Rich, poor, gamblers. Mountains and desert. Stay, Achille, start by tolerating us – and then move on to wanting others.'

'You don't understand what you say, Hugo,' says Achille. 'Philosophy came to an end, and yielded nothing. Now, it's brains investigating brains, tautology and solipsism. Black holes – almost everything's a nothing, and you can be eaten by one, but not know any more about it.... The sky is full of tigers, Hugo, we can't see or smell them, but they have enormous stomachs and their acid is so strong you don't produce a belch, a fart, as you go down: you disappear. Maybe you're born again somewhere as krill.'

'We fiddle harmonics, Achille,' Hugo says. 'Zenia and I. The composing has reached a quiet spot. We hope, though, you're getting angrier.'

'I'm happy,' Achille says. 'It's the rest you don't want to remember, that's sadness and depression. Memory? Time spilt; the fall of Babylon; young girls and boys deflowered: "Don't play all the notes I've written for you," says the musician.

"Don't make it sound so complicated." You'd not want that, running through creation.... There should be no approximation, nothing improvised. There's up and down – don't try to smooth it out. There mustn't be a compromise. If there's no plan, no rules – we're fluff, Hugo.'

'Creation was a rush order,' Zenia says, unconvinced. 'The electricity was connected late, so you didn't see the botch as it was being done. The demolition takes much longer, and there's mounds of broken stuff to go – send it to Nigeria, Benin – they'll unpick it, try to make it new again.'

*

'Your family, Achille...' Zenia starts –

'Forget it,' Achille says. 'We all come out of myth, then get wiped down, are indistinguishable. All stories, you just make them up, until you leave the stage.... There is no script, no line between the lies and truths.'

'Exactly so, Achille,' says Hugo. 'That is what interests me. You've gazed upwards far too long – the starry heavens only fill your mind with zeros, distances you'll never cross. A genius said it right: the eternal blue is sterile, a desert, where genius suffers torments, pain....'

'Oh,' Achille says, 'I'm ready to drop all that. There's thousands working at it, the upward gaze....'

'Then look down at your feet,' says Zenia. 'Think of those guys who pay to start the wars, to make a track, or cover up career and wealth.... Not all is curable – but small vengeance can be yours.'

'This humanitarian stuff,' says Achille. 'It's our space, our universe – it's been examined thoroughly, and – so what? Nothing is changed. It's like a star too far away to reach – it's known about, but there it ends. The earth is dying from a thousand cuts. What do you hope for, Zenia? Justice and revelation – always afterwards, after the fact. Nothing's undone – "Next time, next time" you chant.... And next time is the same or slightly different. Accept it – that is health, recovery. Otherwise, you're sad, lie unconsoled in bed, if bed you have, or else you tramp and maybe there's a tent ahead, will do you for an hour or years....'

'For us, Achille, you're very special,' Zenia says. 'There's tragedy around you.... A crime, a victory, an accident....'

'No,' Achille says. 'The tragedy was Yves. There's something of all of those in what occurred – not even an event: an incident. A set-up, a set piece. What do you want – to lead a hunt, make a fine tale that ends somewhere ... then, silence. Finish. Message delivered, probably deliverance.'

'Yes, in a way,' Hugo says. 'You are our book. But people want a book to be "about" – even an inconclusion.... A story, that is, containing other stories. Many small ones, and the big one like a flood. A purpose, many purposes, possibly not one of them is yours, or is of interest, till it's told another way, skewed so you can see – not a before, and after.... It doesn't even ask what's to be made of it. Even a hero survives and does the enemies down, then folds up into family or temple, exits the chrysalis and speaks the secret name, or finds a brother, sister, true religion. True communism. But – it's not you, Achille. You are a running thing. You are unfinished, not heroic. The hero – defeats coincidence, contingency. The hero finds, by trial and error, then by certainty, that obstacles and friends are situated in an order. There's a reason, there's a plan, a station where the rails end and trains arrive and empty out. There is a rule, a good, a bad, like in a treasure hunt, an up, a down, like in a snake and ladder game. What message is there? That if you're the special kind, the shaman, the magicked child, the one whose blood is streaked with gold – that luck and chance start off as clay, and by your skill can take a shape – a tree that shades you, a cawl protecting, a talking creature that can warn....

'You're not one of those chosen types, Achille. You are our book, our epic, opera, our scribble or our limerick – we set you running as if we'd wound you up. Your story – you don't know. There is no lesson, no message. We don't have one either – you're not "about", and nor are we.... You're ours – but we don't write your plot.'

'It's chance, then,' Achille says. 'What I am, what I find out. And you two – don't dictate, propose. You watch to see – what happens. But – I create, and I am your creation.... You shouldn't tell me, surely, what you have in mind?'

'Oh, we're your friends!' says Zenia. 'We tell you everything, even what you are. We have our positions, which we value, and are known. No secrets, nothing hidden. But neither we nor you have any part in determining our context. The last stand of the species, Achille: mercenaries, fistfuls of emperors, centurions uncertain, mutinous, the squaddies rude, abstracted.... Enemies all round, everywhere. Lurching into battle – against locusts, in black smoke.'

'We will watch you, like the fates,' says Hugo. 'Pay no attention. They look on, they need do no more. Your life is chance, pile chance on luck – sometimes out comes a Ramayana. You should imagine that there's someone, after, elsewhere, who'll watch you, watch you in your story. Like we see the Sumerians, and wonder how they managed to be so intelligent, so beautiful – and yet not see us watching them. Not erotic, naturally – besides, this country, like all this continent, is post-coital. Post-porno too. Other things, perhaps; or none.'

'There's politics,' says Achille.

'No,' says Hugo. 'No one need think of that. Eat what you like, wear any clothes you find, walk, watch your feet – don't stumble. No politics. Don't worry – you won't be sent off – not to kill, not to feed anyone – the action will come here. Or maybe not. In any case, what lasts is ponderous, the run, the tramp, slow motion. Don't worry – instinct will come and tell you what to do, someone else will set it off – bang on the head, a blast, a building falls in quick quick time – all that done quite swift.'

'Don't imagine it'll be that,' says Zenia. 'It can be anything – what's important is going ahead as if there's no one setting it all up, for eyes that you won't see.'

'You must understand, Achille,' says Hugo, 'that when you're away, exploring – we shan't be here. Nor anywhere. You are our bottle in the sea. Never saved anyone – it's pathos. You are our last Mohican, our ultimate rhino, our Nachlass. You are the unfinished symphony.'

'We concluded,' Zenia says, 'that style and design are eternal for our species. With humans gone – they disappear. It's what we have that monkeys don't. But all the detail, the variations – they're just afterthoughts. The precious stuff, the lapis lazuli, the onyx and the chrysoprase – they're exhausted, or they're campy Kitsch. The music builds – to the explosive moment when the sun expands, gobbles us up, turns off.

'We decided, both of us, we shan't be there, not at the end, nor for the preliminaries. Our opus posthumous is you, Achille. You're mortal, you have the fingermarks that show you have been rescued once. Next time – the last. We've had enough. *Assez vu.* Into the waves you go, Achille, float on, and sink. Or drift ashore. Do you whisper "Rescue me!"? No such luck, dear friend...'

'This is terrible,' Achille says.

Alone. What hope remains?

*

Achille never sees Hugo, Zenia, again. No one does.

He's their legacy. He may make a mark – Hugo and Zenia, they won't know, but they have bet their scene, their globe – it will not last. Quite soon – nothing will.

'They wanted me to be their witness,' Achille thinks: 'Of the end of everything down here. The persecutions, strong as ever. That was the proof, there'd be no great change, no turnaround. Best see if there's some persecutors who'll take me in, better than being on the run....'

Hugo and Zenia – heroic. Zenia remembers Fonda's legs – pink plastic – she said she'd probably not make the movie another time, but there it is – the future. Love. Then came 1968, but *Barbarella* had told us all there was to know of space and time, and Zenia felt she herself had nothing more to add. Those women in Cézanne, static but immortal. Do you want a caption? she thinks. For a woman, static's probably the best. Don't peer closer. Wounded in an iron corselet? A bird in the Opéra? Wait, endure the fluttering?

'You can't imagine seeing further than you have,' Hugo said. 'It's unthinkable. Enjoying more? Disliking more? It's true – when you're not here, they know more about you than when you are. But you won't know about the chances you have missed. They'll speculate. Maybe give you a better shake. But, remember – many imposing things have gone – Bel took an unexpected beating.... For what's dug up fresh, something choice will disappear into a safe, a vault. I know – the animals you love, you eat them or you bury them. Better not arrive where you can have that choice. You? you go amid indifference. Then, only then – a judgment. All of us, before we start, we have to know the past. Then – we are in it. Shall I learn from it? All the big names are there – Spinoza, Chaplin, Spohr, Nietzsche – and you'll know no more from being like them in a past than you do now. Less, even. Much less. The past. It enfolds us like a tongue, and swallows....'

It's true – when you have reached the top, there's transformation, revelation. Or there's not. 'And that's the time to go,' said Hugo. 'That's your best shot. You're not responsible for anything – no mistake and no bad faith.'

'... if we were wrong?' Zenia asked Hugo.

'If you don't trust your judgment, you'd never create anything,' Hugo said. 'Cold feet. If you don't mistrust it – there'll never be a follow-up. We're sure – so, no sequels. Cool heads and steady hands.'

Leaving. Everything is clear and bright – you can look it up, as if it's in a dictionary, the best, immortal version. Find its meaning.... 'No,' Hugo said. 'No meanings, just similarities.'

Even so – it's all a something, the leaves, the sun, cat's yowl. Makes you look and listen.This is the best – you'll never see anything like it again....

Yves's death from poison mist: the suicides – Hugo and Zenia blowing their last kiss, a fatal 'plop' or 'smack'.

*

'Let's share a *tajine*, Solène,' Achille says. 'I can't stand expensive things that don't taste, or if they do, they're poisonous.' He means oysters.

'Rich and poor, they'll always get along,' says Solène. 'They're greedy. Everybody is. Even Hugo and Zenia, they thought their understanding was the best. Not to be shared. It's why we fight. More, more – then find a way to keep it safe... It's necessary, I'm sure.'

'They're heroes,' Achille says. 'They left me everything. It's invisible, but worth all the more for that.'

'She's more valiant than he,' says Solène, spurning the *tajine*. 'His thinking about thinking reaches an end. Her stuff – it repeats the instinct to chalk upon a wall. But no reason not to repeat. Hugo could move on – have a project. Empire, invasion, occupation. Those aren't spoilt by thinking. It's a change of job, is all. There's spaces you could dominate – an ocean! You'd claim all the fish and all the bottom stuff, charge for guys dumping. You don't need land – land fills up, there's drought or flood. The sea – it hides. It's a good bet....'

'My idea, Solène,' Achille says, 'was different. Not to have a kingdom, not the algorithm stuff, nor be a celebrity in Yunnan.... Something different. As for you – cohabitation's not enough, it's banal, and it erodes. We're not a couple, but we complement. Different tasks, for heteros who feel the urge....'

'Hugo faced desolation – Zenia, repetition: more of the same,' Solène insists, not yielding to Achille. 'For ever. She would have fit with you, Achille.'

'You're right,' says Achille, wishing he could weep here, tears as condiment out of place. 'We didn't match.Too late now, Solène.'

'Say what you'd want of me,' she says, 'and I'll consider. Not your astrophilosophy, though. I imagine – you want me to make the cash, while you hypothesise. I'm not assertive any more, not militant. I judge. I judge you, Achille, all you say, do: in order. It's not just you – everything needs its judgment.'

'How does the sea stand up?' asks Achille.

'Oh, it's overblown, I think: it appeals to tender minds who see the top bit, eat some denizens. It stands up with the wind, the earth: they move – otherwise – it's flat, Achille,' she says. 'No curative power. I won't eat stuff from it, nor the earth, where all the dirt ends up: there's a tasty grass that grows on mulberry sheets....'

'And me?' asks Achille – no one can resist the asking – 'Your sentence?'

'Blame,' says Solène. 'Not prison. Condemnation. Everyone confesses or justifies. You keep silent. So you must bear everything, as though you spoke.'

'Many causes,' says Achille. 'I've not discarded, but deferred. Good robust causes. Others – we could follow.'

'Not that at all,' says Solène. 'Those deaths – you contemplated them. The lives were pebbles in your hand, they slipped away – you caused nothing, took no stand.'

'I could do nothing. Or – I let people do what they wanted. It's much the same. Consequences and premonitions – that's why there's corners for them to wait behind,' Achille says, embarrassed, but nothing more.

'You advertised for me – here I am. That's your confession,' says Solène. 'I'm in your plot, your history, your being: your continuity, your reasoning. I'm not a new start, I have my own itinerary. You want an accomplice – too bad, you got a magistrate.'

'Blame without punishment – it has a trivial side,' Achille says. 'Though blame implies you are responsible.'

'No,' says Solène. 'Probably you aren't responsible. So – don't expect love, respect, what they say everyone deserves. Everyone responsible, that is.'

'I didn't advertise for someone who would give me that,' Achille says.

'Not I, for sure,' she says. 'Nor anyone, would give you love for being what you are. Respect's the maximum, and don't count on it.'

'That's an easy price,' Achille says. 'Owning up. Being called out. I'm modest, and it works. I never expected even that I'd rule the waves. I repeat – some of the disappearances were accidental, some desired.'

'We're supposed to avoid those accidents,' Solène says. 'Not do everything another wants – although it's true – in that too, you're like a host of other people. Being usual – that's no prize.'

'If I'm not right....' Achille starts, 'I know – there's foot soldiers and there's warriors.... I thought myself a warrior, but it all depends on feet.... Maybe I limp, and can't keep up with you, Solène.'

'We could take the bus, Achille,' she says, 'if that is all. I come from a little island. Your ad said you'd save a beauty from the sea as it rose up to take me. All around there's sea, blue sea, like the sky, and one day the sea will swallow us, and we'll all go into the blue, the blue blue sky. And yet – you can't trust your eyes – it seems we're really living in a huge cool country, our governors are here, our books and language – that's where they come from, and we're already there, there we'll shall end up, homeless, comfortless among those people of another colour, all blue eyes ... you see the smoke from charcoal pyres, they have animals, we had none, there's goats, and caramels that smell of musk.... Paris was the art capital once, so it is that for ever, just like Babylon is always centre of the law.... You see, you must be precise, distinguishing between what you see and what you live in.... You'll drown, but still you'll be a citizen and take exams and tests and have the documents.... On the island, you can disappear, the island with you too, and there is nothing to be done – but here, you're written into laws and graded, passed and failed, photoed too, you've signed, and that will always stand, and never ever be erased.' She slumps, head hits the table and the crockery.

'This, Solène, is whale songs, dolphin elegies. Those enormous hulks will rhyme about you when you're gone – till then, try to escape. Battles are won by the survivors. Whales, if there's some left – they'll win this one. Desert, Solène, don't moralise, it's much too late,' Achille says. 'See – the waiter fancies you – he wonders what our story is...You don't eat – he thinks it's love deceived....'

'What will you have me do?' Solène asks, resigned.

*

'I'm not the one,' Achille says. 'Museum quality – that's what's the best. Museum piece – what you mustn't be. I'm in between,

where there can't be anything. I'm in the forest, so you can bet –
I'm a monster. I'm responsible for being here, for my own
presence: others have gone – too bad for them. Your blame or
praise has no effect – survival, that's what interests me, I'm the
expert of us two. You have to keep up with what concerns us all.
Think, Solène: here are some subjects, objects. A hidden people.
A name – a reputation. An escape. A sacrifice. Those interest us,
civilised people, resigned to the collapse of everything, an
interested distance from eternal struggles of worthy people,
quite unlike ourselves.'

'Yes, Achille, that's you,' says Solène. 'I don't care about
being contemporary, if that's what you're at. Just don't make
me disappear, like you do, like everybody, will.'

'If I wanted, I could sink you all,' says Achille. 'Sink the
island, sink the ship that's coming with your food, your cement.
It wouldn't make it anyway, not in time. It wouldn't take you
off and give you houses – it's not legal. Others would complain,
you're getting it too easy. You're in luck – I'll let nature have
you. I'm one of millions sinking you – all men and women,
equally, each one worth exactly like the other – nothing.
Nothing at all – a liability, incurred from vanity, making a
genetic roster of each one, a jar, bone sliver, a snot, a glass
cylinder, one label each. It's costly, altruistic: – curiosity never
satisfied, the last source of hope. In anonymity, nothing is
forgotten. No intermediary, no author's right, no prying hand.'

'Maybe I was a mistake,' Solène says. 'My curriculum – it's
plausible. It isn't true.'

'Did you imagine no human hand was involved – in
colouring your sky, growing your grass, raising your sea?' asks
Achille. 'Imagine – that it wasn't mine, the hand. We'll get on
well – I've no designs.'

'Long ago,' says Solène, 'there were islands everywhere –
and peoples disappeared: Olmecs, Toltecs, Aztecs – counting
and foretelling – surely, they'd have found whatever any one of

us is looking for. They used whole deserts for their prophecies, calculated when we would all die – they lived tough, but then the whiteys came and cut them up and burned them out.... The cover-up, Achille. The accusations that were made – polytheism and worse, cannibalism, slavery. It's the mirror, like the camera, comes, turns you to replicas. We're condemned to condemn in them, conquistadors, all that we are.... The secrets – they used not to be obscure, everyone was seeking them, for sure, they'd worked it out....'

She looks wistfully at Achille, who says, 'I know the secrets. Like you say, Solène, we all know them. They're banal. Will Spaniards come again, swordsmen and missionaries – come to set us right and send us down the mines and give us clap? Monotheism, slavery and poverty, disease and massacres.... Is this the second better time around? We're closer to the end, Solène, maybe it's getting faster, a music, gopak, dervishes gone vertiginous....'

'I have a little thing to ask, Achille,' Solène whispers. 'It's like a thorn, a sting broken off and festering. The guys don't read, they say, yet everything is read. It's all written down somewhere, if you look, all that you've done or thought. Or bought. I am accused....'

'Stop!' says Achille. 'Are you a heroine, Solène? A victim, or one who fought back – finished in the wrong, repaid an insult, vindicated with a thrust too hard? To be a hero, you must have a cause. You may not wish for sacrifice, but through instinct or calculation, your action, deed, outdoes us all. In you, we saw our higher selves were served: you affirmed our wish, our aspiration.... Is that you, Solène?'

'Maybe all that,' Solène says. 'Except – the law's involved. It's very complex – there is family, perennial, some defamation. Drugs, lots of drugs, and arson and its threat. Then there's the shooting – on the island we're all armed, from necessity, except, of course, it is our culture, carried wherever each one goes, or oughtn't to....'

'Near the entrance to us all,' says Achille, broadening. 'There is a stand – there's walking sticks, umbrellas, a sabre, maybe spears, a sjambok.... When we go out or in – there is our choice.... Peace, or maybe war. Everybody has a stand like this – made from an elephant's foot. Original sin, Solène ... and provocation too.'

'It's far more complicated, Achille,' she says.

'Your island: if it's going under, everyone will go a little crazy,' says Achille.

'He lived with us,' Solène begins. 'I call him brother – but we all had different parents. He was crazy, like you say. He made debts, and laid them on us all – then threats. We'd disowned him – and he said he'd burn the house, with us inside. So, someone took a shot at him – I can't imagine who – a kind of heroism, in our name, serving the principles. We'd renounced him, so he's disinherited – otherwise I'd never get a cent....'

'I understand,' says Achille. 'You need to go to court....'

'Oh,'she says. 'We go to court, and so does he, and every time, someone had some justice, and something that was not.'

'It's finished, anyway,' says Achille. 'To you, it's large – to others, maybe trivial.'

'Oh,' Solène says. 'It's trivial to me. It's that no body has been found or even looked for, and he might turn up every day. There's ways of coming from the dead – the dead hand, that's what they call it.'

'Well,' says Achille, losing patience, 'you're not involved, and if you are, it's just about the cash you haven't had, and never will.'

'You haven't understood at all,' she says. 'I told you it was quite complex, the who, the why – and sometimes when.'

'All wealth will be swept away....' Achille says, in rotund tones, and laughing too. 'Avoid litigious people, on islands or in continents.'

'He cut up all my clothes,' says Solène, weeping. 'More than coverings – they were costumes. Feathers. Tiny. Strass. Immense.'

She talks of clans, parties political and not, manifestoes, soldiers and graves, lone gunmen ... of epidemics and her rights – 'He killed my horse,' she says.

'That's terrible,' Achille says. 'Why'd he do that? Besides, you said on the island you had no animals: there'd be nowhere you could ride ... a cart, a chariot? Apollo? Driving a quadriga, a sacrifice, into the waves at dawn? Asvamedha?'

'Not on the island,' Solène says. 'Here, on the continent. All the lawyers, waiting to be paid, no satisfaction, not for anyone....'

'I'd no idea you carried with you all this baggage,' says Achille....

'We're all like that,' Solène says. 'It takes two lifetimes to lift up all that fills just one existence. Documents, warrants.... Sort it out, Achille, I'll be your slave.'

'I don't offer that much security, Solène,' Achille says.

'You're a good person,' Solène says. 'Though being good's for people who are quite limited.'

*

Achille trips – to Solène's island. There are no crashing planes. There's an old boat, takes you to the island – at most, it might sink, but slow. The island – if you close your eyes, there is the blue – below, you tell the lie, the sea's your plank, you – an upturned turtle, slowly move your paws. No one will come. Above – the blue. One day they'll meet, the blue, the blue: now, you're on the yellow sand, beached, baked on a shell, martyred like a saint.

Open your eyes – there's gendarmes, sullen guys, bedrooms for rent....

'Drink this!' Solène says. 'This way, you needn't go.'

It's true. Drink: it's a hole, you needn't dig, it's waiting for you, just your size, one mouth-full, down a gallery with racks of cheese, quite odourless, it goes. It's dry here, it's very very dry.... There's long tables full of smallish animals, dressed poor in homespun, tucking in – if they roister, you don't hear. It's down! Your belly – lined with twill, and tranquil, nothing churns and kneads. Hours of silence, a cough, hawk in a throat, a copcar far outside toottoot...you, the composer, on a stool, look quietly at your hands. No sound. Public's in anxiety....

'Codeine!' says Achille. 'Once, for sale here, without a dealer. Now – innocence is lost....'

'Not all of it,' says Solène. 'Colonialism! That's where your silent journey's taken you, you smug! It must seem picturesque, that innocence. Maybe you'll meet with fetishists. Knowledge here is fear and terror, they'll take you there.... Smell the blood on the masks, feefifofum.... Don't worry about those animals, I told you, there's none left. You, Achille, are probably a hero, one of the last big idiots to land and scout around,' and she pulls his hand on to her small breasts, and he has drunk and sunk so deep he doesn't feel a thing, and nor does she, but it could be a bond, when needed by either one....

'Look, Achille,' Solène says. 'The house. A flower....'

'If it were Ukraine, it could be a hollyhock,' Achille mumbles. 'Here – hibiscus....'

'Yes, yes, maybe that,' says Solène. 'But look – see the trees? The guys here try their shotguns on them....' and it's so, they're wormy, tattered, bananas full of lead like Bugsy-Mugsy someone....

'Maybe like Che,' says Solène. 'And you see the crime...? Hear the blast, the shot? Over and over it's replayed. And me! Look – me! Outraged. Vandalised. Smoke, thick as mist.'

'Yes, yes,' says Achille, who doesn't see a thing, except the flower – the trademark bloom the famous clown would wave.... Clown and flower, both dead.... How terribly sad; but codeine doesn't make you cry, that's what it's for, to stop, to keep you dry.

*

'For sure, Solène,' Achille says. 'You have a case. But it's all circumstance.'

'Your life, Achille' she says. 'It's had no circumstance? Was it all plotted straight? You never visited the dead, became a wolf, a monster....?'

'Yes, of course,' Achille says. 'We all do that. It's the details, Solène: law is so fiddly if you pay for it. And if you don't, it throws you in the pit. There is no half way court, where everyone means well, and you get paid your due. Like tennis....'

'You are my witness now,' Solène says. 'I wonder if you saw the horse?'

'I'm sure I can,' says Achille. 'I don't dwell on it – I've such pity for the animals. We can duck, they can't.'

Solène laughs – that's quite a grisly joke, the one about the ducks.

*

'It's involving,' Achille says. 'Your property, the family happiness. But – there's wars all over. If you'd report on them, or you think a side's worth joining, you have to wonder, to decide: you're fearful, but would you go there, take the risk? Not necessarily to fight, but make a commentary, save people, put others into jeopardy, kill spies, be a spy, be an advocate, make peace, secede, do deals, sell stuff, run super weapons through the lines – if you don't think you could do this, well, it means you really do not give a fuck, that everything you say is air, passing up your throat and out your teeth.'

'We're at war too,' says Solène, quite sullen. 'If you want danger, stick around, join in the struggle, like in Cayenne: the demos. The Sahel. One side, decide: at least a plan, a big idea...'

'I understand that,' says Achille. 'I don't mean taking cities, avenging wrongs. I don't mean brawling, or handing out some clothes – even if it's like Zenia – just pictures, all that stuff; sitting round, the talk, the drink, and staying up till dawn. I want the further step. She saw she had the power to change, direct, what was created. All alone, she could control the shape of everything: but – it didn't matter. Not a bit. It never has, it never does. She knew, and for her, it was enough. Or Hugo – being some kind of thinker, and then to reach the end, like on a broken bridge.'

'Help me, Achille,' says Solène.

'It's not possible,' Achille says. 'You have your part of blame. and you're unfortunate. Indelible, both those obstacles. Who cares, if you are innocent? Where does that count?'

'You're an overcoat, Achille,' says Solène with a sneer. 'A painter's smock. The painter's making love with his model on the couch, you're thrown over a chair – dirty, full of ambition, an accessory.'

Achille ignores this. 'A horse? Why'd you want a horse, Solène?'

'I wanted a phallus, but I didn't want the man they often come attached to,' she says. 'Once you have your phallus, it's like having your procession regular in the street. You don't need a religion if you've got your gods and goddesses in a cart, bright colours, singing, dancing, throwing giblets at the crowd.'

'Oh, how I agree!' says Achille, admiringly. 'You get a strike with that, Solène – lots of those skittles won't get stood up again!'

'You see?' she says. 'We chime! I bet our souls are made to fit together, like a kit.'

*

'The woman you put the ad out for,' says Mirko. 'She's wild. And have you spent all Yves' cash?'

'I wanted wild,' says Achille. 'Who knows? If she's on my side, I shan't need do her down. The cash? Here, you need think like bankers do. I used it as security, and spent what I borrowed. So, the capital's still live – though I don't know exactly where it is.'

'Those islanders,' says Mirko, insisting. 'They were all shipwrecked, found a cadaver, boarded it, paddled it to shore. The fetishists....'

'I know all that,' Achille says. 'Life! That's what you need – with sacrifice, you're dead.'

'Oh Achille – "Asie, Asie, Asie" – how you romance!' says Mirko, longing himself for romance. '"*Les habits à longs franges*"! We think we explore – no! It's the old will for conquest, for expropriation. Love with an unknown tongue. The sacred flame, that dances ahead of us, what shapes it takes: those Dogons, they've crept into our skulls.... What you are curious about – it enters through your eyes, at night. Your brain – big spiders hold it tight, all round ... it's just a dottle. We become what we see – secrets we can't articulate, they turn our thoughts to crumble....'

'No, Mirko,' Achille says. 'You're right, of course. It's that – but there is much much more.'

'If you're convinced,' says Mirko, 'that the species has run its race – then, at the end, you can do almost anything. For pleasure

or perversion, power, profit, in prick-song or in plainsong – just
so long as you don't kill. That voids your argument. What's
seen to be arriving – can't be accelerated – not for justice, nor
security....'

'Yes, Mirko,' Achille says. 'But there's jails. What is – goes
on. There's slavery, starvation, scabies – every kind of itch....'

'Don't elaborate,' says Mirko. 'Follow the bright silk lines –
they're fixed to where you want to go.'

*

'What can you offer me, Achille?' asks Solène. 'Home has
become a metaphor. No one knows what that might involve.'

'Nothing at all, Solène,' Achille says. 'It's all there, beneath
the sea. Like Alexandria, Atlantis – don't go visiting, that's all.
You lost everything – but gained it all as spirit. I know it may
not feel the same... The struggles, history – all has frozen stop...
Remember – this species seeks out people they can make to
work for little, nothing: do the hard jobs, take the hard blows....
Your colour, gender, school – get one wrong, it takes centuries
to put it right, and then you find you're living in a tricky place,
your army's weak, your gender's wrong again.... Believe me,
Solène, it's true you may expect, some time ... some payment,
some concrete reward, for what you've done – answering my ad
– or for what you'll do, as yet obscure. But you may never find
a person more alike yourself than me, in many registers; the
sediments of wrongs, the strata of offence....'

'I don't believe a word, Achille. As they say – if wishes were
horses... remember,' Solène says. 'I've had one of those, a
horse: the wishes multiply, the damage too. They're strong and
temperamental.

'There is no end, nor a beginning, Achille, to all the
differences you'd wish weren't there, so's you can manage me,
exploit, seduce, traduce me, misrepresent my longing and my

due.... How dare you, anyway, apologise for me, my origins, and all the rest! Your reasons, which seem my excuses – drop it, Achille!'

'I am contrite, Solène,' Achille says. 'Over and over. Take that as reparation, for a start.... If I have fallen short – excuse me, then start excusing all the others....'

'Your mockery,' Solène says, 'is infantile.'

They leave it there.

*

'It's clear,' says Achille. 'Your stand. But – let's not do agriculture – I tried with sheep, it ended bad. With goats, I fear it would be similar.'

'You're right, Achille,' Solène says. 'Enslaving those animals, chivvying, stripping – then eating them – it is a metaphor. The world is hungry for imperialism, Achille. The good shepherd, with her iron-shod stick, her dogs, her shears, the pens, the paschal lambs – she wears the crown imperial. Come! – you're halfway black yourself, my dear. Surely you, the sensitive naïf, you see the parallel, the story, epic, parable – what you will: the yankee movie.... Poor sheep! Evolution let them down – they've grown no venom and no claws....'

'What's to be done, Solène?' asks Achille. 'There's little time, the species' destiny is shared by everyone – except those space-ship guys whose fate is worse; their journey infinite, unchronicled....'

'You see?' says Solène, brightening up. 'It is a puzzle, like I said. There's answers, no solution.'

'It's another of those puzzles that everyone know what the conclusion is,' says Achille. 'The sickness of the father, once limited – it's dispersed; the spores are everywhere. The sickness! The judgments scattershot. We think in ways archaic – classes, hierarchy, and dominance. Evolution's mastered: our defects now are generalised, they're in our bones, in everyone. The shepherds and the sheep! All over everywhere! A massacre of innocence. Where's our enlightenment? Intelligence is manufactured – it's machines, Solène: that do your work and bomb you. Ours is a story with many endings – each one bad, definitive....'

They cling together.

'Of course,' says Achille, 'there were sheep around. I was not a shepherd. I was investigating: my Nothingness.'

'It doesn't matter,' Solène says: 'Not a bit.'

*

'Mirko,' says Achille, 'He drifted by. He wheedled in to be a friend. Now, he gives advice on everything. He's indispensable – don't trust him, and do the opposite.'

Solène's attracted.

Achille goes on, 'He thinks, to survive, you must try everything. No one really survives, of course. He says – everyone should make their movie, post their memoir, drive a horse tram, build the tallest dovecote....'

'Oh, he's right!' says Solène. 'You, you see it all through keyholes, Achille. Rows of brains floating in formaldehyde, suits of wooden armour, warped. Mirko – makes things spin and shimmer.'

'It's words, though,' Achille says, reluctantly conceding. 'Of course, just to say it, let alone spread the idea around, you must forget most of what has ever happened, not to mention, not to think, of what the future and the now can bring. But it's true – most things are tidied up. If the crops rot in the fields this year – the next they're splendid. Late replacement children get the bag's best shake. Some guys will fix the dawn, the spring, your girl, your boy....'

'I'd want to be those guys,' Solène says. 'The rest is crap.'

'The rest,' says Mirko, sailing in on those last words, 'is people paid to fight for you, to represent you on the side you think you're born. They need an enemy – it can be anyone, it will be you. Our side, Achille – it always wins. It has those bombs. They'll fracture everything. Suppose I go and join the struggles – Uighurs, Kurds, secessionists. The potpourri of tragedy, Solène. Lost causes. When I lose, I'll move on somewhere else. Since everything is falling down – I'll help Daesh make it come down faster still.... Except it won't. It takes its time, its own time. It's territory and allies, resources and expedients. The murderers, Achille – are amongst us. The fascists – they never left, they breed, they multiply – in our barns, our schools, our dusty streets.... It's all *us*, what is done – our brothers, sisters. You and I.'

'So, you're staying put, Mirko, here,' Solène says, much disappointed.

Then he's gone. Mirko – dead on the field of honour. A field, at least.

*

'He won't write letters,' says Solène. 'Like everyone you know, Achille – they talk like crazy, then they're gone!'

'Clearly, we didn't understand, not far enough,' says Achille. 'He wanted nothing from us. Not our disapproval either. We don't know, if he joined the good guys or the bad. We've nothing to report him for.'

'Trees!' says Solène. 'Play it like they are a game, the biggest game. Sell little ones, grown high in the hills – people will bet on them, that they'll grow for fifty years, and we shall still be here....'

'Here selling trees?' asks Achille, disappointed.

'It's naff, I know,' Solène says. 'But all your mates – they disappear! They wander on, from gangs to sacred wars and then to prayer, rehab; noble sentiments, uplifting talk. Trees are different, silent mostly, slow moving, if at all...'

When you enter the tree deposit, there are free camels, awaiting you. You ride through the plantations – there's baobabs, sequoias, mangroves, roots-in-the-air trees.... Thorn trees, where the camels linger.... palms immense and welcoming, like the Buddha's hand.... 'Demotics', 'Locals', 'Vulnerable', 'Domestics' and 'Extinct'. There's nothing taller than a handsbreadth.

'You have to hang around,' Solène says, 'for the pricey ones to sprout. I'm for the mandrakes, the swampy ones ... the prelude to the flood. The water seems the softest way – but it leaves nothing, it converts it all, like painting over a canvas, effaces everything, makes it disappear for ever. Transforms totally, erases our trace, stifles us. As you go down – perhaps you see your similars – a flounder floundering, a sole expires, it's all a cod....

'The fire, the wind – they displace, they blacken, but something's still there, is somewhere.... In air, soot and shreds. The earth, it opens, rocks and rolls, but it cannot swallow everything.... Knocks your house down quicker than the wolf. But the bricks and sticks – you see them down the hole. The water – covers everything – you can't go down below, can't wake the captain who has wrecked it all. All you see is scroll, the grey unrolls, not a word scratched on....'

She and Achille – they decide against the trees. 'Too slow, too optimistic,' Achille says. 'A field of cannabis would give more hope, if hope is what you want. Besides, there's no one here who buys or sells the shoots. We could steal our camels, though. Ride off....'

'This heat makes things grow,' says Solène. 'Nothing is solved, but everything is multiplied, the creatures – more and more, more clownish, more specialised. It's life much faster, but it's not for us, Achille. When my island's gone – a country's gone, not just a home, but my frame, my existence too. There's lots who live without a country, some were stolen, some not founded, some absorbed. There's lots who've lost a home or never had one – they lament; it never ends. I shall see it all go under, and all I'll have's a document. Me – a foolscap sheet. It's what I'll have become.'

'It's all you need,' says Achille, unimpressed. 'To win your case. Real things decay – it's best describe them as they were, bind them in the bundle, have the wiggèd ones adjudicate.'

'It's maybe what I said to do,' says Solène, 'but it's not what I want, not at all. I like real things, Achille. I don't believe in countries – but there is land, the earth, the ants.... Real things, Achille. Does that include you? I've my doubt.... You see the forces gather over you, Achille – immense. You're over before you can begin. You must stand up, or else you drown. Brazen it out – there's other guys will decide your case, define what's right or wrong. It's harsh. You must start with little things....'

'You want another island, Solène? Be very very careful,' says Achille. 'People thought in deserts there was just what they could see.... You glimpsed what moved, and that was that. It isn't so. Beneath, there's precious stuff – and maybe not. You cannot see a thing, but in the sky, there's soldiers like a cloud of flies. In the towns there's emissaries. You're a nomad, Solène, a modern one who's unemployed. You drift, air drives you. You're a sycamore propellor, a lost bee.

'There's states. When there's guys not producing anything, and living well, you have its origins. Producers – they produce. The parasites – that's the state. Rich guys, the priests, the educated, chiefs – mistrust them all, Solène....'

'Oh, Achille,' Solène says. 'It was a little island – you saw it on TV – the waves, just four or five – they covered it in half an hour....'

'Look for another island, then,' Achille says. 'You'll find the flat ones have an airport and a base – soldiers come down from the sky. You won't believe it: you think the whiteys come with cash and radical ideas, liberation, all that, and speaking soft. It isn't so – they want what's invisible, they want to make new roads high in the sky, they bring you horrors, Solène, like they've always done.... Hands: that's what they want – everyone at work – or maybe there is none.... No human guy is nice, it's true, but most are lazy, want some other guy bonded who pours their tea and gives them sex, and pays the tax. These new ones – want your bones, Solène – they rig them up to make door chimes, the long ones – make marimbas. They want your souls to make parquet....'

'You look at little things, Achille. Those tiny trees....' and Solène laughs.

'Oh no,' says Achille. 'You'll never understand. This occupation, this invasion – it goes on and on. It's evident, but words are not enough, there's nothing stops it, not machetes, not your gods, your secret places, not your smile, your stare.... Already it's gone into history, a story you will never read, one where your name's misspelt....'

'If there are flat islands,' Solène says. 'All with bases, Americans, Chinese, rolling puttees, bulling boots, let's think, and find a pointed rock, an island that won't sink, with winds so unpredictable only a raft can land....'

'What's there to eat, Solène?' Achille asks. 'Seagulls? I understand you'll find some mates who'll follow you. There'll be a civil war! Your rock, Solène, is like a broken tooth, a Ganesh tusk. It's what is left to write our message with. What will you put, Solène – just "Help!"? Believe me, take advice.'

*

There's no advice.
There's tons of it.

*

'I've had my revelation, Solène,' Achille says. 'In my dream, you loved another guy, and he went off with someone else. We hugged, you and I. And it was clear. The Ark! We are the couple, Solène, the human pair. In the book, the plan is God's. We don't believe in Him, besides, His killing of the rest is genocide. And why drown almost all the animals? – they know no sin, they don't backslide, forget their prayers.... And all the fish were left intact....

'Of course, we'll need some sailors. Carpenters as well; an engine. I'm unsure about the beasts – we want the good life. Stuffed in an ark, those rhinos and what else is left – it isn't right. Not a good life, nor a good death. All those insects too!... Let's forget the literal past....'

'It needs more work,' says Solène. 'Dreams are like that. I have a friend called Vinciane – she'd come along. No pets.'

'Of course, the original tale has faults,' Achille says. 'So we can make ours up.'

'It's surreal,' says Solène. 'That's good. But I bet, Achille, you took advantage of your sleep to spend a night of making love with me, inventing everything.... And was it good?'

'Oh, excellent,' Achille says. 'Apologies of course, but far far better than the real. Or, rather, a better real it surely was.'

'The first Ark.... I bet they ate the bigger animals – the dinosaurs, poor megatheria – "thanks and goodbye for ever,"' says Solène, appalled. 'Disgusting. We'll have to eat the vultures, Achille. Or buy a pizza oven....'

'The good life, Solène,' Achille says, 'is our aim. Don't mock. 'From a small Boat that row'd along' – remember: escape, safety, paradise.... You've a sturdy voice, Solène. No frills, no trills.... Let it resound....'

*

'Don't try for sponsors,' says Vinciane. 'Banks – oh! Ugh! I'll pack a bag – just land me where there's lights....'

She's fun, but doesn't fit. 'Are you the last two, or the first? Or just the heroes available, not coming, not going, always ready for a fight, a flight...?' she asks.

'First or last, it's much the same,' Solène says. 'It depends who's around to write it down. It isn't up to me – the people Achille knows, they disappear. Sailing with him gives you a chance, for he hangs on. But, Vinciane – this won't be a cruise. No destination. No end.'

'Cruises are much oversold,' says Vinciane. 'You end up where you started, and all you remember is the heaving road. The wordless scroll.'

'Nothing will happen, Vinciane,' says Achille. 'Maybe it's not for you.'

'Of course it is,' says Vinciane. 'The animals – are us. We'll dance on deck. Lake Sevan – you can see Ararat from there, we'll have them build the boat and drag it to the sea – could be the Caspian, the sailors in their whites – a vision! It won't rain enough to float us off. Those old pictures of the boat – so stuffy, like a tent and how it rolls! no, not that, not thinking of what to do when it all stops. The sea, the wrath, the pitch and toss.... Instead, we'll frolic – the pure, the sex – the apex, the human top! Not seasonal, in fits and roars, the rut, but on and on, with fouettés, pimento flavouring. Too much of everything, that's what you need. Cannons and Greek fire, chain-shot – excess, Achille! And cut the rain.... Brother sun, wobbling, ever closer, like a blubbery face, our only friend, absent, anxious....'

'Clouds, Vinciane,' Solène says. 'Sulphur and copper. Locusts too: so don't tell anyone about our Ark. If there's not rain, there will be drought, we're in disaster genre. We'll wait in Erevan, and maybe the flood will punish us. The story goes – there's just one Ark. If fashion takes its hold, there will be millions – and that isn't it at all....'

*

'There's suspicion here,' says Vinciane, from Erevan. 'It may be from ordering a boat, made for the sea, when you're in a landlocked place. I have to say it's for the sea – not for a flood! Besides – not everyone is limpid in this town.... There's malfeasance around.They don't know if I'm a hoaxer or a crook.'

'Well, keep them uncertain,' Achille says. 'It's best you're there, you're transparent as a dragonfly. I'm opaque; and I'm the captain of the ship, if it gets built....'

'We thought the sight of Ararat would give symbolic charge,' says Solène. 'But symbols work like jumping jacks – spit fire in all directions. The poor trees, Vinciane, the planks – think, if you give up, they'll all have died in vain.'

'Oh Solène,' says Vinciane. 'It isn't made of wood....' – but they don't hear what the material is, only that it's light as tumbleweed, a truck can take it anywhere, so quick ... a lighter than airship....

'Those silver arms and hands,' says Achille, 'they've always fascinated – in processions, all those popes.... The arms will bear us up. And Vinciane must persevere, work her passage, as it were.... We'll see if she's dependable....'

'Is that my test too?' Solène asks. 'No test for you, you're glass, Achille. You break if someone drops you – sings the right top note....'

'I admire you, Solène,' says Achille. 'You want your land, even if you have no right. If you have a right, maybe you did awful things to get it ... to forge it ... buy it. You want your land, although it isn't there. It's gone beneath the sea. What makes you so stubborn, dear Solène?'

'Our plan,' she says. 'The boat. It's about surviving massacres. The rain, the sea – someone else's murderous plan. Armenians – they know all that. The Ark, landing on the mountain, Ararat – should be in Armenia; you see it from far off, rising from a cloud.... It seems your right's a mirage....'

'I don't agree,' Achille says. 'It's not about survival. In the Book, almost everyone is killed, quite indiscriminate. The boat's a challenge: to the wrath of nature – of circumstance. What they used to say was "Providence". The flood's an unintended consequence of human enterprise. To step beyond subsistence life – leads to catastrophe. Witty, you say; a paradox. The Ark is not a way of saving lives, a test. It's a coffin, a Medusa raft.The end, Solène; or, perhaps, the last resort.'

'It's all a guess, Achille, why we're as we are,' says Solène. 'And why it all falls on our head. We make up stories – but they're not how things are at all.'

*

'They want to make the boat a kind of pod,' says Vinciane. 'I said "forget it" if there is no deck. A pod would spin, there'd be no up or down.... We'll find a barge, a dredger, discard the epic trim, the legend – just sail around....' She's brought a friend.

Boffi only speaks Armenian.

'Boffi says, money's been cleaned up. Everybody wants it now, with no more prejudice, still less revulsion. If you've a voice, it means you're backed with cash,' says Vinciane. 'You need ideas – but not the kind you have to think about. You find them, stacked up on a shelf; your brain has stocked them since prehistory.'

Boffi, thinks Achille, is another one I cannot trust – his thoughts are in a language I can't understand, and written in a script that's worse. We're all in the same boat, they say – but that boat's in a workshop in Armenia, an embryo.

'Nothing between us is a bond,' Achille thinks. 'Not Solène, not Vinciane – besides, on board there's every chance for treachery – the mutiny, walking the plank, smudging the chart, wetting the powder ... the sicknesses, the bunking up ... climbing those trees and hanging clouds upon them.... Being reduced ... eating the cabin boy, and oh! the erotic scenes, buboes and scrapie – no one to help, the lifeboats sabotaged....'

'Save me, save us,' Achille's imagination cries. 'Save our souls, poor souls we don't believe in.... The lovely sharks, they've signed on for the trip. "Port out, starboard home" – their home that's everywhere, they grin eternally, they fuss, they preen – "our shagreen cannot stand the sun" – why, they ate the lady's little dog that used to watch the flying fish, their wings like butterflies' ... they'll get her too, the lady trotting round the upper deck, like on an open bus, except ... all round, there's nothing ... nothing except the sucking waves, a monstrous polyp, stretching from shore to distant shore....'

*

'What have I done?' Achille, a patriarchal bleat, confessional, no father he – asks. 'Watched all those people, friends, moulded in my image, Zenia and Hugo, hours of talk that made them me, made me a part of them, and so I died with them as I made them die.... What have I done?

'What is accomplished? Crumbly figures leaping in a crazy frame.'

'You tried,' says Solène, hearing the rhetoric, 'but you didn't know what you were at. And now, we're in act five, the horses outside restive, the coachmen pissed ... no *bis*, please, the show is at its end. Clap and go home. The piece is repetitious as it is, the voices strained, the new machinery revolves and creaks, the weight will bring the theatre down, the devils pop up through the floor, others are scotched, the ugly sisters mustn't be called that now, but ugliness can be described in subtler ways.....'

'Forget my whine,' says Achille. 'I know I ought to feel more guilty – but there it is. *Sauve qui peut*, that's what they say when the sea is at your throat. Hard to resist.'

'Oh,' says Solène, 'I'd like to comfort you, Achille – it wasn't in the ad. I love dear Vinciane ... too bad she loves the cretin Boffi, even teaching him some words so he can say he loves her too.'

*

'It's payday, Achille,' Solène says. 'You convoked us all so we could realise your plans....'

'The plans, Solène, depend on you. And now, it seems, on Vinciane,' Achille says. 'I have no prejudice, but Boffi can't communicate – it saddens me, but he is on a different plane, at least today he's not in my dependency. To me, all people – they are much the same, until they do me wrong. You hear them, tattling, expressing evil thoughts. In Boffi's case – who'd know?'

'Then there's the boat,' Solène says. 'I hope Yves left a lot of dosh....'

'The boat? The boat....' Achille says, holding out a hand, 'It doesn't rain. The sea is far away, and there's no boat. So, it can wait....'

'The risk is yours,' Solène says. 'In Erevan it lies. There's still, there's always, us. You're a philosopher, a genius, creative, an improviser too. We're all behind you, for that – and also for our own protection. We await your signals.... Meanwhile, there's feasts and music, clothes and shoes.... The bills ... don't differentiate pleasure from necessity....'

'There's money,' Achille says, with disdain. 'It's in the bank. Banks don't have money – only people do. Anyway, that's where it is. What's due will come to you, Solène. Your friends as well ... and even Boffi.'

'Out of this world!' Solène says, growing angry.

'This is vulgar,' Achille says, angry too. 'Start a chandler's – provisions for the doubters' arks. The water'll never go away, once it's come down. At most, they'll have to live on Everest. It's odd – some people won't accept the world has ended! Vanity, dear Solène. Those are the people in the cinema, still sat when the credits go scrolling up. Asleep or dead – they'll see the movie over, and not a word, a frame, will change!'

'I love you!' Solène shouts. 'I love a fraudster with aplomb. I'm with you all my life, Achille – I trust you, you've a face of bronze, a brazen will – I trust you to fight my fight, and naturally I'll cling to you – I have no choice.'

'You know what they say,' Achille insists, '– "only a murderer can be a true pacifist: only a fraudster be a good cop".'

'No,' says Solène, 'I never heard that. You see in me a murderer and a fraudster? I thought you were speaking of yourself.'

'You could be innocent, Solène,' says Achille. 'You could have all the bad before you, still.'

'Maybe the flood will take too long,' says Solène. 'It could be war, with pestilence and famine too....'

'No, no,' Achille says. 'I know I call myself a warrior, but I've no appetite for scuffling in the sand. A war might end with someone claiming victory – their eyes gouged out and limbs cut off. What kind of end is that?'

There's discontent all round. Talk of survival too – 'No one wants a life shut up in the ark,' says Vinciane. 'Especially if there's creatures too. The breeding: and the smell! Then, there is Boffi.... My love is unconditional, but he's a sneak....'

'Boffi's sent from Erevan,' Solène says. 'To check on you, Achille. If you don't pay for work done on the boat....'

'Oh fiddle-faddle,' Achille says. 'I doubt they've even laid the keel. I'm the one who's asked to pay, but if we drown, then no one will.... Maybe they want a seat, a cabin, on the boat, reserved. Meanwhile, that Boffi guy, he learns to speak and leeches on me, on us all....'

*

'I'm honest,' says Achille to Vinciane: she's the one who looks like she can read and write. The others?!

'We come from Nothing,' Achille says. 'Using our brains, that look like tortoises without their shell, slow, slow.... In the old times, everyone went on and on. They were registered. Illiterates were present through a thumb. No thumb? – you used another part. I'm distressed – I'm not yet closing in upon the good. I've had half a life at least, but now I'm nearer to the bad. After those ancient massacres, there were photos, people with memories. It's all gone, of course – first the writing, then the readers....'

'You're mad, Achille,' says Vinciane. 'You can't want to leave a memoir, a stele? For after you? If there's silverfish and lichens left, that read?'

'No, of course not. You are right,' says Achille, with reluctance. 'It's that we all know the game is up. Who'd care that I take steps...? I want a push to do what's memorable. I can't think what. Combat with the worst of guys, would that give lustre, Vinciane?'

'I never thought,' says Vinciane, pulling her clothes tight, protecting against Achille. 'You'd have such vanity. So inappropriate, seeing where we are. First, a person must do something memorable, then modestly await the plaudits. Not the reverse.'

*

'These guys, Achille, Boffi,' Vinciane tells Solène. 'They are unworthy. I'll forget my passion – you, Solène, must battle on,

seeking your rights on non-existent things, a patch of water ...
expecting nothing from Achille.They bring us chains, those two,
and threats, and no doubt death.'

They're a couple now. They walk in step.

'Can you talk, Boffi?' Achille asks. 'We're a couple now,
you and I....'

'Oh, it's easy,' Boffi says. 'I've improved myself. I learned
the dictionary – things extinct, discarded. Too bad for aardvarks,
but there's still zygotes and zyxommas. As a bilingual, my price
has risen – I'm not a simple soldier now. I am a partner.'

'You see,' says Achille. 'Language has consequences – our
evolution shows.... And your Vinciane has left.... She and
Solène have made a compact....'

'Yes, yes,' says Boffi. 'But in the end – talking, we are not
saved. Language may send us faster down. It chivvies evolution.
It permits the pester, persuasion, verbal shaming.... Altruism's a
snare, so's sacrifice unless it's to a totem. The Books ... oh
horror...! Indelible and hectoring. Philosophy can stand alone
and naked, wordless. A rivulet that evaporates, sinks in the rock.
Science ... hmmm ... yes, it must get written down.'

'Slowly, Boffi, slowly,' Achille warns. 'The dictionary – it
cannot speak. The dawn, the dark, separation of the sheep and
goats – call for the charred stick, white stone ... the ephemeral,
written, frozen like Nijinski. A chain, a snake of words, fixed in
your alphabet, but different every time as the ear, the eye, seizes
it.... Chiselling in memory, a draped figure of speech. Or nailed
in rhyme.... A lilting grunt: in strict time, a serenade, a raga ...
nocturne, aubade or fugue....'

'Accounts,' says Boffi. 'That's all it is. War and Peace, and
sacks of dates – it's bookkeeping, all history is. Accounts. In my
example – Providence provides for everything, except the
adding up.'

'Dear Boffi,' Achille says. 'It seems your thoughts come in a
language to your head. Mine don't.'

'I hadn't thought,' says Boffi, stretching, kissing Achille's chin, being short – 'I'm only at the start – I'd say "commencement", but that's another thing.'

'Discoursing, Boffi,' Achille says. 'With you, it's wonderful. My head is in a spin. But – I fear that means we're in a little boat with broken oars.... Which of us might be the owl, and which the pussy-cat? Language can't distinguish what would be evident to anyone with sight: sea eagles, a shark, old salts or cabin boys.... Except, my friend – the waves are high, the wind is solid like a door. They'd never see us in the trough, or teetering on the crests....'

'True. How true?' says Boffi, with a pinch of doubt.

They sit, smiling at one another. Nothing more remains to say.

'Look,' says Boffi. 'Now that we're intimate, Achille – I can show my tool. My old trade, naturally. No civilised relation could have tolerated ... everyone would want one, all that talk.... You have to cover up, conceal, of course, but in yourself, you know.'

'Why,' says Achille, taking it, forefinger, thumb. 'It's a kris. Like in a criss-cross, a double cross. You're right,' and he waves it around. 'No civilised nation could have accepted it. A weapon cheap, easy to hide....' He makes an arc ... a slice....

'My thumb, you cretin,' Boffi howls. 'I should have told you, how my blade was sharp. Now – if I were illiterate, how would I leave my mark, document, and sign, that I am here alive, consent, marry, borrow, have kids....?'

'You'd use the other one,' says Achille. 'In those days they didn't know about the prints.'

'You've hit my weak spot, Achille,' Boffi says. 'Look! There is no other thumb.'

It's like a foot.

'All our species has them,' Achille says. 'We're roughly symmetrical. Wolves don't, and maybe at your birth, your mother thought – like circumcision ... a weak spot ... might be handy too ... God's preference in guys.... Perhaps she's superficial, clumsy. Or doesn't like you.'

'No, no,' says Boffi, toughing up. 'It was my friends.'

'I'm contrite,' says Achille. 'Never heard of such a thing – words can't express....'

'Of course they can,' says Boffi, close to tears. 'Just try.'

'We're a couple, Boffi,' Achille says. 'Accept what happens. If you want, I'll apologise again. Remember, though, the end is coming. I stopped talking politics when it was clear that everyone had learned to talk. I keep my mouth shut now. Where there's bad guys, other guys resist, go bad themselves. When there's good guys – it doesn't mean the rest are good. It's a kind of paradox that's hard to overcome. I understand, when people want something that belongs to someone else. I can deal with that. It's wanting other people to be good, and then to punish them when they aren't. That's something hard to handle, though it sounds quite simple. Anyway, between us, Boffi, no hard feelings, eh?'

'Of course there are,' says Boffi. 'Mutilation's not a thing you can forgive. Even statues, when the ancient vandals had them lopped ... outrage persists, one of two things they can remember. It is an absence. Absences admit all kinds of explanations that shift, change shape. Shape without matter, naturally. Like cosmology, it all depends who you are talking to, and what they have in mind to say. Had I my thumb, you would have no responsibility. As it is – most accusations stand. All guilts, all innocences. What's gone and isn't there – who knows why it went and where it is, how far into intentions you can go...?'

Achille can't remember how he might respond.

'It's trivial, your good and bad,' says Boffi, still suffering.

'Yes, of course,' says Achille. 'Forget your thumb, we'll be profound....'

'I shan't forget my thumb,' says Boffi. 'It's not there, but it exists. Somewhere. A sacrifice. Feel its power, its resonance, my best friend, loyally awaiting in the imaginary. A phantom.'

'You're right,' Achille says,'to rhapsodise. However, you're a crook. Before you had my language, when the order came, I'd have suffered from your blade.'

'Oh, I can talk,' says Boffi. 'Tire the sun with talking. It's you that doesn't understand. Speaking the same language – that's not it. At issue is the thumb.'

'Cosmology is easier,' Achille says. 'I see, for you, the thumb is your humanity, the species badge – without it, there's no maraméo, no thumb-the-nose, no gladiator's judgment.... No off-hand, no hitch.'

'We're on the same side,' Boffi says. 'Just now. But Vinciane – she cleaves to me. Solène will follow Vinciane, so – beware!'

'You and your little shiv?' Achille protests. 'I'm sure it's different for you, a potent force, attracting friends and allies – but, take care! Friends punish treachery and incompetence. Allies are harsher still. What use can you be to me? What can you do, Boffi? Sail? Climb? Swim? Or something in between?'

'Oh,' Boffi says, 'I'm human, more than you, Achille – I've not had these pretensions, your pratfalls.'

'All I've said,' says Achille, 'is, we must stop being monkeys. Be something else. Evolve. Evolve in quite a different way, adapt to the unknown, the inconceivable. Sailors, perhaps. Just for a few years; a year is long, when you're going through. After, it doesn't matter if another year comes along, when you've done what you had wanted.'

'My secret,' says Boffi, 'is that I can do wonders in the Lindy Hop. I fly. I've gone beyond, further than you can imagine. You need muscles, but you can manage without thumbs.'

'Do you do it with Vinciane?' Achille asks, jealous, jealous too of people flying, even a little.

'No,' says Boffi. 'Not with her. Like the signs used to say, "No jitterbugging", in case you broke the lights. Vinciane's jelly outside but stiff inside. It's all things she can do, and things you can't.'

'At least she's not a country or a class,' says Achille. 'Or sexual – that's what you're supposed to know about, and read in books.'

'No, she's none of those,' says Boffi. 'She is herself, not a meander or a reminiscence. Anyway, I'm telling you about myself, that you've invaded so decisively. The dance-hall was my life. The pool hall – was my ruin. You win, you lose, and then you're in the net – except ... the net is yours. A trident too. You have to learn diplomacy, fencing, covering-up. I tried to learn: those big universities – Rome, San Paolo – they must have a course, a parchment too, in doing bad. We are so many.... But, I never found the rooms where something pertinent was taking place. All those lovely people, knowing where to go, oh, the well-kept teeth, the ordered talk – from room to room, even a bus ride up the hill.... There, the Chair of Immortality Studies. Alongside – Mortality. How hard, to transfer from Mortality to the shiny one....' His eyes are travelling far away, under a sizzling sun.... 'Once, I won a chair of Puzzles. I sat silent, speechless, nothing but questions in my head, until the guys sat there on some committee laughed, gave me the job. I never signed for it – I couldn't find the room. That's why the sages went to mountaintops or grottoes – you only can be wise living on your own. No exams, no laurel wreaths.'

'That's a wise thing to say,' says Achille. 'Though I always ask, "If you're a sage, what'd you expect from being wise?"'

'I know what they say,' says Boffi. '"You don't need pay anyone for their advice."'

'More or less, that's so,' says Achille. 'Does it mean I'm wise or not, to ask the question then?'

'I've done research,' says Boffi, quite aggressive. 'The only things possible without thumbs is dance and sex. No pool. No weapons. My sex urge is so slow, it's more a put-put than a drive. I cannot hold a knife or wave a club....'

'You're right,' says Achille. 'I regret. There's nothing else. Not even planting trees. But – there remains the slide trombone – with training, it seems possible.'

'Just mock,' says Boffi. 'I shall do the same. Now, if you have a succinct message, say it now. Me? – I've burnt your boat, and mine, back home – I'm a free agent, radical, you'd say. Be very watchful of me, Achille....'

'I've said it all,' Achille says. 'Everything I have discovered. Walking the byways. If I'm a sage, no one will listen – that's the test.'

'Long ago, that's so,' says Boffi. 'Understand that, and you understand yourself. But I'm the warrior.Your friend today, your ally tomorrow; the next day – I'll cut you.'

'It's mafia, Boffi,' Achille says. 'Money and land. Those are your demanding friends.'

'Exactly,' Boffi says. 'The motor. We are the pistons. You're our pavement artist, Achille, except there's feet all over you, your picture too. Obliterated – as you'd want.'

There's comprehension between those two: hard to call it empathy. Or friendship. They need to prove who's the top animal – a test of aggressiveness, perhaps.

'Here's what Vinciane would say,' says Boffi, unhooking from the wall a pike. 'Have done with doubt. A life in which you lose – it's not worth anything. Throw it away, hope you'll be recycled – leave a sting, maybe a well-tuned organ, some part scarcely used, one careful owner....'

Holding the pike in both his mutilated hands, Boffi lunges – too high up the body, Achille's well-read in the legends.... 'Feet, Boffi, feet!' – but of course, Boffi is ignorant, no graduation, no degree, and Achille parries with the kris – a cut across the forehead, and Boffi's blinded with his blood.

'A nose, a nose!' shouts Achille, like a shark alert for wounds – 'A double cross? Across the eyes and down the face? A pair of lips, an amputation – inflated, cushions for divans, and you'd eat without them like a monster – gnam, gnam...!' and he laughs, 'A pair of ears like the Americans took and threaded like dried apricots? A scalp? A severed head?'

'Pax!' shouts Boffi. 'I give you best. But hark! Listen to your threats! You are the bully boy, the vandal. Not brothers beneath the skin – we're primitives. You disgust me, Achille....'

'Oh,' says Achille. 'It's just ill wind. Mine, everybody's. Here, let me mop you up. It's notorious – old sages with their sticks and stones – strike out... Nothing's intended, nothing permanent....'

The harm is done, the mask is off.

Or – bad guys are warned. Justice is done....

*

'Achille is feisty,' says Vinciane. 'I loved Boffi – but he's been cut down. Will he sprout again, or prove a rotten tree? A poplar, or a cypress – keeping the form, but with dead arms....'

'I trusted Achille,' says Solène. 'But he's a rowdy, a roisterer. Those think only of themselves....'

'I want a buccaneer – not an ancient, a keeper of the animals....' says Vinciane – 'Let's turn around, switch friends, Solène.... Not flood, but heat will come – our destiny's in caves and bunkers....'

'Oh, it's clear, Vinciane,' Solène says. 'The water cure – comes, leaves no hope. A struggle, each with all, the world fried and boiled, chilled and flayed... Boffi's a loser – I need a realist, who'll show me how to live on almost nothing, but with constant change.... There is a new disease, brought on by heat, you lose agility, you're not so dextrous – it's true, some climb the walls on wheels, and train to run like jaguars, but it's useless, it's a spectacle ... there's isolated champions, athletic freaks, the rest of us is blocked, the blood no longer circulates, we cannot stand or walk, the sun clots us, takes our suppleness away....'

'The future's difficult, it's true, Solène,' says Vinciane, 'but you are wrong. There are no champions left, we've reached the limit, and we live a hundred years, but it is dull, all is routine, we'll have exposed ourselves for all our lives, inventing nothing, fighting long battles in no war.... *Accidie* and mediocrity, and pointless torturings....'

'We need more people,' says Solène. 'We're all too much alike; now Boffi's lost his thumbs, his power, and Achille shows he still has his. Time still has infinities to run. Custom and overthrow – neither signify, it all turns round and back. It's tossing of the dice.

'You remember, Vinciane ... we must have been in the same school – about Achille, and how the sea came round the cape of a sudden, and the sun looked over the mountain's rim ... but he was gone. No one to fight for us. How ominous it all sounds now. I'll never win my case and get my rights. I must have made an error somewhere, because the law is always right. It's that they don't tell you how it works, you make mistakes, take a revenge somehow – of course, you're in the wrong.'

'Not the same school, Solène,' says Vinciane. 'The same system, though. All about passing time, keeping it simple, keeping supple,' and she touches Solène's hand.

'No, no, Vinciane,' says Solène. 'No more relationships, there's too much to remember in each one. It's like a book of poems, we all did all of them at school. That was the past, and naturally, it stopped. Achille was much overrated. A narcissist. I never even told him – the guy on the island who did me wrong, and what I'd do to pay him back.'

'Don't go on, Solène,' says Vinciane. 'Father, brother, lover – they all can knock you down. Poor Boffi, though – they won't let him back to Erevan. He's in exile now, like us, our planned salvation all a pretext, all a fix. We'd never get the craft down to the sea, and stock it up. There's casinos all along the coast, and tankers filling up – where would we fit?'

*

'Yolande is coming,' Achille says. 'She'll fix my Diaries. Boffi – can be my bodyguard. Once you start to slice – it never finishes.... It's paradoxical: if you're large enough to need protection, the stronger you are, the bigger army that you need.... Boffi can forage – that will do for me as well.'

'What can happen every day?' asks Vinciane, amused, 'that becomes diary?'

'Not that, of course,' Achille says. 'Investigations. Propositions – then a flight of fancy, into the woods. Escape and enlightenment.'

'Who will read it?' asks Solène. 'The story of the last people on the earth – it should be interesting. Even if we aren't nice guys....'

'That doesn't matter,' Boffi says. 'You think of all the things they did, with hope, conviction. It's that that makes you cry – nothing personal at all. Endeavour, and vanity. Pathos. Like the cat – alive somewhere, dead too.'

'Yolande cuts a furrow,' says Solène. 'Seeded with salt from her own underarms.'

'She's here to watch philosophy, done as I do it,' says Achille: 'You need appreciate the prose, the poems, the poetic prose as well.'

'This crook Boffi stole my tarot', says Yolande. 'I always bring it with me. What does he want with it?'

'What do you want with it?' Achille asks. 'You came to study me and straighten out my thoughts.'

'Oh, there'll be time for that,' says Yolande. 'You who live in religious lands, and plan religious things – arks, Armageddons – you need some magic to whisk you all along. Some foresight too. All the sand here, not a camel to be seen.'

'It's not at all like that,' says Solène. 'Most of the world is crag or desert, and the rest is sea.... All of it, or none, is biblical, I guess.'

'And what does Vinciane do here?' asks Yolande.

'She wanted fun. She organises – naturally, she sought us out. I dare say she's disappointed,' Achille says. 'Especially now you've come along, Yolande.'

'She's a lovely person,' says Yolande. 'She deserves better. Much much better – not just from you, though that's a start, but from her destiny as well. Her story – growing up in Projects, address "One, Death Row" ... it's an important testimony. And the struggles she's been in.... All the creatives she grew up with....'

'She moves along,' says Achille. 'Doesn't dwell.'

'My job too – is not to dwell,' says Yolande. 'But find jewels lying in the grass, and smuggle them back home.'

'Oh,' Achille says, 'I don't do this for money. I know how slow it is to get a cheque, besides, I don't believe in banks. I'm a witness, witnessing before the fact – the prophets do that, even not even quite modest people can....'

*

'I loved Boffi when he was piratical,' says Vinciane. 'His swagger, though, it got cut off. And now here's Yolande – is there fun there? Or more puff and shout?'

Later, much later, Vinciane says, 'Yolande, you know I'm with Solène? She's a rough sort, but the fun is ever hard to find.'

'You live here,' Yolande says. 'With extreme sacrifice....
And there's no animals, no other soul around.' She moulds her
hand round Vinciane's shoulder – she hopes it could mean
anything, seduction or pity, maybe both.

'Oh, there are little animals,' says Vinciane. 'Almost you
can't see them, for they creep and hide from you. They think
you're crap. Then there's enormous ones, like Axminster, or a
moquette – hectares, that lie inert – those carbuncles that you
see – they burst as flowers.... Then there's the villages and
towns you can't quite espy from here.'

'I know,' says Yolande. 'It's terrible, and it may soon be
gone.'

It's tiring to resist her arm, and Vinciane draws up close. She
sees a notebook, by Yolande, 'The Desert Sage'.

'Who are you here for, Yolande?' she asks. 'What do you
think our bodies are for?'

'I hadn't really thought,' says Yolande. 'Having babies, some
of us. Sex, some more of us, like going to war. Dying, just about
everyone, and most of those you've known by now.'

'And feelings, Yolande?' Vinciane goes on. 'We few, we
have a lot of them. The more you talk about them, the more
ordinary they appear.'

'Oh, you're not ordinary,' Yolande says, decidedly. 'None of
you. But all together, you are just a bunch.... Gathered, plucked,
cut off. Bodies and feelings, it's hard not to have them, though
we should be better off ignoring them, and better still if we
could put them in a pattern book, so'd they'd not seem odd – but
then, what'd you do with them? It doesn't make a difference,
none of it. Babies and war – they do. The rest you manage with
a lawyer at the most – Solène knows. Law – it lasts you all your
fleeting life.'

'You're cool, Yolande,' says Vinciane. 'I don't mean hip, if
you had read back that far. I mean – you don't have answers.'

'It doesn't come into my line,' says Yolande.

'I'd love to have a fling, Yolande,' says Vinciane, pulling away, 'But I don't like you much.'

'It's of no account,' says Yolande. 'Concentrate on the design.'

'I look at Achille, Boffi, and I think – 'they're both a little mutilated,' says Vinciane. 'But I'm not sure that being whole has any merit. All those deaths, for Achilles; money of dead people.... Boffi cut up because he has a dodgy past....'

'And present too,' says Yolande, remembering her tarot cards were took.

'Wholeness,' Yolande goes on, ponderously. 'It's a little like Achille's nothingness – a venerable idea I'm sure and one we'll soon see from within – but, wholeness: doesn't it bring to mind a hole?'

'Things can be there even if they are invisible,' says Vinciane. 'Look at the sand and scrub, the squares of someone's ruin, they always take the blocks away when someone dies....'

'What things, for instance, Vinciane?' asks Yolande.

'I hate it all,' says Vinciane, turning wildly. 'The place, the questions, people too.'

'It's "*huis clos*", dear,' says Yolande.

Vinciane hears her say 'wee Chloe' – yes, that would be worse, the mite might have died, or caught the pox, been raped, or turned against.

'There's oceans of peoples just a walk away,' Yolande insists. 'The patterns are not infinite.'

'And Achille, is he a jewel, a prophet?' asks Vinciane, not caring much.

'Oh, prophet!' Yolande laughs. 'Beware – that's fighting talk. He makes a contemplation of what it all has meant.... Suppose it's over – what'll it have meant, our history? Then, when it comes to it, what do you say, and who's to say it? A common woman? Philosopher, king, a murderer?'

'You could say "goodbye",' says Vinciane.

*

'Here's Isabelle,' says Yolande, pushing her forward: she's a tall horse. Elegant and well-financed, a good smell about her and not much to say. 'She takes notes from my notes,' Yolande says.

'I do run on when I'm in touch with genius. And – she organises big events, like when we leave.'

'How do you all do?' says Isabelle, laughing, showing some good teeth. It's civilisation, hers, that one thought had died.

'Our team,' says Yolande, 'sits on this bench. Next to me now, Vinciane, Solène there on the end – make Isabelle feel quite at home, if that is where she wants....'

'When you go, when you leave, and when we all go, can we have poppers, please,' says Vinciane. 'I've always wondered what they are....Balloons: and round us – white silk sashes: in our hair, forget-me-nots, love-in-a-mist, and love-lies-bleeding too. It must go with a bang – no fire, no guy, that is discrimination, but all the rest – marshmallows, jelly in hipbaths....'

'A real-send-off, Vinciane?' says Achille, patronising.

'Everything,' says Vinciane. 'The best.'

*

'Snacks,' says Isabelle: 'And something quite high end – a play, an opera.'

'A music-hall, a circus, a cabaret, a stand-up....' says Solène.

'There's only us,' says Boffi. 'We can't act and clap ourselves. I'm embarrassed, singing and climbing ropes, you need full hands for both.'

'It must be original, and unrepeatable,' says Yolande.

'Really, at the end, God should be there to wrap it up,' Achille says, maybe serious, but the others laugh.

'Oh, there'll be stand-ins,' says Isabelle. 'He has many semblances, it says. There's lists of them, but they stop you having a good time.'

'A solemn good time – usually that's sex,' says Vinciane. 'But ... there's how long, and what to do – then, what's to expect? – maybe a boiling mud or methane, liquid amber – lava – quite undignified.... Stuck eternally in a pose....'

'Sex or sects, Vinciane?' asks Yolande. 'We mustn't seem like freaks who gather on some peak to hear a guru forecast that the world will end: it won't, and then you shuffle off, relieved. Perhaps – some disappointment. Ours must be subtle and low key.'

'Excess,' says Achille. 'What's needed is excess. A blow-out. Regret too. Show life as it should, without the fachos and the mean, no crooks, not even Boffi....'

'Someone is coming who will check you out – body and mind,' says Yolande. 'Like they do before an electrocution.'

'No,' says Achille. 'We shall go with the people, like them, as they do, no special care. Dry leaves, on the pile.'

*

'Yolande diminishes us,' Vinciane tells Achille. 'We can't be organised. We are an epic, heroes and heroines and backsliders, ogres along the way. We are what we are to do: the rest, the universe, it doesn't count.'

To Yolande she says, 'Don't mess with us – we all come from cities burned, our brothers, sisters, children – they aren't here, been stood against the wall, stifled in cellars, hunted with machetes ... there's few left of us; don't write the end, and don't plan living on. We're Congolese, Yolande, too remote for you to notice, so don't be trivial, my dear....'

'Oh no, Vinciane,' says Yolande, boiling up. 'It's me that's trivial, you've no proportion if you don't see that.'

They face off.

'I like that, Yolande,' says Vinciane, softening.

'You'll maybe like my friend Fleur still more,' says Yolande. 'She's on her way.'

'You came down the steps, like it's "*dansons la capucine, Ma patrie est la faim la misère et l'amour*",' Vinciane says.

Vinciane is smitten: not many speak with her as if they're intimate.

*

Yolande sees Fleur, far off – she's small, and when she's near, she is still small. 'I hope you brought your knitting, Fleur,' she says, and they both laugh.

'Achille's the hardest one – he doesn't want to be prepared,' says Yolande.

'Could it have been different?' asks Fleur.

'Totally. And probably not,' says Yolande. 'Achille has no blame, except for what he's done. All the rest – is broken stuff, washed to the shore – a lot of it is carcasses. Who's fault...?'

'Oh, I could tell you,' says Isabelle. 'There's not much point. We'll have our good time here, and then we'll maybe see....'

'Yolande must fix up Achille's thoughts,' says Fleur. 'It's rather menial....'

'Oh, no one would read them, even if they could,' says Yolande. 'They'll read my notes – they're full of life – if Vinciane agrees, they're full of fun as well....'

There's a commotion: Boffi says, 'I'm not going with you lot! I'm cut off here, I'm cut off from my friends in Erevan – the mad idea, as if to build an ark would save us from the heat, the famine too....'

'It's solidarity,' says Fleur. 'We all have work, it hurts to give it up, but still, there is a larger reckoning....'

'Not me,' says Boffi. 'I never sign, and now – look at my hand, I can't.'

'I hear the whisper of a whine,' says Fleur, taking sharp plastic needles from her bag. 'A party's coming, Boffi – be ready to enjoy, and even be a pig, if that comes natural....'

*

'Boffi's lived too hard,' Fleur tells Yolande. 'He's bewildered. He'll walk though whatever door is opened, like an insect caught in a room, changing its mind.... Achille though – he could last another century. He says – "Where did the workers go? Where is the stagnation, the feudal remnants? Augean stables to be cleaned, so everybody starts together, same perspectives, same struggles.... I'm on my own, people all agree with me and no one listens, I don't offend, but.... Who are these awful people, bland and racist, censorious and passive ... self-indulgent and warlike.... People knowing how their empires were all wrong, and yet go on and on, can't stop, picky-pick, rhodomontade, a tic like pig-sticking in your sleep....

'I tell him, it's too bad, as he keeps on navigating on the deep.'

'You can't sail an ark,' says Yolande.

'You'll have helmsmen up there anyway, and officers. They'll do a number,' says Isabelle. 'Maybe there's a lady does that thing with pigeons. Doves.'

'Achille is lucky,' says Yolande. 'He speaks to nothing and for nobody. His world has gone, more ferocious than he wanted to believe. Now there's another – he can't see to set a foot on it.'

'He says his favourite title, his inspiration – is "One step forward, two steps back", that's three steps, and so many someones' toes,' says Fleur. 'Mostly you think you could set things right, going back, into the past – he sees his inadequacy there as well. Never lets it go, always fumbling at his memories. He's a case. I'll leave it so.

'You're right. It's his eyes. They could count the sheep, but now – there's one that's dim, another might explode. The legs and arms are good – he can take walks up on the ridges, where he's very small, almost invisible from below, where Yves ended his existence.... Some people have enthusiasms – the revolution beckons and it sits you on its back, and flies with you, a distance. Your accommodation's left behind. Achille held fast, on to a stump – was never lifted up.'

'Well, that's all of us,' says Isabelle. 'Accounted for. I'll get ready with the party. There's just Solène – her grievance, the judgment. Should we wait for that?'

'You must make them satisfied, Isabelle,' says Yolande. 'Not make them want to stay, no sorrow, and no doggy-bag. Conclude – then finish! Eat everything, throw the plates in the fountain. Then *"Elle s'en va sans rien dire"* – that's the action, sung, not a stage direction. No cheating, no lingering.'

'Solène's only interested in the judgment now,' says Fleur. 'Although, the land – if she had it, what use would it be? She's no will to dig.'

'I love parties,' says Vinciane, 'but I don't want this one to end. There's so much to start to do.... This one – will end them all.'

'Resign yourself, Vinciane,' says Yolande. 'If you were a miner, you'd be quite anonymous, forced to live underground, and when your cage went up, at the last, there'd still be tons of coal left untouched at the face.'

'That's so,' says Achille. 'My father wasn't a miner, but he vanished just as if he was.'

'It's good you know your time is up, Achille,' says Yolande. 'But bad that you've no word on what there was and what you saw. Still less on what you tried to do....'

'You can't have less than less,' Achille says.

'Of course you can,' says Yolande. 'First principle.'

*

'Well?' says Solène, angrily to Yolande. 'Don't I get to leave a poem? A comment on everything, at the least?'

'Who told you about the poems?' Yolande asks.'I bet it was Vinciane – she's no reserve.'

'Who cares anyway?' shouts Solène, much put out. 'Who'll read them? Just you three? And then?'

'Oh, at this point, there are so many questions,' says Yolande, soothing and retreating. 'We didn't ask you, as we thought you'd have some island thing you'd fix up for yourself, want to leave so, ritualised, dedicated to who knows....'

'Feathers and a fishbone?' asks Solène, more angry still.

'It was delicacy on our part,' says Yolande. 'Respect for a different culture. Besides, we didn't ask everyone, not Achille – he's said it all already for himself. And Boffi ... well! Poetry...!'

'You're wrong,' says Solène. 'All our language came from there, Armenia, and then fanned out – it must have come up through Iran, borne on by Sakas, then to Erevan, that was the fountainhead ... those epics....'

'Oh, there isn't room for those,' says Yolande. 'It must be pithy, and in the local tongue. It's really up to Isabelle, that part.... And anyway, whoever reads them will have done so now. Somewhere there's someone, reading – look at the internet – it puts a garland round the earth before you've thought, and then you're answered back, and so for sure whoever's interested will comment on....'

'And no one has?' asks Solène. 'Not even insults...? I hope your eyes boil in your heads,' she adds, more quietly.

A pacifying silence falls.

Yolande asks Fleur, 'Pécine? I thought she'd come and pass the stuff around?'

'She has a newish cavalier,' says Fleur. 'He'll maybe ride her off, into the sunset. It's just us, I fear, for our good time. The pity is, there isn't much to eat, we mustn't kill the birds, the snakes and toads, or even scrape the cardamine from ancient rocks.... We hadn't thought it through....'

'Oh, hunger makes the head spin fast,' says Isabelle. 'Too bad about Pécine – she's a wizard on the musette – the sexiest of instruments, I find. Now, a masque is what we need, with swans.'

'They'll pull the cart?' asks Fleur. 'Who'll ride in it?' She knows she's Isabelle's favourite –

'And after, we can eat the swans,' says Vinciane. 'What difference is there, an hour or so – we may as well....'

'We never know the hour,' says Yolande sternly. 'It could be minutes, centuries – the time's not what's on our wrists.... Our farewell is symbolic....'

'Besides, this is a mountain – no swans up here,' says Fleur.

'Maybe Achille could bring some in,' says Vinciane. 'He's nothing else that's left to do....'

'Achille's the one who set it down,' says Yolande. 'The Master. That we've reached the end. And we – the most exotic, most refined, of all the flowers. A chaplet, the wreath they throw into the sea. That's our last scene. Achille, though – if anyone has said their all, it's him.'

'He could sing the song,' says Isabelle. 'The swan song. I'm sure he has one ready cooked.'

'Of course,' says Yolande, laughing. 'Achille could pull the cart. He already has his chronicler, his archive. His life lived out. He's had his say abundantly. There's always Boffis round – their muscles made the planet whirl. They're useful, but lack nobility. Achille could do the ultimate, be the sacrifice. Besides, what difference does it make – an hour, a day or so?'

She calls to Solène, 'You know about that – you call it "long pig". I've read about it, and respect what you do, so long as it's embedded in the past, your culture. Your normal. Naturally, to me it is abhorrent. But there it is....'

'My island was a part of France, integral and documented,' says Solène, caught off guard.

'Everyone has French names, the whole continent,' says Isabelle. 'We *Franj*. Franks. Even in the underwater parts. You'd say the cultural cordial's quite diluted.'

'I expect down there they all have two,' says Yolande. 'Names. One for the spirits and the shamans, that you mustn't say, and one for writing down. The best ethnographers were French: they had good times! Rampaging, looting – and the sex!'

*

'There's a roast being planned, Achille,' says Boffi. 'With garnish.'

'I know we're at that point, Boffi,' says Achille. 'But there must be someone holding back, someone not traipsing down the path.... Someone who plans to stay, enjoy the spaces, inspiring in the ruins, collecting marbles.... Can it be scientists? – surely, they're too set, they almost all point north into the chill, except the broken ones. No, I believe them: and the moralists, the empty-heads as well – enough, enough, they say. It's finished. Assez vu.... You, Boffi though – you've much left to do, your handicap needs mastering....'

'I follow what I can't resist,' says Boffi. 'That's me. Second thoughts, Achille. That's you, your weakness. Almost everyone's like you – they scribble, scribble in the casket. How tempting it must be! Like frogspawn, a bubbly gel – that's languages! Billiard balls of words – you drive them up and down, and some you pot, and some will metamorphose, jellify, and croak and hop.... You can't think "stop!"'

'The world ends: in the end there too must be the Word. I think the word's "enough". In the beginning it was "action".

Now, "curtain", "in the can", "see you tomorrow on another rock"....'

'You're lyrical, dear Boffi,' Achille says. 'Wasn't it "beginners!" first? – and now it's time to take their corpses off. What isn't done, not properly – is the critique, a summing up, appraisal. Could it just stop, without the chrism of a word, silently ... a planet, ploff! – off like a star...'

'Of course it can,' says Boffi, though that's not what he wants, not now, not yet.

'I know these things, Achille,' says Boffi. 'Believe me, you're not safe – within the big fall-down, there's lots of little ones, unseen, uncounted. These ladies want to honour you, they want a party, and the best for them is elegy. They want their hour, their day – they feel it's owed, the great fear is they could exit, never having sung their song.... It's best for them that you are off the stage.'

'You, Boffi,' Achille says, 'are more exposed than me.... Your friends ... will find you anywhere, forgetting the original, the sin that was a blink, a blank. A nothing.... An order to forestall the wrath, a bill unpaid.... Our handy ark... Every shortfall's a betrayal, there's blame for everything that doesn't turn out right. They'll take it out on you for what you could not avoid....'

And yet, for Achille, Boffi is indestructible – he's the demon on the wall, for the moment held by a leash of service. 'When I'm gone,' Achille thinks, 'Boffi will have everything. I stood for nothing, nothing but my next thought – but he's primed, a culverin ready for its spew....'

*

They watch the sun – it sets, maybe a little slow. It's very red. It's cold, quite uncommon; though it's true, they haven't eaten for some days: there's the party coming, but no food. On the mountain, there's no water, and no fuel – 'It's like an ark had left us here,' says Fleur. 'Except there's no animals to groom, already gobbling each other up....'

The valley – it looks full, but mist, or water? The humans huddle. 'Don't go down.'

'It will have to end,' says Achille, 'when there's nothing left to sing, and no more music on the stands. So, it doesn't matter if you end as Tosca or as Lancelot – but you must do it well.'

The others are too chilled to question this. They don't much care. If you're neither Lancelot nor a Tosca – what does it matter anyway?

'You can't ask that,' says Achille. 'Look where that left Hugo, Zenia, and Mirko.... You have to play it out ... you can't just quit...'

'Those three, Fleur, Isabelle and Yolande, are united,' Boffi says. 'A gymnastics, a party, a story. That's what they represent. It could last a thousand years. You must divide them, Achille. Charm. Lure one to your side.... The fates are three – split one off, they're powerless, and you can write the script. They wouldn't kill you, but you're better dead.'

'You're right,' says Achille. 'That would preserve us, you as well. But – no! There is no resonance, it's cheap and tactical. There is no echo, I'd gain no stature, it's a shallow trick....'

*

They're all helping – building the cart, even Solène, Vinciane has found oak leaves, Boffi improvises wheels.... There are no swans.

Achille goes hop and skip down the mountain. The valley's clear. He joins a column moving along. Free at last?

'Are these the dead?' he asks, looking for Yves and the rest. There's laughter.

'We couldn't wait,' says Giselda. 'We weren't welcome, so we're looking for a place that wants us. Better than being sent back. Onward, onward,' she shouts. '*Vperod, avanti!*'

Achille joins them as they trudge. He fits in perfectly.

'It's a great idea,' says Achille, 'but there's not much time....'

'Time isn't on our minds,' says Giselda, striding along.

'You're all so different, maybe one place won't fit....' says Achille, having to trot.... 'And perhaps it's not a right place we need, it's people.... Class too, since no one has anything to lug along: we're used to poverty and being screwed.... These people come from scrabble; hard jobs no one else wants. Suppose we don't fit, can't work when we get there....'

'See that other column, Achille?' Giselda asks. 'Alongside.'

There's dust, thick enough to be mist. Maybe those are feet beneath, footcloths? – and above, antlers? Branches? '*Those* are the dead. You could go along with them.'

Silence. Then, 'Who are we, Giselda?' Achille asks.

'I think you know, Achille,' she says. 'Of course, there's lots who'd never asked, like you they didn't know, not the now and what was coming, catastrophe or hardship arrived, or threatened – quite fortuitous. And now – I'm sure they know. What they don't know, no one does, is how the column keeps together, since there's no destination and no food. Better not make too much noise. Save your breath, Achille,' and he does.

'We all have an innocent air,' he says, filling a space. 'They say, when the animals have gone, we go too. The column's made of all of us who've lost their habitat. Can we stop somewhere? Anywhere?'

Giselda doesn't respond.

*

'I'm an odd and sod,' Achille says, after a pause. 'I have all the people that I know, expecting me, just a few days march behind. For me, this is a metaphor. When I want, I can go back.'

'Yes, of course,' Giselda says.

They share the same pace, stay more or less together, though each has much varied company, inconsequential chat. Giselda tells him, 'We all think bad things are some misfortune, we don't feel we've been singled out: if only we could explain ourselves to someone, we could all go back....'

'Back to a home you don't remember?' Achille says. 'That you'd longed to leave? If you've a document, it only gives a name, and a single name to everything you are. You can't say you're an onion. Nor a toolbox – things useful and not, broken or unused.... You must keep it simple!' And he laughs.

'It may be true, Achille,' says Giselda. 'You've made yourself protection: a bland accent, colour, origin, and habits, wants, all that. You've made yourself anonymous, and kept out the way of most misfortunes – probably that is why you are not liked. Telling people the world will stop, in the middle of their lives – that doesn't help.'

'I'd not have thought it caused reaction,' says Achille: 'My info was well founded. Info's the balk that stops you falling down, it keeps you on the table.... But – I thought that was all over, the columns, the walking....'

'I couldn't go on living in the old way,' says Giselda. 'Nothing good arrived. So many people round you disappear, you don't know where you are, you lose your landscape. It's best be on the move, even if you're in a group like this. There's lots like me, who've seen misfortune all around, and lots who just are on the move. Better march on than be immobile, a target.

'See – everything that's ever been is present now, even if some of it is shabby and distorted – the caves, the ruins, the frescoes – it's all exposed, all deciphered. We are all here together, living, dead, the ancient, named and nameless, though we don't hear them, each person, singly: we hear them in the choruses: brigands, peasants, men-at-arms, seamstresses, like in the operas.'

'Operas aren't like that now,' says Achille. 'But – it's true. Everything is inventoried. You can see everything in the sea, all the fish, the wrecks, the sunken stuff ... you don't need opera. Anyway, there's actors ready to make melodrama everywhere.... You're right, everything is transparent, everything is present. It's not a good sign. The living and the dead – they are the same....'

'Do you think a song would help us along – all of us?' Giselda asks.

'There's good choruses,' Achille says. 'The masquerade, the one about the roses, but you need know the conventions, if not the words.... Most people here don't know the tunes, they aren't prepared to sing ... the scales aren't in their tradition....'

'Your life,' says Giselda. 'You describe it as all about rules and values – but round you, there weren't any. That's why you're here. For you, it's all seemed trivial.'

'That's what Boffi says,' says Achille. 'That I make it all up as I run on. But there, everybody does. We lived off each others' bones – Solène, Yolande and all the rest. Except Vinciane, who has no hunger ... she's deeper than us, she wants pleasure, that's the hardest thing to find.... We feed on each other, like hyenas....'

'It doesn't sound so terrible,' says Giselda. 'There's people here bombed by their own side, people sold by their parents and their lovers, or thrown out into the street by them.... Droughts and floods – and locusts – that, you can handle, you've never thought of the worse things.

'Probably there's lots of columns like this one; it's better than the tents, though it seems harder....'

'Do we stop and sleep?' asks Achille.

'And lie together hugger-mugger?' Giselda laughs. 'No! On we go! There's urgency – you're a philosopher, Achille, you must have a message – putting things in order, I don't suppose you've answers, but you could lay the questions out....'

Achille laughs, 'Oh no, I don't do philosophy like that.'

'We mustn't stop,' Giselda says. 'You have to watch out for marauders – and be afraid. It takes courage to plod on, but courage is a part of fear. You're not brave, Achille – you're stupid. If you'd been a warrior, you'd have faced them down, your friends – instead, you came down here – not yet afraid, or not enough.'

*

'Giselda,' Achille says. 'I'm dropping out.'

She's reluctant, but they go back, together.

'This is Giselda,' Achille says. 'We did a stretch together in the column – the displaced, the seekers. Animals get resettled – we were tramping on, it seemed for years.'

'Yes,' Giselda says, intimidated by all the others. 'It was years.'

'Giselda's had a life,' Achille says. 'It didn't suit. We should help her start again....'

'Those refugees,' says Yolande. 'And all the rest – they're magnets, they drag up the fluff – they're bound to stop and sink, and then they're wrecks, they pave the ocean floor....'

'To start again?' asks Vinciane. 'Giselda, our lives are finishing; we give ourselves another coat of carmine or citrine, a toad's jewel for the brow.... How can we start to start again, explain our musics, tell where our beliefs became a disbelief...?'

'I'd have walked on,' Giselda says. 'Except the space is dwindling. There's this mountain, and the valley – but beyond, there are only deserts, and the melts, and bombed-out territories and scrub, many places you can't go, and walls and fences – as you know. There's fuss about the walls – but they are not where you would want to go – they pass through wastes, ravines – flat on the map, but in the real, they rise and fall quite mindlessly....'

'Deserted villages,' says Yolande. 'That's where you guys can go – they rock with inspiration and the outline of your room is pencilled in....'

*

'We are the tribe,' Giselda says, 'waiting for the world to end. Achille – you aren't the good, but you're benevolent, a moon, a night – a tiny light up high, your single eye, a dark wing over everything.... Boffi – you aren't the bad, or else we wouldn't keep you here – but you're a kind of mischief imp, who fixes things and has them fall apart as you try to use....'

'If there's no record, no one to come after, no writing or no memory, no tale – there is no good and bad,' says Vinciane, making a duo. 'So – I'm the animal you hunt and when you catch me – I'm your sister, or I'm bathed in moonlight and the drops falling from my hair are progeny....'

'Enough!' shouts Yolande. 'We don't do hunting here, there are no animals of decent size, just mucus blobs and scuttling things.... It's all derivative, false cosmologies: lies, Achille, and you are neither celestial nor chief....'

'I'll be the priestess of you all,' says Isabelle. 'Face-painting, braiding hair and stretching lips – a stick through nose and ears, as you all want, except I need your offerings – a sacrifice, a joint, grilled with herbs and plantains ... a smoke....'

'Tribes like us – there's been a quantity that die of hunger, and the fights that follow when the food is scarce,' says Fleur. 'Except – our food's not scarce, it's non-existent....'

'We must prepare,' Giselda says. 'Prepare for death, and hope it comes from cataclysm as we're told. The world is full of people drawing back, to isolation or in projects to survive. The

ark was foolish, but there's thousands taking refuge in the
jungles, in the sea, in aluminium domes, in prayer in the cities,
or in meditation.... We have no resource, no guide....'

'Cage fighting too,' says Fleur, pressing ahead. 'That's best
of all, it's good for you, it helps you concentrate.'

'You need a simulator,' says Giselda. 'To prepare you all.'

'They're too complicated,' Boffi says. 'We had one in Erevan
– to show us what we'd be without the genocide and no
diaspora: where we'd fit in, and where we'd reach the sea.'

'Oh, it's easy,' says Giselda. 'In my real life, I used to make
them....'

And she shapes a shell, puts the end of – maybe it's a
birchbark – in a little box –

'Yes, it's birchbark,' she says. 'It's for Russians specially –
but it works for anyone. It's where you started from, where there
were once trees.'

Achille goes first into Giselda's simulator – it's swimming,
underneath the sea – in a glass ark, or shipwreck. There's other
swimmers – curious, they flick away. They're breathing through
their ears. Down in holes there's spiky things that wait for lunch
for years. 'Learn from them, Achille,' Giselda shouts. 'You're
clumsy, you've not the shape to hunt.'

'It's terrible,' Achille says. 'There's a bigger world down
here, indifferent....'

'You mustn't breathe,' Giselda says. 'You'll drown.'

City of Nets, says the sign: 'Maybe there's more danger here
than up above,' Achille thinks. 'Come harvest time ... we're all
yanked up to die – it's like the judgment day when all the graves
are opened up and we arise, in new bodies and white clothes –
except ... the fish are suffocated and clubbed, they have no
clothes, and no one cares.... It's a massacre, promiscuous....'

There is a world for everyone – 'Flying makes it all so tiny,'
says Isabelle. 'You could pin on fields and glaciers. Wear
clouds....'

Fleur doesn't much enjoy the fighting: – you find there's no feature you can replace. The noses that they stock you'd not want on your face.

Loving for Vinciane should be the easiest of universes, but she finds it cloys, there's too much spit and sweat; excess requires an effort she can't make – the only one who enjoys Giselda's toy is Boffi. Betrayal is the easiest behaviour of all – there is no punishment, it seems.

'Yield to the stronger,' Boffi says. 'And don't steal. Distrust your friends – be sure they won't trust you.'

It's Yolande who steals. Digging, painting, typing little articles. 'My! It's intricately dull,' says Yolande, 'the excavated stuff is always burnt or broke. Realism's hard – the secrets have been lost – painting feathers, wrinkles ... no one thinks to do it now. "The jargon of originality," it's a delusion. We're all born original, and yet it's clear there's nothing new. Everything is made from something else.... Pillage and loot, recycle the ideas, borrow without acknowledgment, and dig up what you never would imagine could exist....'

'Solène, Solène!' Boffi shouts. 'She must have her world, take her part, and dominate.'

'It doesn't work like that,' Giselda says. 'You're in the world already, up to your neck, and you can't change a thing – the transformation comes when you expire. Already, your trajectory's inscribed upon my tape....'

Solène's the judge. She can't decide – a punishment? What hurts adequately, and what good does it do...? Guilt, innocence? Who understands, who feels, who cares? 'It's much too difficult,' she says. 'Maybe I can confiscate some food.... Someone fiddling their scales.... Some rutabagas, maybe, undeclared....'

They've water, but no fire. 'Your gadget has a limit,' says Yolande. 'It cannot cook, or locate food.'

'I saw date palms up on the crest,' Giselda says. 'And stands of manioc. There's geysers too. The problem isn't mine, Yolande – it's your perception. Beneath your feet – there's fire. There always is.'

'No help at all,' says Yolande.

'What help could you expect?' Giselda asks.

'Your wonder-box, Giselda, brings us nothing,' says Solène. 'Rather – it shows us up: thieves and traitors? Is that how we seem? And as for food – it's like organic glue, we're seizing up. There's nothing new – the world will end, and you've not changed a thing. Maybe you'll call the column and they'll take the food you found for us – vile though it seems.'

'Oh, if I could, I would,' Giselda says. 'They are my folk: it's that there's nothing appetising here.... Your civilisation, your morality – they don't stand up to hardship or uncertainty.'

'We're nothing, Giselda, nothing in particular,' says Vinciane. 'Like you – except that we don't have a wonder-box.'

'We don't have swans,' Achille says. 'That is our difference.'

'How did you meet up, Achille?' asks Giselda. 'These people stranded here, so arrogant...?'

'Solène's island sank,' Achille says. 'My true friends thought it was hopeless staying here. They left. These people – they have no alternative. Vinciane's the sweetest of them all – if I felt I could stand some company each day – it would be her.... She doesn't want that, though.... And then there's you, of course. I feel some obligation, but there is no argument that fits a feeling. Sentiment is everywhere, but you can't know, and can't discuss.... It's all a trace, a fingerprint.

'Building the cart. That is our project: it will be magificent, if it's done, though only we shall see it. We could have people pulling, but it's demeaning, while for swans, it's a promotion. We don't have much, Giselda. We have telephones, that's it. Don't think I'm snide – they're crucial, that's how we stick together and make sense....'

'I see you all from here,' Giselda says. 'In your flesh. Though maybe I do wrong to anthropomorphise you all.'

*

'Let's stop preparing for the ceremony,' says Achille. 'Make a place for the wonder-box instead, the box of sensations, of characters. Giselda improvised – let's do it properly, let's run those strips of bark. The images are what you are, and what you face, your destined life.'

*

The Book says you can live on dates and milk. It must be camel's milk. Dates and manioc – what kind of life can live on that?

*

In the morning, Giselda's gone. Not a surprise – she wasn't liked, and she didn't like. Did she rejoin the column? How could you tell? These are strange times – people move around, shifting the weight, the gravity, as if the globe would tilt and gyre, go into an unarrestable spin, and fall ... in space, you only fall in space – except, suppose you voyage inwards nearer to the sun – heat up, flagrate, after centuries of mist, impenetrable and steamy ... or fall towards the outer edge, and freeze, diminish, heads like specks of mica, great distances of ice beneath your tiny feet....

*

Giselda's gone,' says Yolande. 'What shall we miss of her?'

'She would have become like us,' says Fleur. 'She had great muscle tone. The walking does it....'

*

'Listen everyone,' says Achille. 'Don't go down Giselda's path. It's true, each of you could be a movie, and live within philosophy – all you'd lack would be sensation. You'd react – no one would know, though we could guess – but you wouldn't feel. You'd be philosophers, know who you are in theory – but it would stop there.'

'But Giselda's life is full of feeling,' says Isabelle. 'It's terrible. She left us philosophy – we should be thankful her sensations went with her....'

'It isn't just brains, Achille,' says Solène. 'There must be bodies too, or else we'd grow like our armchairs.... Brains is just your invention, Achille, you and your mates.... That may solve your problem, but there's walking and stumbling too. And swimming – you should remember....'

'I'm sure it isn't like that,' says Achille. 'Look – we've no sodium lights – you can see the stars explode' – and they do, lying on their backs, eating the fat Jordanian dates, wondering when their turn will come, and Isabelle wishes she had paints and chipboard to make a record, and 'Oh Isabelle, you're so picky,' says Vinciane. 'There's stones and flowers – you can concoct some tints....'

No one envies them or fears, no one opens fire on them, or tries to put them in a column, take their documents or burn the huts they haven't yet set up.... But, they're not happy.

'It must be nature, not ever to be satisfied,' says Yolande. 'It's true we're terminal, all of us, as always, but there is contentment even here. It's that – Achille ... can't express it for us.'

'Achille? Too much sulking in the bothy,' says Yolande, briskly. 'Those white cotton pants and espadrilles as if he's about to take a turn along the beach. There's style all right – but far down-wind....'

'It's right you're disillusioned, Yolande. I am too,' says Achille. 'I wanted to be old Karl – leaving you the choice: a bad communism, and a good one. Up to you. If you want money, Yolande, even after all that's been written on it – we could sell each other into slavery. I could have been great. It seems to me it is too late, besides, all the possibilities, especially the good ones, have been said, digested, and rejected.'

'But Achille,' says Vinciane. 'All you've done is usher people – friends – into their grave.'

She reads a lot – '*Les moutons arrivent à fond de train, sur des échasses....* "conceited sheep at top speed" – that's us. See, Achille, that's death, how it ends, or begins. Everything that's real starts and ends, so, deaths can't exist.' She twists her whispy clothes, appeals.

'That's how you see me, Vinciane,' says Achille, much distressed. 'As the crooked shepherd, leading his lambs to the abattoir?'

'What happens in the heavens and the seas – it seems it's run beyond us,' Vinciane says. 'But the columns, and Giselda – who we've seen, socialised with too – surely we must respond to them? Is that the novelty? Or is it in the favelas of Luanda, where people live with no money, nothing at all, it seems, and everything's been stolen from them, and for ever.... And the rest, what you call palliatives, or exposés ... should we go down and take a job, maybe something not paid, to learn the rope.... Telling the truth that way ... starting with absolute disinterest...'

'We've known the truth for generations,' Achille says. 'We can't live up to it, and now, if we are worth it, worth anything at all, they will come for us....'

'There's no one visible,' says Fleur. 'Boffi won't betray where there's no gain....'

'I see peltasts with goggles, almost everywhere. They may come, carry us off, round us up. That is their job,' says Isabelle.

'Of course, they're not your sort, Isabelle,' says Boffi. 'I'll talk to them, I know the type. We've nothing that they want, and we're doing nothing that they recognise.'

'They're special soldiers,' Solène says, noting their movements down below. 'It's a line that pays quite well – except you don't last long in it, you have to live in barracks and there's many things that you can't do. Not to mention – that harassing us is no great fun.'

'Oh, fun,' says Vinciane. 'It's long ago I stopped expecting that.'

'If we were in China,' says Yolande. 'We'd all have jobs for sure.'

'We all had jobs until we came here,' Solène says. 'I was a plaintiff. And I was displaced.'

'I made an analysis,' says Yolande. 'I thought Achille did so too: the exhaustion of old things – things bourgeois and things popular; and our minds concentrating on an end that everybody said was imminent. At the end, there's plethora of artistries, each with a niche. On, on – to nesting holes in cliffs. How to confront that, and calculate the account, and see what we'd accomplished – that's what stood before the species. A reckoning ... but it wasn't quite like that. Nothing is that sudden. And we're in penury now, stuck in this lonely place.'

'It's lonely because we're each lonely, and there's inadequate kinds among us,' Fleur says. 'Solène and Boffi, naming the obvious – and Achille too ... the Master impotent. We forget – impotent once, impotent for centuries.... Why are we fooled? Most people don't even know his name, still less remember what he's said....'

'What are peltasts, Isabelle?' Solène asks. 'They sound over-dressed.'

Yolande and Fleur dress warm – they swelter – Solène's in heels and suit – she teeters.

'Look,' says Isabelle, pointing far below. 'In black, with balaclavas, like legionaries. Soldier-cops. Snipers. Knowing stuff you couldn't dream of, fearing guys we'd never met. It's the right name for them: I know, I made an application once.'

*

Being arrested spoils a party, especially if it is your last. Being beaten with loaded sticks is worse.

'It's Achille's job to save us all,' says Yolande. 'But he has a defect: doubt and stasis. Everyone! – work out a strategy that keeps us safe. It's Giselda left the trace – her box alerted everyone. It sends out waves. It makes us suspects, and subversives.'

*

'Maybe it's us,' says Solène. 'Maybe we did wrong. What do we deserve? Is what we get what we deserve exactly? A part of it? – or just what happens? If it's the last – there's nothing you can do except wait and submit. My own struggle – it's too complicated – I give it up. The law – is infinite: it started early, it will last till we're all gone. Shall I get the justice I probably don't deserve? I doubt it.'

'You don't want justice, Solène,' says Fleur. 'You want compensation.'

'So, if I don't get that, maybe I'm guilty, maybe we all are – me less than you....' Solène says.

'How can we have done wrong, Solène?' asks Yolande, irritated.

'Oh, you might have a needleshaft of perception,' Solène says. 'A glimpse of peccadillo underneath your story, repeated till it seems the truth. But it's other people usually who tell you how, and how much, you did wrong.'

'Well, I don't see it,' says Yolande. 'Giselda showed us each a challenge, and if we would survive by overcoming it.... It means nothing, naturally: everything's a test to face until it happens. Then it's instinct. We know everything that might occur by looking round, but we ignore it. Let's do what people do – escape the soldiers, go down to the column, march away, and pinch and punch Giselda for bringing it all down on us....'

'Take it all as judgment, and accept,' Fleur says. 'We've all been to school, sat at desks, had parents, it means we all have imperial pasts. We don't contribute to the looting, but we sit on sofas stuffed with it. There it is. Once on the winning side – however smart you are, and slick your innocent expression – you've much to answer for.... Colonies – they stay on us like an itch.'

'But, Fleur,' says Isabelle. 'The guys who come to beat you up – they're on the winning side, you can't say it's right you suffer so's they can have another win.'

'Is that what I said?' asks Fleur. 'Anyway, we are disarmed, we can't resist, and if we did we'd lose.'

'That doesn't help at all,' says Vinciane. 'It's up to Achille to get us out of this bad place.... I shan't offer love and peace to guys that come to do me harm – we need to make a distance between us and them.... Achille's a warrior – maybe he'll hold them off while we all run away....'

Boffi's not around. He knows it's better not to wait, prepare a speech, and talk. He knows there is no place where he cannot be found. That is the flaw.... You may not get what you deserve, but your side's been written up, your photo's in a file somewhere with all your mates, clowning with weapons, it doesn't matter what your sister suffered, it's you they'd like to catch....

Achille compromised with him, a useless deal, humiliating. In the end, poor Boffi is exposed. And on the run. Dear Boffi – if an ark could bring salvation, everyone would order one, the price would fall, the world – entirely under water always.... Catastrophe.... A genocide avoided, or playing in slow wave motion, in the bosom of the ocean.... And – wait! the literature is unreliable. It couldn't happen, never did – there'd be a get-out clause for sure.... Doing it slowly – doesn't count, could even be just war, or a defence....

For Boffi, these genocides are hard to contemplate.... He alone seems to recognise ... the design, the movement, the repetition, the build-up ... the will to exploit, the slavery, and then the will to eliminate.

Boffi in love – his affection is secure, it doesn't need live subjects, he'll be happy taking his sentiments with him, wherever he decides to go.... Achille – he turned out bad, a procrastinator ... not to mention thumbs, slicing the human into proto-animal....

The image is impressive, though – arks everywhere, bobbing, yawing; and starvation too.... This time – all saved, but then, no port, eternal rain, all drifting, or driven under sail, the oceans eaten out.... And Ararat submerged eternally.... An aimless voyaging, until we all are dead or crazed ... and must we pay the shipwrights too?

*

It's a mystery – between them, they have all human qualities there are. Each has a brain, identical – to a profane eye – to all the rest.... Perhaps Vinciane's is shaded nicer, pink and yellow.... But.... they don't, singly or together, not even adding Achille, who has a hero's name, tall body, self-conviction, reading of tomes ... they don't seem able to solve the puzzle of extinction: not their own by lassitude and nature, nor of everyone's, by explosion, collision, or a conflagration.

'Author, author' – no one cries.

It's strange: all organic stuff – it ends. Relationships, ideas, a voyage, even hair-shirts go matted, brittle, unwearable, you'd say.

*

'Come, shining prince!' says Vinciane, mussing up Achille's hair. 'Our champion! Take your tombak shield, chased with racemes, and "Spare me"s!' circling round the rim: you only need to spar and fence ... but make the bad things go away,' and she ogles Achille, although she finds him frigid, strange. Love, they say, you can bring to anyone. Often, it's disappointing.

'You can't expect extraordinary force from me,' Achille says. 'I could have been a humanist – or humanitarian. Everybody is. Quite unavailing. Or a communist – no one is, and all those countries disappeared, no fence is left. I chose not to be a human. Not knowing how to be immortal, I was left in the province "in between", where no one else frequents. The project, the human epic – has collapsed. An enormity. Can you grasp it? Evolution ends in disillusion. They – the bosses, chieftains – couldn't manage, steer, our little rock. Left alone, it's on automatic! Our brains are grafted on machines, and on they sail, down to the other stars, round us and around, bringing louche stories to our hearth....

'I'd suffered, I had losses – and I had a recipe, or an analysis. The purpose of existence? When existence is terminating, what's the purpose then? My contribution – was essential, even if I stood and roared alone. I was a stag: you were the dogs. You sought me out – Yolande, Isabelle and Fleur: I was your work, and you were trained to leap upon me, lacerate my back and pull me down. And eat.

'I am a shepherd without sheep. A slave without a master. Those are good, honest lies. Nearly truths, a way of eliding the real slaves, the real masters.

'Our time is up. There is no taste, even, in making a bull's eye at dear sweet Vinciane, with her cow eyes swivelled over me. Another relationship? Where is the point? All the intrigues, the pairings off – promised, not realised, the lawsuits and the ceremonies, gymnastics, scams – planned, not undertaken.... You all were not worthy, I was not capable.

'Why did they fail, our politics, our philosophy? So much time spent crafting them ... our self-portrait has become grotesque, a faceless suit, from Magritte, over and over, legions of us, troopers ... or a silent circus number, tumblers and climbers all bespangled ... after Beckmann.... Before – it wasn't good – but it didn't finish so.... It went on, always another chance....

'I know I haven't understood, but understanding wouldn't make a difference, and does it change the plot?

'Is this the end? The soldiers? That means not the other ending, then. Not the fire, the twilight, the splitting of the rock, the bubbling of the seas, the dust, everywhere. Dust we are ... briefly wetted into clay.'

He rocks and keens.

'The ending – for us, it is the soldiers,' says Yolande. 'Not cataclysm, nor the Armageddon – just armed men coming for us, up the track.'

The five women – Solène, Yolande, Isabelle, Vinciane and Fleur – peer down, down as far as eyes can penetrate.

'Oh no! I think I see the soldiers go away!' says Fleur. 'It's worse: disaster! An end without a finish.... All inconclusive, while we age and lose our teeth and eyes.... Must we wait some more? More travail, more emergency?'

'Oh, it will end,' Solène says. 'Soldiers, or the sun gone mad – but patience: it will happen slow....'

They gaze down – the valley's misty, but you see the cops, the soldiers, mustered, starting again to clamber up....

*

It was a detour after all – the soldiers hadn't gone away. Slowly, patiently, they climb up, towards the crest.

SUMMER NIGHTS

'The only thing we're born with is virginity,' he says. 'When it's gone, it leaves no trace.'

'I never had one of those,' she says. 'I was taken on the helter-skelter before I was born. Maybe that was when.... You want to start again, is that the plan?'

'There's planes over,' he says. 'Too early.'

'That's good,' she says. 'They're ours. Anyone else's would be later, when we're off to work, if we have some.'

'Ours? I didn't know I had an air force,' he says.

'You don't,' she says. 'It's mine. You can't fly.'

'No worry,' he says. '"The living being is the universal power over its outer nature which is opposed to it." Our being alive is a guarantee....'

'Yes,' she says. 'That we aren't dead, that our body hasn't given up. It's a great comfort. I know it all by heart. What can it mean? Or do you use it as a hook to pick people up?'

'Everything gets hooked,' he says. 'Sheep, fish, beef carcases, addicts, sport freaks – people who remember Cream.'

'I can't swallow that rusty bunch,' she says. 'No one's mouth is that wide.'

'Lie here beside me on the bed,' he says. 'See if we can swap. Each other. I'm not sure if that disproves the Master,' and they laugh. 'Philosophy is a finite province. The only living thing is time.'

'It's what they say,' she says. 'That it's difficult. It's easy, instead. Changing over. To and fro, if you want. Though I'm not sure what the gain is.'

'Yes,' he says. 'I can do it too, but for me it's a bit harder.'

Each lies there, becoming the other – it's a game, gymnastics, one multiplied by one. One into one, nothing times one....

'Your brain's not in as good shape as mine,' she says. 'You should go biking. I've wanted to try changing places since I read "*si j'étais vous*".'

'I don't speak foreign languages,' he says. 'I understand, though. I can't do clicks.'

'You miss nothing,' she says. 'It's all the same. There's no special things carried in a special tongue. It's just like flowers – different colours, that's all. They can't help it.'

'Anyway,' he says, 'it's clear any story lies in brains, even if you're not of the idealist persuasion, as no one seems to be. Brains as it were, though. Not what there is when you peek inside, but when they're whirring, making smoke. Bodies are fragile – pour a little water in, hang them up by a foot, plug them in to your wall – and it's over. Compared to carpet sweepers, their solid parts are crude.'

'The money you spend, trying to get work,' she says, 'you'd do better with good shoes and that guy Cavallo, Mister Horse, make you a good summer suit. Walk up and down the beach and wow them. Or I'll do it, if you're shy.'

'I'd do politics,' he says. 'But look what free voting does – the odds and sods they elect – thieves and murderers aren't even the start.'

'Just lie here,' she says, 'and wait. You're too angry. It makes no difference. You must give everyone what's expected.'

'Naked, saves money, and it's Vedic,' he says.

'Not if I'm you,' she says. 'I'm the shape of something else, not yet familiar. Wear clothes for my sake. Decide the colours; be me too if you want.'

*

I feel free, walking along the front, in tan and red, the sea green and red. It's true – philosophy made a bad shot at telling us what freedom is, and it's true I only feel it. Can't hold it in my hand. For the little that it's worth, everyone is free and not. It might as well be psychological – anything else more complicated, more satisfying, doesn't fit what we, as it were, decided we would be. I am, for sure, in nests of cages – unfree, if freedom has to do only with restraint. Constraint, though – is central to freedom, that too's for sure. Self discipline. It's like sacrifice – killing animals to please inexistent deities ... and also being altruistic, or maybe throwing oneself into the pit, for some reason still to be explained....

When the Impressionists were here, they built a piece of Japonnaiserie – a temple: there's a crowd today, all looking up. In the rafters, there's a bird, trapped – a spectral owl, the owls' grand-duke...

Is it empathy – themselves – the crowd sees pinned up there? Or is it the dark couple – death and wisdom, trapped and contained, in a single flap of wings? In that case, whose is the death, and what the wisdom? Bizarrerie? – that always gets a crowd. Incongruence, anomaly? It isn't fun, that's certain. Maybe it's idealised, the image of a fear, of being trapped, quite without reason, without exit, without purpose – trapped in the flatness the impressionists had left us. What you see is all you get, no second glance, nothing moves, not ever.

'Hi, Tanguy,' I say – and tell him about the owl, the unresolved, the trap, the question-mark.

'You're late,' he says. 'Maybe we're finished. We must start....'

We load all kinds of boxes on the truck. It's late out, misses a day.

The boss says, 'Here's your cash. Tomorrow I'll have someone else.'

'It wasn't me,' I tell Tanguy, 'Blame the owl....'

*

'Now you're free,' says Piers, the boss of bosses. 'Tell me now. Tanguy – a solid type, dependable?'

'Totally,' I say. 'My victim, by mischance.'

'I don't want that sort,' says Piers. 'You're what I had in mind. You're my beginning. It's my project.'

'In mind,' I say. 'It's all idealised.... You and me – we're both an "I". The external's internalised in mind, in the "I". You might say, "since everyone is an 'I', we only say something quite universal" when we say it.'

He's impressed: 'You made that up yourself?'

'No,' I confess. 'But I should have – could have – done. Except – the universality of mind is not a thing you can make up.'

'Listen,' says Piers. 'The task I have for you is the most important in the universe. It beats loading trucks, and climbing to free the grand-duke. The trees here' – and he points out over the sheds – 'Are full of owls. The owls are full of mice. It's nature's plan.'

'Sure,' I say. 'You must be patient, but it's a plan where you can't fiddle the figures.'

'Come in,' says Piers. 'Have an absinthe, something stronger ... a pill, a powder.... I've a movie to show.... It fits with nature's plan.... Oh, and you can bring your feminine side....'

'I carry her always,' I say. 'It's become essential.'

It's a tiny movie: a child waves a cab farewell – its coat gets caught in the door, it's dragged off.

'See!' says Piers. 'A little child. Dragged like those heroes to a memorable death....'

'Where do I come in?' I ask. 'Where did the child?'

'Oh,' says Piers. 'The child was mine. That is, it lived with me, I was the father, I suppose. It all counts – the biology, the affect....'

'So, you want to know who was in the cab?' I ask.

'No, it was me,' says Piers. 'You'll ask me – why, then?'

'Conventions seem exhausted,' I say. 'Questions begin, answers end. Maybe you want an editing job done on the sequence, on the film?'

'Nature's plan,' says Piers. 'It's not a snuff movie. I want to know the plan. I don't have time to do the meandering myself. You've read the books. Don't make the answer tedious, no footnotes and no feet, no trudge, no rousing refrains, no ho-hum....'

'It's a great job, Piers,' I say. 'Except – I don't believe there is a plan. Not about anything, and nature's just thrown together – weeds, clouds, and animals that eat each other and the grass, and stand out in the rain, and we, like them, act opportunistically and instinctively. Maybe what we have that's more refined is shifty memory and regret: but once a thing is done, it is unchangeable. If you want, I'll make a story for you – it might make you laugh or cry.... I'm good at making up these things.... You, and the child ... a fiction, naturally.'

'Oh, I love the philosophy stuff, the talk, the rhetoric, the "might just be", the "only if"....' says Piers. 'It's my compensation while I hire you guys and skim and scam.'

'The cranes on Hokkaido,' I say. 'They could fit a plan. A dance, chicks, people bring you fish to eat. Otherwise – it's all a warning, quite obvious: what to avoid, what precautions. Where not to go, where to look twice.'

'It's dull, then,' Piers says. 'It's the dullest thing, and the only way out is to ignore – roll down the mountain in a barrel, hit the tree and fall unconscious in the sea, on the lonely island eat the

only nut and turn into a hairy rock, immortal and blind. Dumb
too, I expect.'

'Yes,' I say. 'Risk is dull as well, you know how that turns
out.'

'The "something more",' Piers persists, 'that we say lacks
and must be somewhere – *that* we can add. It's pyramids and
human sacrifice. Learning whole books, putting guys in camps
and starving them.'

'Those are things you need money for,' I say. 'Fear and faith.
That's your province, Piers.'

'I rage,' says Piers, 'but I'm tolerant. If I get out of hand, I
take some drugs. That way you get to know people who take
risks. It makes you strong.'

'I'm kind,' I say. 'But it doesn't come from deep. People who
cause accidents, even when they are before me, vulnerable – it's
not my hunt, not my prey.'

'Find who killed my kid,' says Piers. 'What, I mean. Before
he could grow, evaluate, judge, despise me. I was innocent
then.'

'To make your money, you need a gang,' I say. 'Maybe they
do the books, maybe they're different guys from the accounting
team. But underneath, everyone who has the cash like you –
they have a gang. They sort out your noirish side. Ask them to
give a motive to your accidents.'

'Books, books....' Piers laughs. 'They make books, they
fiddle books – they don't read them or write them, that's for
sure. I'm someone else inside as well. Like you, Yuri, like all
poor grimy guys. We've other selves like socks rolled up inside
a master sock. For a peg-leg. Maybe I'm a gang – it can't be a
religion does it – I don't believe, so for sure it's not a better, nor
immortal, self. Nor a country. I live here, it's not mine, but I've
nowhere else to go. I squeeze its money out as if I'm making
cheese. A philosophy? A physics? Those don't bring you friends
– think of it, "I'll be late back, I'm brothel-creeping with some

philosophers"... It isn't plausible. Yes, I must be a gang too, with special clothes and a snickersnee, and a chaplet of peonies.'

'I know someone,' I say. 'Living life as it should be lived. Talents innate, exploited fully. An elegant life, gifts quite bountiful – a sage.... But in the end – too good to be of interest.'

Piers is enchanted, 'Yes!' he says. 'A sage! But earthy. Each word will resonate. Imagine, a sheaf of arrows fired upwards – they fall, unfold – each hand outstretched receives a tulip, a carnation. Each arrow blooms.... The words, each becoming flesh or flower, you take your pick....'

'No, no!' I say. 'No pick! It must be chance prevails: besides, those flowers are dead. Some people will contemplate them till they wither, others will burn them on to tiles and bowls, to last eternally....'

'Yes, yes!' shouts Piers. 'Just show me how. A sage! I'd be comfortable, up here in the bend of this fine tree, its white beards reaching down – wisdom lives by letting it all grow long ... in jail they crop you....'

Each of us proceeds by error, error after error. Chance favours the exception, the unusual. The rest blunder on, and on and on.

*

I'm discomforted. Piers insists we meet up in this baobob.... this fever tree; the sloths, they creep around, a wonderhang of ruggy sluggish things, the lemurs hopping far below, a pangolin discreet, it must have known how much it costs to eat him in a restaurant – a snake, painted over, skin in rungs, that droops from boughs and crawls by the intermittent stream that's run down from the mystery mountain top where we hear distant skittles fall, black balls cannoned off....

'The costume suits,' says Piers, adjusting his.

'It's authentic, Piers,' I say. 'It's hot here, and just a penis case to wear ... it's maybe what you need, for comfort and display, but with you, quizzing me, I find I'm fiddling with it all the time. Your office, now – that has cool air, racks for your modern clothes....'

'Oh,' he says, 'it's true. Wearing just a cover for your prick – it's all you think of, though no one could peep, besides, the casing's uniform, no one can guess how neat or lanky you might be.... I like to talk to colleagues unadorned – body to body, face to face. Tattoos – they show a lack of trust – a barrier of nothing much, except it's ink. Remember – officials: ink is their tool.... Avoid them, and the artists, masking off the truth with "nearly so" and "better thus"....'

*

Modernity here – it's new, attracts the capital. It's a delight, this system. No one's read Kapital, sees how it ends, and who falls underneath the wheels, what happens to the horses....

Piers says, 'Outside, my dear, it sparkles. But within – we're happy savages, just beginning to forget all that we knew.... Solitary walkers...'

'It's not so, Piers,' I say. 'We have no knowledge to forget. We came from everywhere we couldn't stand, and ended here – in tiny rooms where nothing works and serpents lay their eggs in our hot beds....'

'You will look back,' says Piers. 'When the end, the crash, the soldiers ... when it all comes down, and that is good and true. You wouldn't want to penetrate the looking glass and see the nails and glue that hold it up?' He laughs. 'Don't fidget with your bit that's covered up, you'll draw attention....'

'That's exactly it,' I say. 'I feel I am a soldier on parade – keeping my shoulder's-length....'

'It's not just clothes, not having them,' says Piers. 'It's having all the rites and rules that govern the not having them. To preserve the nothing, you must have your carapace. "Nothing" has an argument as long and wormy as does Something. Believe me. I read the book.'

'I'm not comfortable, Piers,' I say.

'Maybe you're ticklish,' says Piers. 'Your feminine side. Take off your penis cover, if it irks. Maybe my other side is you....'

'No, none of that,' I say. 'My clothes contain me, I'm a thing that needs containing.'

'Your body's full of every kind of grotesque stuff, that no one needs to look at,' Piers says. 'Think of yourself as something that's not there at all – a Mind. Like me. I am one too – it can do many things, although we're fucked, the species has just about reached the Thule. The gruesome parts, where nature reaches ends, you have to make them up. On your map, put space guys and the monsters, the lionmen, the men with heads beneath their shoulders. We can have fun as gardeners, fiddling old tunes, crossing a yak with cows.... But big inventions? No. Those Greek dinner tables; chiselling out laws; the technique of the *cire perdue*: those were the big steps. Once done, repeating, doing the variations, is banal. There is no more. It's all laid out – you just need look it up and do the maths.'

'A mind,' I say, 'must be a kind of ghost. This tree – doesn't belong here at all – those lemurs are all ghosts, of people we don't know, from far away. The book said tattoos despoiled a body and its destiny. Its fate was already coiled up, primed and timed, a dragonfly's transformations – ready for the flight in fig that lasts fifteen minutes, not a second more. Our last flight, up from the grave in shining suit of skin – but now, I'm not so sure. I thought it was a desecration, scribbling on the skin, our memberships, the sailor's art – but then, why not? I might have tattooed on – a suit of clothes. Ghost clothes. The style must be "new school" – it's not what the Yakuza has: there'd be puffy pussies and the classics, Kuniyoshi-style....'

'You could have penises, tattooed all over,' Piers says. 'Since you're so delicate. I hope you're not a softie, for I had a project for you. Explore. If it's all accidents, why should I strive?'

'Yes, it's true, all that looks new here is really just a corpse dug up from somewhere else,' I say. 'Here, what's died elsewhere, it flourishes, makes millions, builds these facades we live behind, the roundabouts that don't go round, the widths and vistas. For a relief, pastime, there's life, the greasy alleys where we buy our food and sex, our magic....'

*

I feared the gang would be an ugly crew. Instead – they're charming: slender, elegant, the youths, the girls that walk like serpents. It's a joy.

Suppose the world was going to end – it would be kindest, just to give us notice of one day. One day when we would all be frozen, together, with familiar people all around. One day, when we would all be free. My female side – I try to accommodate, be nice, but I've been terrible, in my time. One day: free from her, from me. But what would freedom mean to Piers? He employs, he has a plan, he didn't drift here, not like me, floating to the margin of the atlas page, he saw the opportunities, new life. And the gang: they couldn't be more free than they are now. I heard them saying how it's best to hit a guy straight on the knee, not on the side, don't bother with the ligaments, just the cap, like cracking a saucer, a toy plate. They use a club, an iron bar. Free trade made freer still. Freedom, what would that mean to them, or to the market people here? – undo forced marriages, some trading of the kids? – people fetch much more than radishes, and you can eat them many many times. So, no freedom day before the world will end, although it seems so right; another casual day, instead of taking stock invisible, just plodding on: lie on the bed with your own or someone else's self.

*

'I love you, Yuri,' Piers says to me. 'I feel an obligation, giving work, or cash, to people I find here, waiting for some luck, coming like me from off a voyage, a ship, a plane, thinking the same languages, not mixing in in case they can't get out again.'

'I'm here because of what I couldn't do,' I say. 'Not for what they say I did. You are the sage – all I can do is brush dead leaves off your balding dome....'

'It's true,' says Piers. 'I'm at the point where I possess more than I want, and so I can renounce. Start off a stretch ascetic, moralist. Gnomic – that's permitted. I could enjoy my day of freedom too....'

We sit in our tree's fork. There's hard brown fruits that hang – no one, no human, ever eats them, or finds out what's inside.

'All the Chinese people here,' says Piers. 'Came here as sailors. It started with that huge ship, it could easily have sailed around the world, over and over; it was unarmed. But someone had decided – they'd follow the alternative adventure: not sail anywhere, not even in a paper ship. Was it the wrong choice? It's useless asking.'

'I was a sailor, Piers,' I say. 'I wasn't classified. To get your pay – it's been agreed. There's stokers, oilers, greasers – though now, no one does those things. The ship's unarmed, there's five of you, you sail a continent of boxes, chained-up on deck. I wasn't classified, and so I wasn't paid.'

'I'll go to law,' says Piers. 'I'll sue for you. The owners. The union. Everyone.'

'I can't wait suspended all those years,' I say. 'I'd have to take ship and move again. Let it be.'

'There's lots of laws,' says Piers. 'Things are illegal here that aren't elsewhere. And what is left, is punishable. We are fish, swimming in and out the ribs of wrecks: we socialise, we flourish. We can't stop being fish. You see – this place is built on islands that did not exist last week. They crawled up from the sea, or else were laid down in grids, set squares. It's wonderful, dear Yuri, but so perilous....'

'Tell me, Piers,' I say. 'Where those old wooden wrecks come from.'

'Old politicos, my friend,' he says. 'Venerated thieves, assassins with a million fixers – they're the wrecks, layers of them, they rise, they bob, they sink, there's always more...'

'There's need, more, *my* needs....' I say.

'Oh yes,' says Piers, 'there's opportunity. That's how I buy your services....'

'My ship was Chinese,' I say. 'They were right not to pay me – unless there's pirates or you sink, there's nothing you can do.'

'Money,' says Piers. 'Your ship was full of money. Enough's enough, they say. Well, I have enough, I think. I'm not a spiritual guy, believe me – but I too feel the need. My spiritual side. Help me, Yuri. Help me develop it.'

'Sometimes, the big mosques,' I say, 'when there's no prayers, you can feel the emptiness, right up to the sky. You're clean, you can't read what's on the wall or in the books ... nothing of you's attached, the universe is beautiful that you're in, you knew that, everybody says it, but that's all. So what.'

'Oh, I know,' says Piers. 'I've no faith, so I am faithless – that's what I am and you can work on that, but I am not unfaithful.'

'Why me, Piers?' I ask. 'I look around, that's all. I feel curious, I feel oppressed – I feel bad when there are trapped animals. That's all. What you want – long long ago, there were people asking the same thing, but they had hair flowing like rivers, they sang, their bodies lightly used and bright.... Now....'

'Yes,' says Piers. 'I'm going bald. It happens to us all – at twenty nowadays, there's rust marks on your hands. I should work out. Massages – like you are in a muslin bag and they are making cheese....'

'Well,' I say, 'I've told you what there is, outside of prayer times. Maybe you are not the type.'

'Horseshit,' says Piers. 'Everyone's the type. Meaning, purpose, lying beneath appearances ... find them for me.'

'Spiritual opportunities?' I say.

'If that helps direct you, yes,' he says.

'Forget sex, Piers,' I say. 'That's off the table.'

'Oh, I do,' he says, quite eager. 'Forget. That's how you can face up to more.'

*

'Sara, you're with Tanguy still?' asks Yuri.

'Oh, when you made him lose his job, he lost me,' she says. 'I cost. He's had to find himself – doing the ordinary bad things.'

'Maybe Piers could help,' Yuri says – and she holds his arm tight –

'You know Piers,' she says, 'so you must know his plan.'

'Nature's plan,' Yuri corrects.

'A dream of stone,' says Sara. 'Nature giggles, doesn't smile on you, not kindly, not in any other way. He wants mastery – they all do, they all have a plan and call it nature's. He wants to be so many things, and in so many skins. A *tombeur d'anges*.'

'No,' says Yuri, laughing. 'An angel-fucker? No, Sara, you'd not say that seeing him perched up in his tree.'

'Well, I bet he never falls,' says Sara.

'Oh,' Yuri says, still laughing. 'It's a broad tree. There's his child – he wants deeper into that....'

'No child,' says Sara. 'It's his hypothesis. One child would never do to make a case. They'd need to multiply among themselves: kids – a skein of bees, grubs begetting grubs: it has to fruit, it has to bring forth multitudes.'

'I can believe there was no child,' says Yuri, quite alarmed. 'So – just a scenario, a plot that starts, out for its walk, its jog? A platform.'

'Yes, of course,' she says. 'Piers is a dark thing. He roots, he's tendrils round the world – casinos, luck machines. Ships each bigger than a peninsula. The world – it spins, you'd think it flies to bits. If you, the chiefs, want mastery, you have to make it stick, like a mud ball; you bind the crust, you keep it smooth and round. We others, we're glued here to the earth: the masters' gravity, their power, stops us from sparking off. But – they're mortal too – they climb the trees, they question and they doubt, they want the "something more", being a captain's not enough. They have to launch, to flap their arms, but – what then? No one flies, no one has ever flown. How does it go on, how does it end? The answer? It's us that they bring down. And, there is no end.

'Masters – they're all born again. Down *we* go!.... Then we plod along, we limp. They're up the tree once more. The desire's all on their part, Piers, and the rest. Wanting to fly – is always about the flying, not fear of the eternal fall.'

Yuri hears the passion, he's impressed, he doesn't grasp.... 'On the ship, they show you the street sign for "women". That's your reward, it is benevolence. They say you do a favour, going there – it's money for the children, the women send remittances,' says Yuri.

'Oh it's not that,' says Sara. 'Not routine; not desire for nothing in particular. Piers wants to be recognised, among the masters. They own all the children, living or dead. Millions of them, trillions, all off to school with textbooks on their heads. Some go this way gladly, some are dragged. They're all his. They're raised to work for him. Lots have an early death, but still it all goes on – the catastrophes are his and we survive, all thanks to him, his kind. We're born to work for him, we fall and die – he lives again, he climbs the tree ... he fools you, drags you in, makes up your story and your task ... he pushes you, of course....'

'These masters, the captains,' Yuri asks, amazed, another universe a glimpse before him – 'Who are they? Shippers? Couriers, transporters, middlemen and top and bottom women, procurers, facilitators, spinners of the globe, truckers and trackers, stockers and storers, makers, disposers, miners and refiners, dumpers and humpers, fixers and mixers....'

'All those,' Sara says. 'They make the world's veins, its arteries; theirs are the beetle tracks across its deserts and its seas, they make the capital, build capitals, they deal, they auction and they price – and it's us that they employ, as men, women, children, soldiers, artists and carters, mimes and quacks, preachers and leaches....'

'I hope you're not exaggerating, Sara,' Yuri says. 'I hate exaggeration.' He lightens up – 'There's rare things everywhere, owls, vultures, captains of industry and sloth – they bring catastrophe, some wisdom too – but disasters? – those are rarer. Every day, catastrophes – the disaster that's foretold – it never seems to come, to give its warning call.... A grand-duke – isn't an archduke, see!' And he laughs loudly at his little joke, trying to pull her in....

'What's exaggeration?' Sara asks. 'You have to have a standard, a measure, before you know if you have overblown. Yuri, you're naive. I have the wisdom, almost everybody does – your owl was clueless, all its wisdom didn't stop it sticking in the roof and dropping shit on all its sympathisers....'

'Tell me, Sara. Tell me what to do,' says Yuri. 'It seems, so far I have no choice – serve Piers, or be a poor man, thief or beggar....'

'Oh,' Sara says, and laughs, 'Don't expect from me! You got poor Tanguy fired! Rot in the dust, Yuri, eat your knuckles till they've bleeded out ... steal a cute dog who loves you, and when it's dark – roast it, eat it all ... enjoy!'

'There's countries, Sara....' Yuri says, not knowing if it is significant.... 'Some people say they love them....'

'Oh, there are boxes for the lookalikes,' she says. 'They have their wars, but those don't last – and then it's back to things. A mass of things, eaten and growing, landing and floating, round the world and down your throat ... and on and on....'

'I know,' says Yuri. 'Tanguy and I know everything about the boxes.'

'Imagine,' Sara says, 'when we left home this morning, we were children. What are we now, going back, hoping there is something left?'

They don't know what to add to that. Sara goes on, 'Look, here's my new man, Mackie. I still work the bars – behind, in front. Bars for foreigners – like I am too, we're all high born in Tunis, here we're floor-fluff. All behind bars!'

Mackie is olden, he rolls like a tarry lobster-pot, all ribs and spaces, soft roll of bellies, mantis arms, some spiny stuff hoping to find an exit. He sputters as he talks. Not a good catch, thinks Yuri, neither the cage, the outside, nor the brittle squeaky thing within.

'Yuri,' says Mackie. 'Avoid Piers, don't serve him. With Piers – there's history, to avoid. With Sara – an idea, that sings, up on its branch.'

'I wasn't sure,' Yuri says. 'What either was. Neither has shapes you'd recognise.'

'Sara sees commodities everywhere – laced up in boxes, travelling the seas, like albatrosses, whales, that stuff. We killed the animals and fenced what's few alive in parks....' says Mackie. 'Boxes is what's left.'

'That's true,' says Sara. 'There's rangers here with guns, there's poachers too – I bet the beasts are scared, can't screw and reproduce, can't eat or sleep....'

'Be quiet, Sara,' Mackie says. 'These articles, the ones we trade and pack on ships and sail them up and down, the food that no one grows but everyone imports – these are now our animals, the seas our jungles, and the ports our woods.... The earth is barren, Yuri, sterile; parched or bog. What moves, what makes us live on – is the commodities. It's true, what shamans say – we put our life to making them. They are our better hours, our younger efforts, our hunger and our satisfaction.... Once, making stuff was alienation, now – it's life!'

'I didn't know I'd said all that,' says Sara, squaring up and poking Mackie in his gut. 'Nothing has changed. The stuff in boxes – it's what it always was – a spectral dance, illusion of a life, the things, they do not live, our labour dies when – before – it is expended. It dies the moment we go in the bar, put on our espadrilles....'

'You're wrong, Sara,' Mackie says. 'Stuck with the fear of bosses: I would say, stuck in a rhetoric of freedom and oppression. We're far beyond that, Sara. The only power that used to matter – was the power to make our habitat ... uninhabitable. Power over each other? Who cares, what does it mean? Oppressed? It's antique stuff, all that; tradition, elite. In jail they feed you, outside – no! In jail you're healthy, outside you putrefy.... Inside there's torture: outside, the bullet and the gas. Besides, there is no guilt, there is no punishment ... only instinct and suffering, wanting to be loved, to be hated, to love and hate yourself....'

'Mackie!' Sara shouts. 'You're guilty. Understand? You are not innocent!'

'Tell me, Sara,' Yuri says. 'All about Mackie.... Declamation. It's the old stuff....'

'Labour is dead,' shouts Mackie, interrupting, in a pose. 'That's what power was all about. Ransoms and loot, taxes and rape. Now – life is traffic. Power is macabre, it is the butcher's shop. What's preferable? A muddy pig, or thick neck chops? Life's beautiful, but when it's your neighbour's – you want her cut up when she crosses you: rump, skirt and shank. That's what the philosopher asked: "What's better – be a pig that frolics in the orchard, or the swine cut up, laid out in parts, like a plumber's box of snakes and wrenches...?" Each one of us believes that life would be better with those others – rivals, arrogant, ungodly – lying dead. Or maybe just in jail on hooks ... or maybe working in the fields, the mines, and selling us stuff cheap, that's boxed and rollicks round the world and brings us cash ... or in the frigo languishes, ready for our lunch.'

'You're hopeless, Mackie,' Sara says, frustrated, laughing....

'Normal people, Sara,' Mackie says decisively. 'Prefer a table full of pink and white, of ribs and patties, mince and tongue, to some clapped-out bovine, smeared with crap and milked to death, stood stupid in the grass.'

'You twirl them round, Mackie,' Yuri says, coming to admire him. 'They don't lie still, the words, the arguments, you don't bring peace, they are not tesserae cemented in a frieze....'

Mackie smiles, since he's in charge.

'I always go where Sara works,' he says. 'Come! We'll have some drinks and theorise.'

The bar is like a piece of street – there's no inside: 'Pouring and fucking,' Mackie says, downing a blue-green drink. 'That's power, old-style. The last. Machines can't do it.'

'Not yet, I guess,' says Yuri, warming towards Mackie.

'These drinks,' says Mackie wisely. 'Are mostly seawater. That's where the wind and spray come from – we're on the deck, but we can't leave our seats and dance or pee – or someone else will come and sit in them....'

'You know, Mackie,' Yuri says. 'You could be on to something good, a new aesthetic, a new theory of everything that's present. We might need get inside the things – the boxes, yes, the contents too. They're not subjective nor objective – they make no claim, not to liberate, nor represent – and yet.... the boxes – contain everything. Inside – there's what we think are thoughts, our instincts, insults, blasphemies perfected in the womb. So – they're nothing. Empty. Messages. That nothing – it's packed with spiders' eggs, messages from nowhere from no people. They're what we started with – the words, the wavering lights that take us up the mountain to the stones, the chiselled laws the goat scratched out, that we don't read.... The everything – it's shards, granules – everything in particles. The particles are all the same and everywhere – and yet we don't see them so, we see hogs and mountains, elephants and dragons. They're energetic, Mackie – the particles. They dance and sing, no words, no movements you can hear or see – they buzz, conspire, drill through your ears into your calabash, your sounding gourd, twangle the tin strings, night and day the kora – they are our darling and our twitch....'

'You're telling me, Yuri,' says Mackie, holding on and rocking: 'Leave Sara alone, and do what you want with Piers. That's my conclusion.'

They quaff the krill – Sara pours more. The two, the mariners, watch on the little screens the bargirls jog and jig their customers –

'Oh, I'm not there,' says Mackie. 'Sara is reticent. Wherever she has come from, maybe it was Tunis, who can tell – she wouldn't show our tumble-fumble. No video exists, I can't etch those primals deep down in the dark parts of my eyes.... We have no recorded past. Besides, the record – you can't touch or smell.

'I told you, Yuri – she is the idea. I mean – she *has* them, the ideas. In your head there's shelves and your illuminations are disposed in rows like periwinkles. Traps opening, and closing. Free to air. You see,' and Mackie twiddles round, his barstool comes about, he yaws – 'We rose up to the crest – now comes the curl, the trough, and back we go, down on the shore, beached, panting – see! our toes expand, our lungs grow out.... Gills, flippers, Yuri – water in, and out the arse, our motor puffing ... like so many put-puts, squids with blond curls.... Back to the beginning, what we were, crawling from the sea and slowly learn to stand, to hurl the assegai and whoop.... Except this time ... nothing. Into the deep. The sea, the sea – always full of drowning thoughts, whoosh! whee! and splosh! We're back in there, somewhere among the sponges and the filmy stars.... When you reach the top, dear friend, you're in the crows'nest. Where's the crow? It's flown – and so do you, and down you go, like everyone – the species, when it's seen the panorama – down it goes. It is air. Everywhere, nothing. Is that it, the all? A desolation. Waves, and waves invisible. Hello, goodbye, say the waves. Sea changes, Yuri. The fine old wooden junks, sea wrecks, sea wracks ... all gone, long gone, gone by....'

'Hearing you,' says Yuri. 'Brings on the sickness, I see the rocks, I roll.... I have a tale with Piers, to finish off....'

He slides away. All down the street, there's bars like windows, all lit up, the high-born ladies pouring krill – a twist of bladderwrack on top ... rewind, the videos of suck and sex....

*

'Piers won't receive.'

It's good old Binkie, head of the gang, inventor of the martial arts: of bat and paddle.

'Are you in my class too, Binkie?' Yuri asks. 'Spiritual exercises? Maybe your hoods would help – I see Laoula and Aloès size me up – they'd go ape for metaphysics.'

'Oh,' says Binkie, dismissively. 'We're hunched over our keyboards. Unlocking every door in a long street. We aim at gold – no one keeps cash in the house. Buy, sell, hump the huckster's pack, tap with the stick – we're peddling and pedalling away.... Information – that's how you get in. You knock – "Tell me," you say, "you think..." and your foot's in. A look around – buy or sell? Is the bracelet silver? white metal?'

'I understand,' says Yuri, having heard this many times, not grasping once. 'Thieving and speculation – it makes your fortune at your desk....'

'No, no,' says Binkie, irritated as always. 'We're always on the move. It's quicker than Ariel....'

'Never heard of her,' says Yuri. 'Tapioca and Zalzal, yes, but Ariel must be a new recruit.'

'Forget the names,' says Binkie. 'I've lists of those. The trouble is – it's all mundane. Those doors are locked, but there's a million keys to each, they've all been robbed so many times, there's nothing left, not even doorknobs. We've gamed, bought arms and pills – we are spirits, Yuri. We have a million names, a million homes – none of them is true. What more can there be, what can you teach us? We've been everywhere, in places that don't exist, that are invisible, dark and deep. We pried in every library shelf, in every armoury, in every cave and tent. Piers, our master – to us he is king Ouf. He asks us each day what we have found ... an enormity. Oh, how we climb, we hide and seek. Sometimes through our screens, at other, still darker times, with masks and gunny sacks – hunt out treasure for him. We scale the ladders of infinite length, and we are monkeys of an indeterminate weight – we find, we know – just about everything. See no wrong, report only to Piers. And yet – we are not wise.'

And Binkie turns away, hand on brow, and seems to weep.

'I understand all that,' says Yuri. 'But for sure, for you, there's always the mundane? Some guys whose legs need breaking? It can't all be knowledge without insight? Going everywhere, sleeping a second here and there, but at the lowest price.... Yes, it's a bore. The shape is all the same, always and everywhere, like photons ... like Mackie says....'

'I didn't know that about photons,' Binkie says. 'Maybe we should find this Mackie, give him a taste, the old-fashioned one-two-three.... If you're his friend, you'll stand beside him, we'll give you a tawsing too....'

'No, no,' says Yuri. 'You're all spirits. Stick to your genre.'

There's avenues of lime trees here –

'We do research,' says Binkie, 'to eliminate their stickiness.... We're a consortium....'

'Of course,' says Yuri, tears starting in his eyes. 'Now, all's so advanced.... My school – they didn't keep us long. A day or two. We learned to play the shell game ... now, they shoot rockets to the moon and Mars. Sometimes they land plop in Arabia, or on Isfahan: those splendid oases for the mind....'

'Oh, we're traditionalists as well,' says Binkie. 'We sing the melodies. We use their names, the characters warbling in that epic opera: *The Star! L'Etoile!* What vision! We'll hide behind our names, and do our dirty deeds ... for sure, one day we'll black our screens, load in the pod and – off we'll go! The star, its spar, the red the blue – sighted some centuries ago, and now within our grasp, our destination, destiny....'

*

They stroll along the yellow path. 'I'm sure,' says Yuri. 'Yesterday this wasn't here. A here today without a there, yesterday, tomorrow, no place at all. Day by night, all changes, this was water, now it's clay – it's evolution playing out for

kiddies – see, there's little wrecks out in the skimpy flow.... So
tiny now, the flux, just mud and twiggy stuff – it can't be
floating houses sunk ... the nomads sail them up and down, they
catch the crocodiles and feed them snakes, and then they take
the fish the crocodiles would eat.... It all changes, Binkie, *o
saisons!* – do we change with it, the time? They say it all does,
all passes, but we change slow, so slow, forgetting all, our loves,
our hates, wearing unchanged the same old mottled skins.... The
eyes, the gums – they sink into themselves, it's true.... And are
there transformations? Are our houses moored, and then
untethered, floating, trailing our lines to catch ephemeral and
slippery preys...? Times change, we surely change, Binkie – but
we're not like them, the times, our rhythm's different, we
impose a fractured beat, and yet we seem to stay the same
inside, the skin goes smooth with wear, the brain stays always
wrinkled in uncertainty, the folds ironed in....'

'Yes, it's seasons, Yuri,' Binkie says, impatiently. 'They
change, and so does everything. Things disappear, others grow
old, and others still fall wet and naked, powerless into nests...
There must be season in Siberia where you're from?'

'Oh yes!' says Yuri. 'There's a song about the ash – the
tree.... I've never been there, wouldn't recognise one – but of
course, there's meadows, flowers that last an hour or so, white
cities invisible when the snow has come, ice palaces that melt,
form rivers broad as seas – the Amur, we love it so....' He weeps
– the beauty never seen....

'There,' says Binkie, hugging him. 'Bear up, dear Yuri....'

'Yes,' sobs Yuri. 'I'd forgot the bears. Though I have never
been that far. Mother Russia – she abandoned me on someone
else's doorstep. I have never been....'

'Those little wrecks,' says Binkie, much irritated. 'Not ships.
Those are bargirls' ribs. Toy boats – that's what they seem, it's
what you want to see. The women – drive a guy to anger, and
some jump, and some are pushed. They're worth a lot, it doesn't

help them. The flesh, the word – we can compute it all. The web, Yuri – it all falls in the web, and we're at the bottom of the strands. Then – it's bosses take it all, the profit that we make....'

'Yes!' shouts Yuri. 'Bosses. Just like Sara says. The permanent vendetta. The weakest ones will pay....'

'The fish escape the mud,' says Binkie. 'Go to the estuary. Here, there's only business left – the little skeletons, and now the yellow paths solidify where you reflect, philosophise, wait for the snow up in the mountains, the north, maybe Siberia – to melt and fill the river here... And so, we call a temporary end to all philosophy!'

'And everything is covered up,' says Yuri, calm and serious. 'With water. Fish. And crocodiles.'

'Yes,' says Binkie. 'The circle closes. Another one, maybe the same one, begins.'

'My search,' says Yuri, 'could be eternal. It *is* eternal – the search for something more than is that is.'

Binkie nods – he hasn't understood. 'If things had been quite different,' he says, 'I'd have joined the armed struggle.'

'You did, you're in,' says Yuri. 'With all your gang. You hack and pin. The cause, any, every cause – is like a cardboard box packed with lead balls – you push one side – the other bulges.... That is the sphere you're in – the public, Binkie. Push from the right, the left, indifferent – you give the other side its chance. Smart operators prepare for that – look at the Russians. Destroy the left, espouse the right, and then destroy the right....

'The people – now, that's the cause. In rags or uniform, in smocks and cassocks. Remember the police chief – after, when the revolution was the state, he said, "In general – I was on the Bolshevik side."'

'Ah – in general!' says Binkie. 'How I love rank – and I have none. Not field-marshal, not archduke....'

'You've better,' Yuri says. 'You have a squad. Siroco, Patacha – Zalzal, Oasis – the whole cast. That shows your genius, dear Binkie – a wink at middlebrows, a sense of humour....'

Binkie laughs. 'Not gallows humour, Yuri.... That ropey trick – always creates a mess! You're such a cynic! But you're right – best stay in shadow. We're recognised: we're a militia ... everybody uses them. Soldiers? There never are enough. Strange ... you'd think they'd all enrol. They don't. It's the fear. It spreads. Instead of turning, facing up – the people run.... Someone has to stop them, Yuri. Before they reach ... conclusions.'

*

'Might Binkie's idea be of use?' Yuri asks Mackie. 'Politics, armies, intelligence and electronic theft? They all sound solid stuff....'

'Forget it, Yuri,' Mackie says. 'I know your task for Piers is difficult. You clutch at air. But – no! Binkie's messages are precise, and unforgettable. 'For your eye only,' they say – and bang! your eye's knocked out! You can't mistake the sense. What I mean is, Yuri – the meaning in a message is what you give it when it comes. The sender has no say. It's jelly, flying through the air. You gave it shape when it left you. But, it cannot last, Yuri: it cannot gel. The shape, flying through the air, which is not air but metaphorical – is jellified. The shape, when it arrives, jiggers helpless on your screen. The meaning – is up to you. If you don't give it meaning, just press the button and it disappears. It's those boxes, Yuri, on those ships. What's inside? No one knows. They have fake manifests. Many are empty, I suspect – an enormous honeycomb with no bees, trucked round the South China seas. It's like Binkie's names – they're names on a list, take one – you're anonymous. Thugs, Yuri. Watch out!'

*

Piers says, 'Yuri – I ask you to suspend the search – my search – a big deal's coming up.'

'Oh well,' says Yuri. 'It's chasing butterflies away – thinking maybe they'd get tired....'

'No net, though, Yuri, no killing bottle,' says Piers. 'What do you do, Yuri, you, your friends? All beggars, I suppose.'

'Oh, we talk, you know,' says Yuri, irritated. 'Astrophysics mostly. Girls....'

'I'm your friend, Yuri, so forgive me if I say that's dull,' says Piers. 'I have a way – of voyaging. Relax. Pictures, and going deep in space. Of course, I can stop it any time I want.'

'That's your thing, Piers,' says Yuri. 'I see it nestling in your eyes. They have everything their way. Their own wide way.'

'Oh, I have real friends,' says Piers. 'They're a prop. That way we're equal. Even you and I. Let me guide you....'

'I've to be careful, Piers,' says Yuri, backing off: 'I've an addictive personality – everyone must have, in my family, that's why they aren't around, I guess....'

'Oh, tish and tosh,' says Piers. 'There's no such thing. No thing like personality: it's choice. To stop, to start. Besides, addiction's to impurity. Take stuff that's chemically pure, you can stop any time you want. You need a friend, dear Yuri. Not want: I tell you, *need*. It's in your skin. The skin is like a skein of silk, we're worms, Yuri – start and finish, we eat the purple fruit, we gambol: we are worms and what we spin is what we are, extruded from a thousand bellies – all is joined up, we do not die, we're dyed. Rainbows, Yuri. That's us, up there – we are the sign one day the rain will end, the zebus and the prairie dogs will come together, and there'll be wordless communion between us all, and we shall leave this sterile lump, this rock we're exiled on....

'Who did it, Yuri? Why the punishment? Who? Who marooned us here? We are all innocent, we pay for someone else, the sinner, we're plonked down on this frigid shale, there's fire, there's all-consuming fire within.... It's terror, Yuri, freeze or burn. Hell: with its choice, a chance, of Hell, my dear....'

'I can imagine it,' Yuri says. 'Tell me, Piers, about the deal.... And, really, my head's already full of shamans, princesses, talking horses, all that stuff.... I don't need more, already I relax too much.... I have a friend, she lies beside me when I don't quite wake and don't quite dream....'

'Oh no, Yuri, that's the propaganda, "all hallucinations" – no, it's not like that at all,' says Piers. 'We're stars, Yuri, stars in exile, fractured and fragmented. Pieces of the puzzle: somewhere it's incomplete, it waits for us. Naturally, that is a metaphor. We don't travel in our body – we are messages. Transmitted, like they come to us each day – banal and misdirected, or peremptory, seducing....'

'It's quite what Mackie says, but from you, Piers, all seems different,' says Yuri. 'And, what I cannot understand....' He pauses, thinks – how was it possible, the big owl, wisest, largest of the birds, got itself stuck, high in the rafters....

'There's heaps of spirit,' Piers says. 'It just lies, inert. It may look like rubble, but – call the dogs and have them sniff....'

'What's the deal, Piers?' Yuri asks.

'You know what impresses here. A tower, to scrape the sky, or give a nudge to heaven. You could call it an attempted goose....' says Piers, laughing loud.

'There's hundreds of them here,' says Yuri. 'Monstrosities.'

'That's why I made mine different,' says Piers. 'For a start – it's golden. Ah, the sun! See how my statement glisters in the dawn, the dusk. Second, but not less apposite – it is an arm. And at the top – there's fingers. Not a fist, which might be your idea – but reaching up, still higher, tickling the clouds....'

'They say these grotesque buildings,' Yuri says. 'Spare us. Without them, there'd be rebellion – people fearing they'll get less, and those just wanting more. The towers, they are a resolution. Instead of people making revolutions that go in waves and roundels, destroying themselves and us – the fans – and what there'd been for centuries ... there's architecture. The grandiose, the pomp.... Innovation and stability. Wealth and show.'

'Culture?' Piers asks sharply. 'You mean, that old-time revolution? – those charabancs of guys with flags, chanting, and waving at the clouds? You can't think my towers destroy the local culture? There was none, Yuri. Not here. No spirits. Nothing to destroy, no culture, nothing to modernise, to vilify, to petrify. All the Chinese, for instance – they were sailors, they'd signed on and off, abandoned all their custom ... if they even knew what it had meant....'

*

'I'm confused,' says Sara. 'Even more – I'm desperate. Two who were high up, their men in prominence – they're coming here.... Abnousse, Charlotte, both demoted, cashiered, thrown out. They're tall and arrogant – they may be too lofty to fit behind the bar.... Then, there's the hours – mine were excessive, and it suited me – now, shared out, a pittance remains for each of us....'

'I can do nothing,' Yuri says. 'I'm sided with those animals who don't know the plans we have for them. Maybe we'll ship them all, lodge in some island where they strut awhile, and eat each other, and we'll have finished with them save in pics and fossil rocks....'

'These two don't need speculate,' says Sara. 'Philosophy is out. When things were florid – there was no need for doubt or dialectics. When things went bad – still less. Their men! – oh

Yuri, what a plague, a flail, is genuflecting to the great god Hetero.... Their men, hanged, maybe, dangling from a dump truck; or shuffling in the line to aeroplanes and exile.... Not even a migration offered with return. Even the big birds get welcomed back.... These gentlemen, suited, uniformed – they're finished, for good or bad.... Charlotte, Abnousse, they tumble down from quite another world – the world of Piers, of towers.... Towers, Yuri; your storey seals your end, they push you off your floor, you flap, you fly, you flop; perhaps with a turn of wit – take-off from the thirteenth floor....'

She keens.

Sara is right. They're very tall, these ladies are. As well – they're slow, and snippy too, with serving booze. The very worst of bargirls, they are dignified, they slop the hooch and overcharge. They take offence. They think they've still some dignity, some rights: they will not play according to the rules.

'You know the worst, Abnousse?' asks Charlotte. 'My fear – approaches realisation. Up we went, and down we go – there is no respite. These are the Russian mountains, the big dipper, the biggest scare, the scream.... The worst is – there will be no end. It's our design, the "what goes up...." We treat the world as we've been treated: the worst way that we can. And still it doesn't die. Indeed – we think of taking ship and sailing through the universe, and that will be the same. It's far too vast to kill at once, though you'll be sure there's germs and dirty globules, parafin and dandruff we shall spread throughout. It will be poisoned; in a hundred years – that universe will croak. But – Bang! Here comes another universe, the shards go skittering, here's a rock, a perch for sages – there a pond for narcissists, huge lizards grow from gobs of snot.... It doesn't end, Abnousse. That is our destiny – down, then up, and up then down. Except – the down is long and painful, the up – full of decisions, louche individuals, butlers with swords, majordomos bearing poison pills....'

'I'd become,' says Abnousse, 'an expert in the death of cats.'

'My speciality was currencies,' says Charlotte, chattering to hide discomfort....' Now, I can change from one to tother, but I can't access them, not one, not one at all. Moneys: it's a religion, Abnousse. Make the right choices and it's paradise....'

'Such beauties,' says Abnousse, not listening. 'My animals – they came in crates ... my Big Man was a minister in charge: the cats, all colours and all temperaments ... they didn't last. I loved them all. They died, all of them, reluctantly. Who now shall I love? You? Sara? Mackie? It seems a downward shift – you're unpredictable all of you, you lie, exaggerate. And it is clear – there's turmoil coming – all those sentences, the condemnations. In the dark you hear them clambering up, they make careers, they take some loot ... and in the morning in your flowerbeds, big poppies broken, faded, torn ... your intimates, even your servants, people you could speak to, tell a joke ... down, down they fell.'

'All that is gone,' says Charlotte. 'Now, there's rats – more of them than ever there were cats. This is the beginning ... on and on it goes....

'I was optimistic, Abnousse, to think an up will follow every down. For us, this is the start eternal...There is no "next". I shall write poetry. If there's time.'

'Maybe for us, the worst has come,' Abnousse says. 'After all, we're just the concubines. Ours is the classic fate: humiliation – what does that count? Who cares? Except – if they come after us, they break our hands. It hurts, I'm told.'

'Well,' Charlotte says, 'I'll write haikus. They started so – inspiration fading out in pain. The right mode for a broken hand.'

*

'Everybody's here,' says Mackie. 'Except for Binkie, but he listens to it all. So, I was right. We're modules, boxes. There's enough of us here to do anything that comes to mind....'

'An opera, a militia,' Sara says. 'Anything. If we had the cash for drugs, we could go in rehab, all together – or run a hospice for small animals. Shall we be bosses? Never!'

'I have a job from Piers,' says Yuri. 'It isn't paid. Of course, it is the ultimate – arcana. Everybody can have one of those employments – or several, even....'

'You idiots!' Abnousse says. 'The bar! That's what we do. There's nothing else.'

'Already, we're a gang,' says Mackie. 'Looking for a guy to roll.... Maybe one of us already has tattoos, is part of Binkie's crew? Now's the time they should confess, before we all strip off and verify that who is who....'

'What can you mean?' Charlotte asks. 'Clothed or unclothed – we are who we are....'

It seems an argument may start – to Mackie it's quite clear that centuries and syntaxes divide 'you clothed' from 'you as nude'....

'Peace!' says Yuri. 'We're too few, too primitive, incipient, to question who we are.'

'Well,' says Charlotte. 'Before we get to towers and spirits – I want to ask Sara.... Bargirls: we have a name for sex.... How do we manage it, to keep our distance, our frigidity?'

'Oh,' says Sara. 'It's easy. If it's tourists, Europeans especially – say you're respecting local culture. No matter where your fancy lies. It always works, it's their soft spot.'

'Except for Finns, I hear,' says Abnousse. 'We're tall, though they like taller still, cuirassiers. Fir trees....'

Charlotte hears fur trees. 'I'm more confused,' she says.

'When virginity has flown,' says Yuri, 'all that's left's frigidity.'

'This is not it, the nub,' says Mackie. 'These nothings – messages, they're everywhere, they're systems, structures, inexistent but we live by them, with them, insubstantial, they're the law and the police, the work, the pay.... We are a language, words in the wind and from the clouds ... words: they're a flapping of our wings, us tiny birds the size of locusts – to stabilise us, chacking if there might be nectar in a flower. Faster than heartbeats, so fast they are invisible – but still nothing, stasis, no move, staying in the same place while you put out your tongue and hope it finds the syrup in a golden calix.....'

'Sometimes,' Sara says, 'I wish I was in the tower, and could jump off. Sometimes, though, the suffering holds you here, more than the void, stronger than free fall – even when the void is under you...'

'What suffering?' says Abnousse, angrily. 'About the shifts? Hours, Sara? Hours and hours? Our hours? The powerful ones thrust us here – we didn't wish for it. For them it was a favour. For us – it *is* the void.'

'It's Mackie, I dare say,' says Sara. 'Brings on the pain. His sailor hat. His crap about the messaging, new age of immaterials that last for ever that you never need to read, with prizes arbitrarily allotted, cups made of foam, you can't collect....'

'It is the sun,' says Mackie. 'I wear the hat because it will get hotter still. And I'm a sailor; I know, the weather burns your brains.... It's the repetition, Sara, everything over and over, less and less, first Tanguy, then me, the almost ancient mariner.... Your bed, Sara – we, the dirty sheets.... Time's sucked all the juice from me, I know,' and he weeps.

'The tower,' says Yuri. 'If it's ever built – will promise a platform to jump off.... It's a relief – to know that there's an elevator, no sweat to climb those stairs, the fingers curled above you, they protect, shade; you sit there on the palm, take off your espadrilles, lay them side by side, a couple, faithful, rounded to human use.... Someone needs them, like you did.'

'It's not the hat, Mackie,' Sara says. 'You're an addict.'

'So what?' says Mackie. 'An addiction is good. Where'd you be without one? Just floating, nothing to hold to. My addiction isn't yours, it's mine and precious ... you're full of prejudice, Sara. Now Abnousse and Charlotte arrive, even fuller of cliché, even worse than you and even emptier.'

'This is taking us apart,' says Yuri. 'Though I suspect that I have an addiction – to spirits....' And there's a laugh, and Mackie says, 'It's all salty water in your glass, from where the sea creeps in to meet the estuary. Drink, and your eyes turn inward, it's a going home: oak spoons and bead curtains, eels boiling in a pot, rowan berries on the stoup, the pier where you hope for journeys long and landfall among fine folk....'

We all drift away.

*

It's late, time to open up the bar that's never closed.

Yuri lies on the bed again: he is alone. She says, 'Here, you can't do anything. They say "you can do anything" meaning that you can't. All the people here....'

'I know,' he says. 'I'm part of the rot. Imported rot. The natives have their own. I should get out.'

'I have a plan,' she says. 'I found a note: "A hidden people. A name. An escape. A sacrifice."'

'It sounds like an adventure. Those notes are everywhere. I'm not sure,' he says. 'Already it ends bad. Being Piers's tutor in things immaterial – that gives me access to the bar. I could stay here always. That sea water – makes you thirsty – you could drink it all, all the oceans. Walk to where you want to go.'

'There's ships,' she says. 'Leave. It's the only thing to do.'

*

'You won't hear from me, Yuri,' says Piers. 'When you've gone. But I'll be thinking of you. Science! What a quest! How up to the moment. You're pioneers. Don't go East – they moved the animals there, so, you can go West. No animals, but you'll get lost and sick, all the same.

'I'm busy with my business – the tower. If it burns – imagine – not a flaming torch, but an arm, flames at the fingers' tips. These huge buildings – they burn so easy, we might just set ours on anticipated fire....

'Anticipated. To satisfy us all. Bring me something back, Yuri, not alive: a juju, a chief's skull you've shrunk. Something – that only you could do it and won't be done again.'

'Everybody wants this,' says Yuri. 'An adventure, a trek, with people that they know and don't much like. Hoping that love will come.'

'I've never felt that,' Piers says. 'Nor heard it from anyone but you. It sounds – a fantasy. Discoveries aren't made so. Love? What there is, you have it or you had it all already. Be satisfied.'

'We could stay here and watch the revolution,' Yuri says. 'It would be good and right, but – they end. Some are big, you live in their new building, the new concourse. Some day it will be perfect. Most are fevers, revolutions; that leave you weak. If they went on and on, you'd die. They don't do what it says on coins and medals.... You need killers, Piers, like they were harrowing, thinking of the crop, not of the beetles and the fieldmice sliced.'

'Oh shit, Yuri, you disappoint!' says Piers. 'Your bestiary! Those aren't mice and beetles, they're grenades and cluster bombs. You have nothing, and you want nothing, for ever after: happy to be a shit like all the others in the street. I possess lots. I want the rest. I take care to have the power, and it's insured: my arm, my strength, my tower.... If it falls down – that's good as well – better, that's how people will remember it, the idiots, as if the building up and falling down were both the same, the one sequence, same impresario....'

'You have Binkie....' Yuri says, not knowing how it fits.

'Binkie's an oaf. Never considered suicide or vagrancy as a career, not for himself, nor the children he won't have. Every night he bulls his boots and so the moment of procreation slips away,' says Piers. 'Those toecaps. I see my face in them: he sees his own dark knees. Mine, the vision, like I see you and your band, stumbling up the watercourse, looking for the source.... It's a hole, you stupid! Water comes out. That's it! And those beautiful women, Charlotte, Abnousse, you drag them to a fanciful demise – their fear, their optimism. Their bodies eaten from within by strips of poison flesh that hang from trees, sliding in their trusting ears....'

Piers in his mind contemplates the band, abandoning its boxes and its canvasses, syringes, pencils – wavering and hacking on through greens and browns.... 'I admire you, Yuri,' he says. 'You could have led the world, into a hell with no way out or up, a skyless universe ... a Trotsky making us form fours, then fives, then sixteens, sixty-fours, and march, march, march.... But, in the end, you're small. A small guy, Yuri.'

*

Someone sets a fire, and burns the arcade roof. A day or two, the bars will open up again. It's not a serious threat – it's just a tarradiddle. It's unsettling though, like the future changing hands.

*

'An expedition!' Mackie says. 'It's exactly what we sailors do. We want to get away – first, from the place, the work. Then, when we've got there, from each other.

'I have a way to get some cash. You send a message, with a plan, it's for science, even mysticism. They send the money back at once. The animals were cleared from where we go – so, if we find anything alive – it is miraculous. Or else – it is new life!'

'If we find nothing?' asks Abnousse.

'Then the next lot invents a better claim,' says Mackie, laughing. 'Finds a jumping molecule with young, that hibernates.'

'And if we die? Or else they take our heads, or ransom us ... no one knows who we are or who we've been....' says Charlotte, and she weeps.

'Oh,' Mackie says. 'All the better. If we're a mystery and disappear, they'll paint our faces on a mug, or carve a mountain, name a street.... No one who's been forgotten is forgot for ever.... When you're dead, they drop a hook, up comes a memory, behold – a bit of you!'

Charlotte whispers to Yuri – 'I shan't go. I don't want to leave here – it's so awful, somewhere else could only be worse. No, I won't go. But if I went, where....?'

'Oh, the forest – the jungle rather,' Yuri says. 'Will take all our time, but I should like to exit in Iran. To see the people walking round. Round and round, some busy, some reflective.... There's China too, all walking faster still....'

'It's Mackie, Mackie's science,' Charlotte says. 'It's so dismaying. He's so hermetic – he promises so much – keys to those containers – what do we do then, he doesn't say. Open them? There's millions, and they're all full of fusty air. But – he's a scientist....'

'I never thought of him like that,' says Yuri. 'He's an exotic. How do you see me then?'

'Oh,' Charlotte says. 'You're a protector. I need one of those, though it ashames me to admit. Besides, you've a commitment, you love beauties, women. Sex with you – you'd fit it in to yourself, and there'd be nothing left for me. You're gravity.'

'The birds have gone,' says Yuri, 'but think of our expedition: quail steps. A passacaglia, the start of a great trek. If we don't return, or if we don't cut through – we shall be celebrated just the same. It's too leafy there to think of sex, you must be complete yourself – that's all you ever have, yourself. There's Abnousse too....'

'Oh, Abnousse,' says Charlotte, laughing. 'She has family. Not yet, of course, but it will come and then she'll be away, adrift with several, gripping on to her as if she were a raft.'

'You both had ships that sank,' says Yuri. 'But you've not drowned.'

'Oh, how you understand me, Yuri,' Charlotte says, as if she'd wanted that. 'Yes – I see us forcing through the jungle – it's music written, scored, but never played. The finest quail steps in the world. It's genius. But – I still don't want to go.'

*

Someone will be Binkie's spy – a Youca, a Koukouli. It makes no difference – the others want to be spied upon, so if they're lost – might they not be betrayed and found?

*

'Where are you driving us, Yuri?' Mackie asks. 'Not to salvation, that's for sure. There's a green wall to penetrate, bound tight. Not to escape Piers – enough to tell him already he has more than he can have, and he'll forget the wanting more. We aren't loved here, it's true: we're envied for what we didn't want. But – the jungle. What might be on the other side? A desert?'

'Oh,' says Yuri. 'I don't have expectations. If I wanted an item, I could order it from here.'

'You're wrong, my friend,' says Mackie, coldly. 'If you think you'll find something in your nothing. I'll go along because of Sara. There's no union here, she'll have to share her hours. All is lost, Yuri,' and he melts, embraces his friend.... 'Days of speculation at the bar ... gone, gone. Others will take our place, they have the right.... They say we're born with rights – maybe it's like virginity, there to be lost....'

*

'I can't stay here,' Sara says. 'Not if Abnousse and Charlotte take my hours. I support Mackie – but he's a thirsty hole. Into the green – it's science. That's what he says. Use the right technique, you discover something.'

'I don't want to discover anything,' Charlotte says. 'I want access to my accounts, and I can't have that here.'

'I want space,' says Abnousse. 'If I had a cat ... but in the city it's forbidden, and there's eagles, vultures on the balcony and those lizard things that crunch them up, dogs too, supposedly our friends, not that I care for them, bullies and incontinents....'

'Jupiter loves us,' Yuri says. 'That's what we're told – but by now, he's very old. And the Greeks are all so literal. You don't discover spirits, they're always round. So, what is new, a novelty? Your early songs turn out the most antique. It's primal stuff for you, but not for griots that you filched them from. The first, the earliest – always the oldest. Pinning the butterfly, sticking the pig, hanging the cat – they die when you paste the opus number on your works: opus, *fatica*, chore, day's sweat, the job. Science! It's quite indifferent, whether you use it on a foetus or a skeleton, it needs no people, no future and no past.'

'That's true,' says Mackie. 'But the green. Wouldn't it be more convenient if it wasn't there? An hypothesis, a metaphysic

waiting for its physic? There's nothing to decypher or transmit
... it's a hedge without a field behind....'

'If it is that,' says Yuri, losing patience and the thread.'Then
it is so. So be it, then.'

*

I've tried it all, thinks Yuri, betrayed, got wrong, and what is
left is me and me. Tramping after other peoples' armies and
campaigns, their wrongs and everybody's rights.... I'm the
outrider, wavering off.

*

The green wall – that is left. Through it? A wall. Insubstantial?
A green thought. Into it? Green oilpaint, you finish in the blob.

*

'If there's no animals to eat,' says Mackie. 'How shall we
survive?'

'There are stuffing contests, Mackie,' Sara says. 'You could
stock up before – donuts, dumplings, kilometers of noodles,
spaghetti.... You could do the same with booze....'

'I have my doubts about our Yuri,' Mackie says. 'I
understand he wants to lead us in – but does he want us to come
out? What's the end? Do we survive?'

The world – won't end, not in a hurry. Its kidneys die, but not
the circulation. Almost everything is known; only the green, the
screen, remains. Better leave the secret so – present, and never
opened. A door that leads to other doors.

*

Sara tells Yuri, 'The world won't end. Not for everyone, just for each of us. Doesn't it seem the same thing? Everything is present, always, every consequence – it's all a question of time, of how fast its various wheels and spindles turn. Whoever takes over here, they'd be wrong to pull down these towers, these tombstones. They're like the lines ancient people drew in rocks and deserts – those were calculations, to make life go better. Here, they're monuments for workers who fell off – fell off their thirteenth storey,' and she laughs.

'They weren't our confidants,' says Yuri. 'Where did they sleep? Does it matter?'

'I know you want to leave because Piers shouldn't have the secrets, to add to those....' she says.

'Not from me, anyway,' says Yuri. 'Slaves can't give everything to masters – it spoils the plot. It spoils the setting, the casting, the "who knows what".... The "what the butler doesn't see". It makes things uncontrollable take place. It's been tried – it doesn't work for long, it ends in shouting – shooting too. There's those whose talent lies in power, and those who play the kora. The first bunch – some end up on gallows, the second – your fingers lose their sap....'

'You know' says Sara, wheedling, 'I've finished here. The city's bubbling – so much success that my hours have been reduced to nothing – they're cut, cut to my bones. I could leave with you. And Abnousse, Charlotte – they could stay. Things can get better for them. They're shocked still. Their fall – like Icarus. They want at least that someone notices, as they hit the wave and penetrate, grow gills, a wavy tail ... seduce again....'

'If we left them, Sara,' Yuri says, 'there's still Mackie. He's a genius, but not for doing anything.'

'Oh,' Sara says, 'I have an obligation. I can't start something unknown with a betrayal.'

'That's the best time, Sara,' Yuri says. 'He's sneaky, I'm quite sure. He crept so swiftly into Tanguy's space. We're all double here – part obeys the rules, the other part – breaks them all. He's the same as all of us.'

Sara pushes on – 'Anyway, Binkie will know where we finish up. The strongarm always knows, and always tells – they don't believe in disappearance. It's small-change knowledge, but it's stored. If Mackie wants, Binkie will tell. Mackie could even be in Binkie's squad right now....'

'It's dangerous,' says Yuri. 'So – the fewer of us take the risk....'

'The green,' says Sara. 'Who knows ... soft, hard or liquid? Scratchy? Sticky? Can Mackie manage it – if there's hills and rivers.... The hot, the snow. Pulling the ship over the mountain....'

'You see?' says Yuri. 'In an adventure, in a dare, a drama – you need to have the right characters. Forget the plot, the script – the stage ... it's a boat, a crew. If it looks leaky on the quay, you don't sign on.... Mackie feeds off you here – in the green, how could he change?'

*

Tomorrow, it all starts. He – Yuri – lies on the bed alone. 'Mackie's a problem,' he tells her, as if she doesn't know.

'You have to take me,' she says, and laughs. 'Leave him, one more's too much.'

He laughs too.

'I have the answer,' she says. 'Sara's not right for you, but she has courage. She's dull, that's why. She's a good mate, captain! But Mackie – he can come, and carry the boxes. Besides, he's got the cash. The boxes – they're science. They're all empty, but they weigh. It's hot and steep. He'll be no bother, except to himself.'

'Yes,' he says, 'that's it! That's genius.'

She goes on, 'Abnousse and Charlotte – forget it! They can run the bar. Then, if we don't get through the wood and come back here at once – tell them a story, they'll give you a drink – and we shall be friends "just like before".'

'Yes,' he says. 'That is one way. And you and me – we're a good team, an "I" invincible.' And they both laugh again.

'It won't happen,' she says. 'We must not come back here. It's all changed. Everything is cruder, rougher – regressing. Military. A sleeker kind of fascism. You won't survive. You must get out – everybody must, all of us who've grown up here, on that familiar earth – we have to leave. Where, where next? That is the problem....'

*

'I'm not carrying those crates,' says Mackie, quite determined. 'They're empty, but they weigh.'

'It's science,' Yuri says. 'Light science at that.'

'And Abnousse and Charlotte – what have you done with them?' asks Mackie.

'Oh,' Sara says. 'They'll have found new friends.'

'It's true,' says Mackie, holding Sara tight, and tapping on his nose. 'They know the road. The future's here. Only idiots run off, too scared to make their fortune and their name. I'm tracking with you, to carry forth the word: this is the nub, the *foco*, the holy garden, of what's to be. It's monotheism,Yuri, come again: the big idea tht sweeps the old away, the differences, the localism – the little gods that look and feel like you.... This place will loom and boom, the universe must love us, we're its favoured nook. The other continents will languish till they're converted too – by fair or foul....'

'That's what Binkie thinks,' says Yuri. 'Are you by chance with him?'

'I've seen you two together, in cahoots,' says Mackie. 'He pays intelligence in cash, and on the nail. Of course, we all know Binkie, I do too. Chabrier – hah! What rusty taste! His hackers and his whackers ... stage bandits every one....'

'I'm finished here,' says Sara. 'And Yuri won't survive.... What if the world ends while we are away? It's in the news it may....'

'Nonsense,' says Mackie. 'Even if it does, there is the universe all round – they'd help us out....'

'We're so pleased you're here,' says Sara, hugging Mackie. 'Yuri was afraid you'd be in danger on the trek – he has such concern....'

'Nonsense,' shouts Mackie. 'All bluff. He knows there is no secret. The spirit! It's supposed to top out Piers and his tower. Mind, held lightly in the golden fingers. It can't. It's inexistent. Yuri'd be in trouble with Piers, if he'd brought him nothing. So, he'll run! I know his sort....'

THE GREEN

It's easy getting in....

It's a curtain. In a room with curtains, you've made a world outside, and when it's dark, a whole universe lights up.

'Monogamy – was another bad idea,' says Sara, making conversation. Mackie drops another box. Without animals, it should be easy to march on. He stops:

'There's something I shouldn't tell you both,' he says. 'The city's – being sold. The Golden Arm attracted them. In the city, there's a base, a quietly occupying power; but the other guys – they told the locals, 'Another base would suit. That way you're betting two of three. You're sure to win.' Our guys said no.... The guys behind the other place, they raised the stake, Dutch auctions to and fro ... and so, we're being sold. It's hard for what I do.'

'What *do* you do, Mackie?' Yuri asks. 'Apart from drinks and playing the machines?'

'Oh,' Mackie says, straightening himself up – he's tall, a string, a piece of rope – 'I demolish things. I do appreciation, then I blast. Babylon....'

'You're Babylonian?' Sara asks, quite thrilled.

'I went, and opened up the gate. What was raised up – I brought it down. What was flat – it fell into a hole. That's how I understand the towers,' he says. 'The Vedas had it right – things grow upon the death of what comes in their way, and looks like it was edible.'

'I'm amazed at your learning, Mackie,' Yuri says. 'Why didn't you stay, and maybe you'd be asked to blow up Piers's tower?'

'You shit!' says Mackie, and he laughs. 'When guys take over a rich place, you don't want to be around.'

'You're leading us, then,' Yuri says. 'When we thought we were stringing you along....'

'First, let's settle the question of the box,' says Mackie. 'This is the last one. It's for the survivor, or the new shoot.... A creature, scampering, and hunting. Maybe it's already very large.... A saurian, no doubt, a rooted snake, a beast that looks like mud, with wings and smelly excrement. We capture it, we tie its feet. You'll need to take your spell at carrying the load, Yuri....' and he hoists the last empty box on Yuri's back – 'See how it rests on you. Inside – a prisoner. Beneath, and lugging it along – another captive. Reflect on this, dear Yuri. Feel the weight ... it's science, naturally....'

Yuri staggers, beneath the empty crate. Just a few steps....

'"Winter comes knocking at our hearts", like the song says. But here, the winter is the hottest part,' says Sara. 'I love you both. I'm strong – but maybe, Mackie, you could carry me a kilometre – for love, of course, also because you owe....' And so it goes. Mackie's the old school type, takes on the burden, though he's now no lobster pot, so tall that Sara's head goes banging on the branches, soft fruits that dangle, waiting for the birds that never come, or the sloths, stirred, prodded, crated, dumped somewhere....

'No, no!' she shouts. 'This doesn't work. 'To carry me, you'll have to stoop.'

They stop. 'What bases, Mackie?' Yuri asks. 'What are they for, if there's no war?'

'Soldiers,' says Mackie. 'For the war that they don't want. What the soldiers want is drink. Then, when it's all a blur, they remember – there's women too, or kids. Their fancy. They're sentimental, and the drink drives out the fear. The bar is trashed, they clash their horns in rut.... They trumpet, like they're elephants with must. Better stay clear, Yuri, till they're all locked in their room.'

'How'll you know when all is calm?' asks Yuri.

'Abnousse is devout, Charlotte's avid. That ensures there's sharp information, true, precise,' Mackie says, scratching at his groin. It's hot.

'By the way,' he says. 'About Sara.... Maybe you're my rival there? What is she worth, young man? I'm going on in life by smell and feel, heavy with my years – you've still got your eyes and promises....'

'I'm appalled!' says Yuri. He really is. 'We don't hawk women, Mackie.'

'Oh,' says Mackie. 'She doesn't enter in. It is for me: you give me something to avoid my jealous fits. Then it's a fair contest between us two.... Love conquers all, you know....'

'No, absolutely, Mackie,' Yuri says. 'I'll not play.'

They sit exhausted. Sara wants to chat –

'The place back there,' says Sara. 'There's corruption all around.'

'When there is socialism,' Yuri says. 'If a guy's corrupt, and not a friend of some big boss, he's put against a post, and shot....'

'Oriental despotism – that's what we had,' says Sara. 'Now it's banks and capital.'

They stumble on. It's very hot.

'Those soldiers,' Mackie says. 'They're not the socialist kind. They're pros, they do the sums. Enough that the protector's not too stupid and does deals; or else the edifice falls down ... or rises up in dust. That golden arm, imagine! uprooted, torn from its socket, and lying on the ground – looks like it's a beggar's act ... those fingers plead....' He chuckles.

It's even hotter.

'Sleep!' says Yuri, making a deep nest in the grass. It's still daytime – he can walk no more. Sara slides in and cuddles him. 'You've finished with that boys' dull talk?' she asks.

'Your offer, Mackie,' Yuri asks – he's not the brawling kind.... 'Say what it was again....'

'I'll give you the bestest deal,' Mackie says: 'No haggling. Six hours a day, you cart the crate. And if we find an animal – the discovery's all yours. You bear it all, the prize, the box. We'll hope it's light and doesn't bite....'

'Suppose we don't find something that survives or has evolved right now?' asks Yuri.

'We'll find a guy that sells,' says Mackie, reaching over, shaking Yuri's hand.

The sun is high, it wobbles in its haze, as if it's sweating too.

*

The green goes on for days – sometimes it's trees and grass, sometimes it's rolls of worn-out astro-turf, or used green grit from tennis courts.

'It's going home, home to Siberia,' Sara says. 'Yuri – you'd be a political, those exiles took their women too. But, of course, they had a destination, somewhere to arrive, and stop. Convictions too – in every sense,' and she laughs.

'Without animals,' says Mackie, despondently. 'There's nothing to be top of. Ours – the only intelligence in the world, and here we're ponds of sweat and blood....'

'Well,' Sara says, 'the blood is good – it shows there's bugs.'

'No one could doubt the bugs would come – but look up high – there's birds, they overfly,' Yuri says. 'Here, they must've treated in some way. This green, it doesn't feed, it doesn't grow, it doesn't taste....'

'Well, we can't put some tiddly thing with wings in this great box and bring it back,' says Mackie. 'They'd laugh. They'd say we hadn't gone at all, or else it's evident – these pesty things, they see flesh move, and in they dart and prod.... No, we're here to find a curious beast, large, even cute, robust enough to live in dark confinement, carried in a bumping heat....'

'Suppose it doesn't want to come? These creatures almost always don't....' says Yuri.

'It's science, Yuri,' Mackie says. 'And science never asks consent.'

*

'Here,' says Sara. 'This will serve until we're back. The problem's solved.... You're useless, Yuri, not a trekker, not stout Cortès, not Pizarro....' and all three laugh.

She holds out a length of string. 'Here,' she says. 'This will do. The creatures – they are used to this. But Yuri, how'll you face the crowds? You are a spirit guide, you know the shamans' routes, heaven and hell – just two stops on the underground for you.... When we get out this green, our discovery needs to make our name.... You need to be the showman when the box is opened, you the Mago in frock coat, the great illusionist.... Illusion, Yuri! It's not a dirty trick, don't let it seem so. An unexpected wonder, not a paper duck, a rubber rabbit up your cuff....'

'Sara, you're wrong,' says Yuri. 'Science – is that the universal mind? Are we its slaves, not worrying where the green will end, not seeking hospitality, but truth; not sustenance but plausibility.... At home in desert lands, salt lakes, karst plains.... If we get out – there may be no crowds. No celebrities. Pure altruism, Sara, drives me, no showman's trick. If we should die – over our heads, we'd hear humanity's feet go marching on, our duty to the species done.'

*

'There's no way out,' Sara says. 'An animal is safe, and so it doesn't want to leave. An exit is a threat. For us, not getting out is death. There's nothing here to eat. No stalls; stuff rots or doesn't grow. Why should it? There's no customers. It's lucky we're so tired, but in the end, you have to eat. Outside, if you've no cash, you starve – maybe you scavenge. In here – there is no cash, nothing to buy and so – nothing to throw away. You can't sell drugs, there's no one buys, can't steal, or threaten, no one wants your body, even for an hour – it's misery complete....'

'I'm going back,' says Mackie. 'I did good deals with you, but.... There's no way out for you, and no way back for me. Science? If we found the animal, we could eat it – then, the science would pass into its taste, the recipe, and whether people want to visit here – as tourists, see where we caught the beast, maybe there's a plaque, museum, viewing platform with a guide to tell you what to see.... But ... there is no animal.'

'I understand,' says Sara. 'I know you well, dear Mackie. You want to ditch the box.'

'Well,' says Mackie, laughing. 'We cannot roast or boil it! What's the use?'

Without the box, they walk faster, further, for days, without the crate, they find more strength – but still there's green around; it doesn't rain, there is a breeze – it's like being a picture except – there is no frame, no wall behind, no figuration, and no flat.

*

'What we see in animals is sex and violence: that's us!' says Mackie. 'We are the topmost animals. Here, there's no animals except us, so all the sex and violence must be ours.'

'No, Mackie,' Yuri says. 'All this walking and sleeping – there's only violence. There must have been so much, to lay it bare. Eruptions and fractures. Maybe it was the earth....'

'There's selling too,' says Sara. 'Without it, there'd be no sex or violence, and with selling, it makes both normal, ordinary, and domesticated.'

'There's also nothing,' Yuri says. 'That's here as well, and we've been walking through it. The rest is seasonal, sporadic.'

'Not if it is building towers,' says Mackie. 'That's violence, permanently. Sex is much too small and wheedling to fit in towers.'

'It's bleak,' says Yuri. 'If we get out, or stay, go forward or go back – that's all we have. No dinners served by slaves and waited on by slaves and slaves to clear it up – no talking of justice and equality – just violence pretending to be sex....'

'And selling,' Sara adds. 'Which is not pretending to be anything else but what it is.'

*

'Where's the difference,' Mackie asks. 'Between "there's no way out", and "we can't find a way out"?'

'It's that a way out's not something you can look for,' Yuri says. '"There's no way out, and then there is" – for you, it's a surprise, but of course, it's planned and planted. It's always been potential and you haven't seen them making paths and filling ditches. Cutting lianas....'

'Yes,' Mackie says, admiring. 'That's good! You're a wordmaster, Yuri. That's what's happened to the country, to the place. It's unchanging and unchangeable – and then! Everything is different and transformed.

'Sold and bought, a little place merged into, becoming, a much larger place. Abnousse and Charlotte – they've not seen it happening.... In retail, your eyes are on the small change – you don't see that you've been bought. Absorbed – a little place, it disappears, it makes the weapons now, and sends them out, it's protected, no little war awaits. There's the big, the final one, perhaps.'

'Then, maybe there are people making exits from the green,' says Sara.... 'What people? Out to where? Who will we be to them?'

'Just persons. Getting out. Just to see. See what we are,' says Yuri. 'Where we are. All we've done so far is get out of eating, and it's not doing us good. There's no animals to eat or keep us company.... There's trillions of us, Sara, and we're all alone....'

'This is banal,' says Mackie. 'We're a trio. That's something.'

*

It's obvious, what they must do. Climb a tree – over there's the golden tower. Head for that – or go the other way. Simple. Essential – a tree, a tower. Standing on each others' shoulders would do too.

It's a revelation.

*

'This is a unique situation, with a unique solution,' Yuri says. 'You can't say it's physics, and if you set aside the mechanics and the axioms, it lies in a new region, a discipline – you might say it lies between exploration and reflection. Seeking, finding, and insight. We've pioneered a new science – maybe carrying a philosophy in its pouch. Let it not become religion! A theory of endurance and change – like the great Master found when he withdrew into the forest, except – we don't know where we're going next. For us, contemplation is no use – we have to eat, decide, and be very very careful which way we leave the green.'

'Exactly!' Mackie says. 'I can claim my intellectual share. It's the puzzle naked: what is in those modules, those message boxes. Ethereal freight, meaning in invisibility, intuited through cellophane.'

'Well,' says Sara. 'Which of you will write it up? It can't be weaponised or monetised, so you won't be paid, but it's so large, we'll all be made to suffer – first with fame, then with derision....'

'It's true,' says Yuri. 'We don't want to create a superstition, a fetishism of the quest, nor of the solution – a slippage to a study of walking, not of the walk....'

'Wait!' shouts Mackie. 'Yuri, you're drifting off! Keep it brief and simple, then move on, away.'

'There is no other side,' says Sara. 'We shall go back. We saw no more. Where we were and started from. That's all there is.'

'There is another side,' says Yuri. 'We didn't see it, that is all. Now, we know it's there.'

'Make the story,' Mackie says. 'Conceal yourselves somehow, like I've done. Or we'll be punished, you mostly, that's for certain.'

They walk on, deep in thought and apprehension.

*

'We'll work it out quietly,' says Mackie. 'It's good that your idea changes nothing.'

'You don't fit, though, Mackie,' Yuri says. 'Not with me.'

'I'm not with you,' Mackie agrees. 'If we all go back together – I'll be the modern – no, the new – and if I can, if I feel so, I'll protect you ... I'm wanted. You are decoration.'

'It doesn't sound like much, Mackie,' says Sara. 'Your help.'

*

'It doesn't sound much, Sara,' Yuri says. 'The new theory. But, it beats the withering of the state! It's a wonder! Another, better, philosophy of movement. The solution and, on its heel – another question. You walk along, you talk philosophy – then – it's like gravity! The apple falls, the universe bends, sparkling like a butcher's knife. But – take care! It always falls, that apple, not a bounce, never a flight back on up to the bough. The universe bends back to where it was, and you are inexistent at the start and at the end. You remember what they say – does consciousness enter into eclipses of the moon? We don't suppose so.

'"Description and edification" – that's how minds trudge along. That's movement, and its pace. As we make what we call history, our consciousness develops. Movement is automatic. Time spools out – but our minds evolve. We've been in training, our mental legs should prosper, we're quicker, sneakier....'

'It's true – we got into the green, then we got out,' says Sara. 'But Mackie thinks we are more vulnerable than before.... Worse still, we left the spirits in the trees, just wormy fruit: Piers will be sad ... grubs and blackbirds, they have the lot. He gets nothing, except for contracts and hard hats.'

'Oh,' says Yuri, 'fruit is fruit, and knowledge, knowledge. Rarely conjoined. There's life in fruit – especially the pomegranate. In knowledge? Hmm. I'm not so sure. Good and evil? In neither of them. Remember, though, as our thought blooms, it gets more poisonous.... No one knows what I am thinking – but they know it isn't deferential, it's nothing good for them, about them. I just don't write it down – that way they'd jail us ... but we shan't confess.'

'"We" and "I"? – be very careful where you cut me in,' says Sara. 'I nestled with you, but I shan't share your cell.'

'If we go back to where we were,' says Yuri. 'It means worse: worse suffering. The new people coming in, with cash, crap jobs ... my delicacy regarding Piers, his spirits ... all will have changed.... And maybe after all there's nowhere else, lying beyond the green....'

'It's not about the suffering,' says Sara. 'I suffer. Abnousse, Charlotte – they live beneath their flails.... Don't imagine Hegel was preoccupied about the guy who swept his chimney, suffering.... Old Karl warned us: suffering – it's not enough. You act as it all moves: the history moves and so must you – there'll be more suffering, maybe multiplied. Don't flinch. Stop your ears. The religious – they offer palliatives – suffer now, peace later. There is no remedy, Yuri, not for suffering, even if you are the only one, or if there's trillions. We were in the green. We're out of it. We could return. We haven't finished suffering, for sure. No one beneath the wheels is saved by what we've seen and done....'

'I understand all that, Sara,' Yuri says. 'I knew it all before.'

'I'm hungry, and I need a drink,' says Sara. 'Where can I do my shift and earn? Tell me, Yuri....'

'Don't be banal, dear Sara,' Yuri says. 'Relax! I've all the cash that Mackie took for doing science, finding the new animal which we didn't see.... A slave can serve our dinner here – then we decide. Forward or back....'

*

Mackie has slumped. He's half his height. Once more a tarry ball, trundling from chancelry to treasury, picking up the confidences – no longer secret, their authors confident no more.... They hadn't found the animal – who cares? It wouldn't change a life, unless it stings.

He sticks himself, his buttocks, firm in the barstool. Before him – Abnousse, the faithful, the devout: and Charlotte. For her, the best days went for good, the better ones – they surely have to come.

There's secrets revealed all round. Mackie prospers. Life here is tough, but full of promises of wealth. Yuri knows in theory how to change it all, but if he tells – it could be tougher still for him.

'There's always something for you, Sara,' Yuri says. 'Ingratiate and stoop, then maybe you'll need bribes, and slithering down the rungs – but it's in no one's interest to see you starve. Someone will find a use for you. Life is a well, and you're the bucket – tell them above to let you down, it's cool and damp, and in the end there's maybe toxic slime, but you're immune by then. There is a bottom to all descents, dear Sara,' Yuri says.

'I want to sing and dance,' says Sara. 'I'll go anywhere for that, anything to escape my life behind the bars....'

'Then there's Binkie,' Yuri says. 'Him and his cast. Our legs could be at risk....'

'No,' Sara says. 'This is the future, there's no good running from it, there's no option, it will catch you, wherever you hide out. Here, is where the world becomes one. No more big war, nothing, no irritant, no cause Binkie cannot deal with.'

'Which is what we don't want most?' asks Yuri. 'You being wrong, or right?'

'You don't want the big war, Yuri,' Sara says. 'That's the worst, there's many around who think they would survive....'

*

If you know where you are going – entering the green, running, hand in hand, perhaps – you're out the other side. It takes no time at all.

THIBAUD

'That's a fine ship,' says Yuri. 'There's no water, though.'

'People still need ships,' says Thibaud, handing Yuri a large adze. 'Untie some knots – this tree longs for the water, hear its spirit wail.....'

'This ship is what you'd call a dugout,' Sara says. 'A dead tree.'

'You'll find something to explain to me in time,' says Thibaud. 'This place business, and the authorial voice – they're not needed here. I know exactly how this ship is made ... what it's intended for.'

'You're optimistic,' Yuri says. 'Where we came from, there's talk the world will end. Maybe the towers they build are ways of getting out and up....'

'Perhaps it's ended,' Thibaud says. 'And time goes on but doesn't catch on solid stuff – like a clock whose hands don't turn, a car – the motor's fine, but the transmission's bust. History's not circular, but churning on ... it all works, but the connection's lost.'

'That is my philosophy,' says Yuri. 'Or a small part – "how, and why, things change". That is my speciality.'

'You could be valuable here,' says Thibaud. 'We don't have socialism – just elements of communism, primitive, like us. We celebrate when sober – the rest of our lives, we can be drunk.'

'Well,' Sara says impatiently. 'Dancing and song – will there be that for me?'

'Of course!' says Thibaud. 'No one can stop you, and if they do – you just go on, inside. I bet your friend, protector here –' and he points to Yuri, 'is well equipped, he'll have a feminine side to give him strength, advice, all that. A couple is a bind, a threesome brings more options....'

'What interests me,' says Yuri, 'is how you're organised....'

'It's naturally of interest to us all,' says Thibaud. 'There is a science, even where you're from, that tries to find it out. But tell me, dear,' and he takes Sara's arm, 'What is your song, and how's it connected to your dance?'

'Oh,' Sara says. 'I'll have to learn. The will is stronger than the deed, you know.'

'You cite our only rule,' says Thibaud. 'A question, to you two, beautiful young people, slogging towards old age ... which is more effective as a punishment – money, or the knout? The whip is quick, the money gnaws, corrodes. It's a shapeshfting beast, that comes and goes. They say it's taste, the preference. What's better, quick or slow? The knotted sting, the hectoring mouth? Ah, maybe – the purse: the soft tongueless craw that holds you, while acid spittle burns off your face, your prick.... We are unsure. Whose should be the choice? We felt that laws beget corruption. It's judgment of behaviour – that's what counts.... But where, and who, and how....'

'There can't be many of you here,' Yuri says. 'Laws are scattershot, for where there's too many folk to be judged in other ways....'

'Oh,' Thibaud says, 'we've nothing. We are poor. So we are very few. What do you expect? We mostly work at things unfinished, that will sail around the world – like this grand ship. It needs some other steps before it's ready for the water, if we find any. For now, it is a hollowed log, that's difficult to work.'

'It is,' says Yuri, sweating, throwing down the adze. 'You may be on the right track. You'll need a shanty in due course. We'll see what culture you guys admire when Sara gives her gigs....'

'Oh,' Sara says, 'I'm far from that. Besides, I'm sure you've got your pros equipped to play in every genre....'

'Well,' Thibaud says, 'you'll never be a griot – you'll just have to find a niche.'

'And the spirits?' Yuri asks.

'This tree,' says Thibaud. 'Died wanting water. Well – maybe it will get some. Eventually. I assume you'll be a sailor then, my friend. You'd be its spirit – a jolly jack, a tar, I'd hope.'

'I realise that is the norm,' says Yuri. 'And – hope drives us all. Spirits – they are weak, and contrasted by their lookalikes, their twins. But still, the weakness of the driving mind, it disappoints.'

'That's to be avoided,' Thinaud says. 'Disappointment. That's why we mostly do things that make us active now, might have a future life. Think of purpose, not of end. Ends are inevitable when you stop.'

*

It's to be contemplated, that conclusion.

*

Sara, Yuri, wander down the slope: there's people growing things...

'That isn't so,' says Nadia, a youngish crone, in flowered apron and a wind-stretched foulard.... 'Things grow themselves. What you do is kill the weeds and beetles.'

Yuri thinks, 'Oh no – they're literalists. I'm out of place. standing there. But, after all, if it is true the world is round, there's really no place anywhere – India is there, China beyond – or else it's China first, with India behind.. It spins, the wind swirls round, but changes tack, it's hot, then cold – nowhere is ever where it was. And then there's space and time ... the yin and yang, coupling and circling round – how fortunate, that what I'm sure of, nailed down – is fragile me, and her, of course, my faithful, my feminine side that lies beside me on the bed and knows me better than I know my voice, which changes when I have a different need or different person standing there, to kiss or hit, flatter, insult, buy from, sell to....'

'You're the thoughtful kind, I see,' says Nadia. 'You'll do well here. We don't bother with that stuff. So, you'll stand out. Before you two start your act, you need submit to the big chief. Me,' and she takes a bottle of vodka from her apron, offers it to Yuri....

'Do they obey you, Nadia?' Sara asks.

'Of course not,' Nadia says. 'Otherwise everyone would be a chief.'

'I don't need much,' says Yuri. 'I'm a sage. I need a tree, a rope and a basket for the food you will send up. Sara needs less – some planks for her to dance on, nothing for the song.'

'You'll need a lot of vodka, Yuri,' Nadia says, taking the empty bottle from him. 'Sara can dance on grass – that's what we make the vodka from – it gives a rhythm....'

*

'It will be difficult living here,' Sara tells Yuri: 'You have to concentrate, they say exactly what they mean.'

'Like those poor penguins,' Yuri says. 'Before their island was submerged. I remember how it ends – "Fifteen millions of men laboured in the giant town." It was a fiction then, not even science.... Then we lived there, in that city. You can see the scaffolding from here, the tower that ends ... a fist? protecting fingers? The gold finish, gets in your eyes. There's poor Charlotte and Abnousse, they said nothing memorable, they're on hold, whole lives – stasis, Abnousse fixed in a dark frame, Charlotte waiting for her letter, like when they came by hand. The repetition, Sara! Only the rain distinguishes a day from day. Routine is wishful thinking – it slows things down, but in the end, the handle breaks, the dog runs off, your heart gives out on the top step.'

There's other people down the slope, tending rutabagas and themselves.

*

'The good part,' Sara says, 'is people will always stop and have a drink with you. The negative – when they're sober and they celebrate – they tell you – "Sara, you can't hold a note...." or "Yuri...."'

'I know,' says Yuri. 'My theory. How is there change? Some things, it's true, I underestimate. There's laws and particles. Waves, deaths, explosions. The wearing out, the foetuses. That's why things change, and how. Virus and collapse, pustules volcanic, aneurisms like the wave in Hokusai....

'Rousseau, Kant and Marx.... In our universe, which is the smallest in the matrioshka set, theirs was a twitch, a spasm, hardly perceptible ... theories of movement that can't wind a clock.... Will this poor place become rich? It could, it won't, is that the point? – the same we say of the rich place going poor, as probably it will, it is....'

He weeps....

'The noise a thousand sages make – is of a crumpling ball of silk, each brain – transmits a rustle, at full stretch. Their tree is motionless when it's pictured on the scroll. I have exaggerated, puffed myself, the best idiot my tiny village had.... My theory – how the future, where we lived, will end – who hears, Sara? Who even listens?'

'You're one of them, the gardeners, that's all,' says Sara. 'You're right. These are the best of people. You are on the right track, Yuri. Believe me, you're great, not that it counts, but that is what you are. You think it's unavailing? Anyway – you're up there with the best....'

'I'm sure your voice will reach the top, dear Sara,' Yuri says. 'Keep on, keep on trying it.'

*

'These celebrations,' Yuri says. 'All the emotion.'

'They feel in control,' says Sara. 'Critical. Things as they are. You weigh them up, and they go on.'

'I have emotion,' says Yuri. 'But where does theirs stand? It's theirs, not mine.'

'It's empathy, being in the species, an understanding,' Sara says. 'I'm nearer than you to being here, staying put. But I don't want. You – want it still less. If things won't get better, they can be worse. But here, they stay the same.'

'What are we supposed to look for?' Yuri says. 'Happiness? Its pursuit? That's in a document they make you learn – if you live over there.'

'There's no books here, Yuri,' Sara says. 'Don't you need to check off milestones?'

'I'm indifferent to stones,' says Yuri. 'And it was never books. Here, there's no cinema – it's a graveyard. No one's buried there. Movies. That's what I lived for. The movement. Start and finish. Colours, people always young. The proletariat – it mostly wins, wins good and clean, or else goes down in heroism – the audience always cheers. Who'd want it otherwise – once, there were even usherettes....'

*

'We've no right to be here,' Sara says. 'They were born here, we don't have a document.'

'We can't leave,' says Yuri. 'We've been everywhere, there is nowhere else.'

'I'm not happy,' Sara says. 'We've no right.'

'That's a tricky point,' says Yuri. 'They could expel us – we've nothing they call work. We're not even unemployed. But maybe they will not. And Abnousse and Charlotte – they're in trouble now.'

'No, Yuri,' Sara says, starting to cry. 'They're not in trouble, they're in jail. What did they do – plan rebellion? Talk bad? Or try to link with their big men again ... stir up acquaintances, talk down Piers's tower? The winds change, Yuri, guys have lots of kids and suddenly minorities become majorities, and what are we? We are just us....'

'Those two would do a deal,' says Yuri, irritated. 'Besides, a year in jail, soft, no rude shocks – you learn a trade or to be real bad. It's not so different from Neon Walk, where they were.

'Here, when you're moribund, they send a squad – you hear them on the stairs, their iron-shod boots, and then you hear the whistle, the last train – the iron-shod stick, sings through the air ... your last concern and melody ... and then you're gone. Like with the cat, the Cheshire cat, disposal is the puzzle.

'They call them the ambassadors, the *embajadores*. It's the right work for a philosopher – being, then nothingness, the rictus, waiting for the wheel to turn, maybe your number or your fruit will come up to the top, you've lived the perfect life according to the book, it must avail, you say.... And then you've said it, and your moment's passed....

'If I join the squad, I'll stay. But – do I wish for that?

'Sara, it was not for that we breasted through the scrub.... Wrestled with Mackie, fought off Binkie's crew and faced down Piers....'

'It's up to you, Yuri – movement of things, of nature ... or of people?' Sara asks. 'Their material conditions, Yuri, determining consciousness, remember.'

'I know,' says Yuri. 'It's all been muddled up, and maybe me – the fiction and the science.... Both hypothetical, that's true. I should insist too: there's matter, quite insensate, then there's plants, animals, then us. What we make, we call our history. The other species that survive – must make what history they can.

For their struggle, they must need a splash of consciousness... Anyway, what's made here, aside from vodka? They're all good people, though they don't move forward as they should.

'I can't do anything at all for Charlotte and Abnousse, even if I knew whose consciousnesses were involved.'

'I think you're not so interested in what comes about,' says Sara. 'It could be a big problem for us both. There's no hope of sacrifice – you for me or vice versa. Our loves – anonymous, long gone. We're on the road – feelings ephemeral, deeper than love, but not to be relied on. You will dump your disciples when it all starts going wrong.'

'That's why I don't have groupies, Sara,' Yuri says. 'Disappointment. They bring it copious.That's to be avoided. Love? It's falling down a well – you don't try it twice. Don't talk – it breaks the rhythm. Don't share bad news – that too's a precept, a thesis, if you like. The deeper an individual goes into herself, themselves, they should be disenchanted. Deep doesn't lead to deeper, with more mysteries unrolled. No mystery; no deeper depth. The more they cogitate, the more an individual they become. The collectivity's limited – it doesn't care what happens to each one. The individual has prospects – it alone can see and hear, suffer and die. But, that's it, everything to know. We reach a limit, a limitation, permanent. Only one-self can act, only you live in that vivid way, hear the birds in descant, see the rats play in the street.... And then – you're not there, not anywhere at all, and all the rest go on, and you can't feel for them, nor they for you ... no itch, no sting.'

'All true, Yuri,' Sara says. 'But that's the end. No mystery, no quiddity. And no philosophy, no more....'

'I'm sure I never thought, I never said, there was,' says Yuri. 'You're my disciple, Sara, and herewith – I cast you off, as you cast me: not into a longboat after mutiny, but like a line of knitting, obsessive, repeating over and over, extruding an enduring comforter, extra-large, of infinite length.'

*

'It feels all the same to me, whether I'm your follower or you're mine,' says Sara. 'The people here – they don't have kids. That way they avoid imperialisms of every stripe. There's no one needs feel sorry for them. No one seeks to educate them so they can do new jobs.

'No one bought me either, so I am out the game. Sagery and vocalising – it's what you do when you're waiting for your future that most likely will not come. Watch out! or else the stream, your Lalesh, won't be the centre of the universe – just in the way to somewhere else, that crude guys can pollute and dam.

'And, Yuri – you're not sharp enough – your female side: virginity? Is that your topic? I despair.'

She does. It doesn't count, it doesn't count at all.

*

Obviously, the tower falls. If it has a significance, what it is depends on Binkie. He takes his net, his butterfly – his butterfinger – net. He's cool about it all, catastrophe. There's many explanations, and you emphasise one, and then another. You know the real reasons, everyone's real motives, the ones that underly and every now and then they surface – but that's the individuals. How a collective reaches its conclusions – he knows he can't quite decide on that....

*

The fingers, the heel of the hand, the golden hand, come down on Thibaud's patch. They dig right in and make a golden shelter, like a shed, quite low, but he can sleep in it on humid afternoons. Nadia has so much work to do, keeping abreast, and keeping out of things, and making all go back, familiar, to nothing in particular.

If there's a structural fault, Piers would be angry – not that the complexity of the design was his. Better if it's sabotage, better still it's vandalism or terror ... not that he is terrorised.

There must be casualties – people going down, captains at their desks – dying *for* something, not just dying – that's important, that is what they say. It's a difficult conception, but it's travelled, and it's always fresh.

Mackie wanders in the corridors – free-lance. Sometimes he canters, somtimes rolls, like a bowling ball, guttering out, glimpsing in, or sending off to have you all knocked down. This is his home, here, and in the bars. There's love, too – just behind the door ... there's Sara, needing a protector.

Just now, Sara and Yuri – they're in a holding cage. That is its name, but it is cells:

'There's two of us,' Yuri tells Binkie, who thinks Yuri's playing mad – a trick.

'There's you and me,' says Binkie.

'No, I mean there's more than one of me,' says Yuri.

'Yes, of course,' says Binkie, who's used to this kind of talk. He says, 'Piers has suspicions – all who've ever been as close to him as you – you must know something that can help us pin it down.... "Pin down the tower!"' he shouts, and there is laughter up and down the line.

*

'Piers. I was his mentor,' Yuri says. 'Seeking the spirit. Perpetual motion. We should have a class, a book. All the great liberators have one. Listen: "the possibilities for all motion to cease at some time or another ... for the dialectical conception, are excluded from the outset".'

'I understand all that,' says Sara, 'but it's true only till tomorrow. There's so many ways – the hot, the cold, the bang, the water and the bug. The motion stops.'

'It's not there's no ending to the world,' says Yuri. 'It's like my theory of change. It needn't end, just roll on and on, a sea ... tides, return eternal, "The new age begins with the return to the Greeks – Negation of the negation!"'

'Back you go, so's every end looks like the start!'

'They tell you not to use an exclamation sign,' says Sara, quite sceptical. 'I remember long discussions of electricity in your book.... Now, Charlotte and Abnousse, they are suspects. Guys drink, you serve, there's rhetoric, your customers run off – and you're accomplices. Those two won't want to hear about electricity, how it moves, is it inherent, part of a substance. Let's hope they're earthed.' Then suddenly she asks, 'You don't suppose they shock you here?'

Yuri doesn't know – the new age is a mystery.... Will there be room for him, also the female side that takes up little room and gives advice?

He says – 'The Greeks invented electricity. They invented genocide as well, then they thought better of it when it was about the Greeks ... though when it was Iranians, I am not so sure.'

'They invented everything,' says Sara. 'Art and religion, and the rest they had a theory for. That's true for Greeks – probably Iranians too.'

*

'We're only here to answer questions,' Yuri says. 'I have the big one. We know all changes, flows: but why a transformation? Is the old world truly pregnant with the new – what will it be? Another world, a monster or a twin, a toddler, a Pinocchio?

Things falling down, guys transfixed, incinerated at their desks?'

'It's all your fault, Yuri,' Sara cries. 'I know nothing. I'd go back behind the bar – that's my home, not in the green, or on the slope – not here....'

'I can't stand it in this cage,' says Yuri. He shouts, 'Sara, how long....'

'Patience, Yuri,' Sara shouts. 'It's been half an hour, no more.'

'That's my limit reached,' says Yuri, beating at the wall. 'Abnousse – may never see a cat again – and Charlotte – her cash unused. She can't buy the stuff it brings in prison movies: a lobster thermidor, a silver bain-marie.... Escape! That's the priority....' He scrabbles at the door.

*

'Slowly, you Wozzeck,' Binkie laughs, and pats poor Yuri. 'Your drama's not today! Sara – she goes back to Mackie – she's a spy like every citizen should be, though each avoids the name. Poor honest Tanguy – who remembers him? For shame!' he laughs. 'Bars and more bars – my best resource! High-born ladies – they're the best. Abnousse and Charlotte, they will learn to pour straight in the glass ... and smile and chat with customers. But you! You were a confidant, Yuri; Piers trusted you: you failed. Attach yourself to me instead – life can be good. Nothing's assured, of course – but in the street, these summer nights, the lime trees! Cicadas, and the watercarts that lay the dust. A paradise, with a cayenne pinch of warmth from hell...!

'In here, you'll find the summer nights are tough. Bugs love them – but you won't. No owls, stray sparrows cheeping in the roof.

'Tell me, dear Yuri – why did it fall, the arm that reached to heaven, caught all the rocks and flashes that came down – a provocation, and protection too. Was it the spirit, Yuri? Something slightly wrong? Eternal return to Babylon, its tower? Does the secret live in there?'

'Well,' Yuri says. 'Trying to outguess old nature, trying to make it seem like us, with dialectics, features you can understand – forget it. It's too big and slow. That book was a mistake. Just – when you walk outside, watch out! No malice. just catastrophe, nature grinding on...

'We humans, we are different. I believe – we all have souls, or spirits – when we die, they die. They're us. Forget them. They absolutely have no function, Binkie. Politics. That's what counts.

'But – you're right, of course, dear Binkie. You need a guide. It's clear the tower fell because the spirit failed. Maybe from the start, it lacked ... the quiddity, the mystery: commitment. We're all seekers, Binkie – I can offer you the longest journey, the journey to the light, and one day, maybe you too can plan a tower, and this time it will hold, and you will be King Ouf, if you wish, or any name that comes to mind.'

Both are fascinated – with each other, with themselves.

'Yuri,' says Binkie. 'I'll take you on. You are my shaman, my spirit guide. For now.Tell me the mysteries of everything you see, and you will have the liberty you need....'

And he unlocks the door.

And Yuri scampers out.

THE ESPLANADE

'A flourish!' Chris shouts, shouldering me away. 'Thirty musicians. Ancient instruments – the best of the west – in front of the esplanade, where the empire held reviews. A spectacle, my world covering the world.'

'Chris wants to know,' says Rufus, 'What you can do? Why you are here.'

'Oh,' I say, 'I know something about everything, but not so much. I had a one-way. I do that, and look for work – then I track on. Onward, you might say.'

The parade ground of the elephants – nature's natural trumpeters. The grass is coarse, like stakes.

'Beware the snakes,' says Rufus.

Who are these guys?

I say, 'I never saw one.'

'That's how you know they're there,' he says.

*

Stay or go? It's a fine point.

*

'It's a huge event,' says Rufus. 'To bemuse, enthuse the locals – a spectacle: armies dancing, fantasy motors made from junk. A carnival, new empire, soldered together from worn parts ... old glory, now humble subjection.... Modernity high-kicking....'

I've read the guide: it's about Yama, the judge, the lord of death and hell.... Each temple, each king builds one, then at the end, a pyre, time comes, it's covered with neglect and soil....

'Don't fuss me with history and ignorance,' says Chris, who knows it all. 'It's my stuff, my coverage; if you don't like, aren't enthused or sponsoring – then, off you go! You're casual – perhaps you want work: – I give revelation. For that, you need guys with credit.'

*

I'm not wanted here. That's rather good. They've stuff with wires lying in waiting, women hooked, intent, not trusting me on sight....

'It sounds like Macedonia,' I say. 'Fruit circus.' No one reacts.

Full up, no room.

*

There's a bus, and lots that look like buses. Same with bicycles – some will take you, others not.

*

Rich people, sympathisers, give me a ride.

'We go everywhere,' Raoul says. 'So far, Yunnan was best. Colours and differences! Those matriarchs! We do good, usually by being somewhere, casual good, not industrial. Not tourists, not just curious – rather, seeing everything there is, and binding people who can't move. Giving them a value, by gazing at them. Being extraneous spirits, giving, taking nothing. Pressing them like decals, convincing them they have a stickiness, can adhere, to a globe you don't fall off or need to cling to. A world that doesn't crumble ... we construct one ... travelling with friends, lovers, partners, sometimes staying. At other places found unworthy – a sandwich and it's off at once....

'It's better than pretending. You bring communication, not aid or cash. Respect the poor, don't linger with them, everybody has complaints ... make a video if we must....

'We take in the suffering we see, it makes us strong, and we move on,' Raoul talks on, practised. 'We're pampered animals, we're on the hoof – everywhere, just as we please. We rent the vehicle. Our tent – it has to be a kind of prison, an open prison, and we are trusties, or else the empathy we feel for real prisoners – race, sex, poverty, chance, aggression – would not calculate. We share the feelings, not our capital. Really, it's more like prison visiting, but nonetheless, it's a situation not to be condemned. It is rewarding, not so easy, and it costs. It's our link with a past you couldn't otherwise feel nostalgia for ... We're the enlightened ones, all's tumbling down, we know enlightenment has failed.... You have to be grown up....

'Your neighbours – they can kill you, kill their millions. But – it's guys like us, from outside – we think big, our fathers did, in tens of millions and feet cut off the prisoners ... we photoed, we had albums. After that – what can you say: "oh, so sorry, can we pay?"'

Raoul and his mates – the ride they give me, free... That was a good turn too. I'm moving on....

*

The airport guy says, 'They told you wrong – the planes are only for officials. You leave by walking through the trees. How? You'll have to find a guide.'

I hang around. Write it all down – somewhere, they'll pay you for your story, possibly. It's a big industry, after all: travel, hamming, touching up, the pics....

*

After some days, the airport guy comes up – 'Raoul and his guys have gone,' he says. 'Daphne is different. She looks poor – or maybe she pretends. It's good.'

'When you live wrestling with the land, each plant needs a story, someone to live in it,' says Daphne.

She gestures often, strong arms and neck. There's other guys sat round, no one belongs, it seems; they're not a chorus helping things along.

'When you drive animals – you need something to drive you too,' she says. 'It may be a song, a book or bullets from your gun. We're not like that. I don't know what we're like, people like me, if there are some. There's been no one like us before – we're intelligent but if we're not, it makes no difference. We eat the same food as the crudies, the primitives, take the same transport.... Give sweeteners. I don't leave, I hold it together, I've escaped. I am the tendrils binding up the stones. Can't leave.'

'I need out,' I say. 'Will you help me?'

'I help everyone,' she says.

'Here?' I ask. It would be tough, doing that: so many at their edge – a mountain of them to be levelled off in ladlefuls.

'I find a tree that's not in lines, not like those clay soldiers, drawn up, waiting for the battle in the earth,' she says. 'And I shake it. It may give me seeds. Dead fruit. I shall bear a tree – I know.'

'I want to leave, Daphne,' I say. 'Don't say I don't know about leaving. I'm an expert.'

'Don't believe in Yama,' she says. 'I'm sure Chris and his spectacle guys do not.'

'You should believe in everything,' I say. 'I do, it doesn't cost, it's not insurance.'

'To leave, there's burning sandy wastes to cross,' she says. 'No indication and no help. It's thirty kilometres – take enough supplies to get you through. And if you lose your way – it's sixty. You can't carry that much stuff, and if you sit and ponder – it's over a hundred, even two. Mostly we don't see the guys who try. I'd help you, but I'm busy now.'

'I could stay here, harass you, Daphne,' I tell her.

'Impress me,' she says. 'I'll find you a short cut.'

'I was a genius at school,' I say.

'Poor thing – did you have to go to one of those?' she asks.

'Those distances,' I say. 'Usually it's states that make them so elastic, not knowing what to do with strangers, not knowing what country to send them to. Nothing in it at all for anyone, best have them wander in the sand.... Have them find infinity, a waste.'

'Here,' says Daphne. 'I am the state.'

'That's fighting talk,' I say: 'Look at the flags ... hear the music ... and the dancers, each with a prize. None of those is yours.'

'Nonetheless, for you, I am the state,' she says. 'When I die, you can have me stuffed, sat on a throne, enoble people with my sword, ask them a civil question. Must be always the same one. Obeisance – I want it, love it.'

'I'm not illegal, Daphne,' I say. 'I came by plane.'

'Look at your visa,' Daphne says. 'See the date! You've overstayed.'

'You're a joker, Daphne, I can tell,' I say. 'I've had enough. Cultural superfetation – that was Chris. Paternalism – Raoul. Now you, statehood diffused – I've met them all. I'm finished with all that.'

'Then you shouldn't travel,' Daphne says. 'You shouldn't drift. You're a ball waiting to be kicked, a wasp waiting for its swat.'

'Anyone can have engine failure,' I say. 'Far from port.'

Just humouring, to banter on.

'Listen,' Daphne says. 'I told you. Here, I am the state. I fix. I fixed Chris, Raoul, their show, their meddling. Now you want a fix for free. I am the state, I do things as I wish, and when I'm fixing, like states I can be mad or drunk or full of dope, and no one cares, and if they care – the worse for them. I know this universe, the twenty-seven kings, the elephants, the grids, the train time, and who gets out by plane. And who meets who. That's all there is, I am the Lord, the spiritual – that's all that you can be these days. Having an army makes you vulnerable. It costs, or I would have one, but I can't raise tax because we're poor, everyone is poor, and that's my guarantee. I'm needed. My living comes from fixing, and what I fix – you pay.'

'Out, just out,' I say. 'I'm talking freight. Load me.'

'Everything you've lived or read, or put together and imagined,' Daphne says, 'is now of no significance at all. I'm the author of you and everything that droops around you: your despair, your ignorance. I'm not your spirit guide, my dear, but I'm the pilot's friend, the bearer of the compass, I draw up the manifests.'

*

'It's hot,' Daphne says. 'And hotter. I'm bringing Chris's embroidery in, his show. Musicians. They'll deck out the ruins. It's cow music. The old rich guys kept musicians, a whole herd, and milked them. They're clean, don't mess the cathedral floor. And – they kill themselves, no need for an abattoir. The music – it goes round and round. No one knows what it is – you hear it and it's gone. Or you don't listen – and it's gone. An immortal flitting. Chris knows a bargain.

'Hey!' she shouts to me. 'It's hot. Wait, wait here. Make a nest in the grass – there's no snakes, no one's ever seen one. It doesn't flood here any more – so, there are battalions of white trees, like matches in a box.'

'There's stuff around they can make music from – whittle and scrape....' I say.

'These are rich old cows,' Daphne says. 'They bring their stools and pails, and a herdsman too – probably maids to milk them.... States fund it all, the cheese.... goodwill – not especially mine.'

'You may be right,' I say. 'But though they say the world will end quite soon – or make us flee to somewhere else, I feel this place has far to go. It can take a lot more pain.'

'It will all happen, as I say, as I've arranged,' says Daphne, happily. 'I have borne more fruit. They'll come – play their *wheen wheen, bomble bomble* – then go, bemusing everyone. I know what it all means, and I'm protected. Here, it will be then as though they never were. After, I can think for you – transmit you if you still want to go.... Most people settle where they are, even if they're where the world will end.'

'Anything can start again,' I say. 'A line of kings. A full house. An empire. Make this place an island, float it somewhere safe. Promote some values. Fraternity? Or *luxe, calme* and the rest?'

'Or you could take ship. Surabaya, loading salt fish in Senegal, Bilboa – then New Brunswick....' she says.

'It'd take for ever,' I tell her.

'Just as long as you would like,' she says. 'People don't want you nomads, wanderers, enchanted or not – don't like your colour, your smell, your luck, your stories, your baggage or having none, the camel songs, the tone deafness. Think of staying, not in my sight: everybody has a use, it just takes time ... take, take – take time, there's always more.'

'You're a bobo, Daphne,' I say. 'What they call a bohemian bourgeois....'

'No, no,' she says, 'I'm much much older. I was never a phenomenon. I'm too old to be afraid of soldiers – I've seen lots, and in the end, other ones arrive. Too old for world's end – mine will finish, maybe tonight, or tomorrow, walking through the grass – you never see it, but it's there, waiting.'

'That world is to be cancelled,' I say. 'Like feldspar pounded in a mortar, just glimpses left. Thousands of worlds continue.'

'That's a beautiful thought,' says Daphne, pinching my cheeks as though I were a melon. 'Banal, but always welcome, like a cow-symphony. You'd hate it to sound too new and strange.'

*

'The people here,' Daphne looks up from her screen and says, 'Rejected socialism – the bombs, and then the shootings, put them off. Now they want the capitalism that brings them wealth, with the equality that brings security, they hope. Whatever comes, I shall survive, my dear. Forget the trees. When the trees go, there'll still be grass. Our tradition rests on fire – cremation on the farewell pyre. Something combustible will be found.... If I can't turn into a bush – I'll be a phoenix, an eternal flame.... I don't much care, I don't discriminate....'

'This boat,' I say. 'To reach the sea....'

'I'll point you where to go,' she says. 'Tell me, if you decide to stay – do you have sex on your mind?'

'The rule is "don't touch their women",' I say. 'It sounds presumptuous. Summary.'

'Don't imagine me,' says Daphne. 'You're free now, don't spoil it. Free, in a tiny space. It's the best! The best you'll get.

The worse, you'll find, is a door, a wall, away. You'll be free –
if you scale and scrabble. It's a risk. It – nothing – ever lasts, of
course. You'll want a double, too: a person, one you thought
you fancied. All the rest is fluff, stuff unexpected that falls from
trees. All the denunciations, betrayals, bribes and flights – all
are hummocks. Leap over them. But being unfree – born under a
flag, skin coloured all over, chained by an oath, your prick, your
promise – do you want that?'

'Of course not, Daphne, and thanks,' I say. 'I see it like that,
but never in immediate words. You mean, I'm free, but can't do
anything with it, anything at all. Maybe it wasn't what I wanted,
maybe it's inscrutable. There's better things around....'

'That's how it is,' says Daphne. 'There's never any more.
People want more of it, but there's always less – you need more
people, more rules, more cash. The result is less. Be content.
You're free. If you want something else – you do the sums. Free
means complicit and harmless – but then, you don't know
what's what, where the stink comes from, who it is that you
don't want to harm.... At least, stay away from me – be sure,
that's what I most desire.'

'Just one more ask,' I say. 'What's your plan for all the other
people?'

'Oh, you crafty little sod,' she laughs, holding my head
against her bony chest. 'You want a life of questions! Now, do
you think those guys will bring their music stands?'

*

The festival's a *festa*. The guys imported – they're not docile.
They stamp and rut. There is a fire. There's deaths, and
clubbings, sex in the grass.

That's the way – kick into the frame, lots of frames and fill
them. Try to get out again.

It's a great show. Daphne flies them off.

'Now,' she says, 'I can despatch you. Be very, very careful where you put your feet – under the grass, there's every form, every pitfall, *feux follets* ... they're called *snakerijen,* snakeries. Not snakes – just grotesque shapes and depths. Where there's been empires, everything is overlaid – the frontiers, jurisdictions, the religions – what do you need to rub them out and start again? Sacrifices, then meditation; god-kings, then magnates – and that's just you, my dear. You're not even one coming from a people, you're just people landed who've stayed on ... massacring for bucks ... over and over, children's children....'

'I know all that,' I say. 'It's history, culture. A minestrone – people like you, Daphne, vaguely New Age, you see it as a presence – mash it up, paint it, chew it over. Everybody else – ignores it, lives it, does it at school, then comes to see the ruins, takes a pic.... It doesn't bother me in either way....'

'I told you, silly boy,' says Daphne. 'It's not at all my thing. I'm a despatcher, not a judge. My advice is the same for anywhere and anyone: be very very careful who you meet, especially the cops. And where you put your feet.'

'I must be on my way,' I say. 'I didn't know I had one till I met you, Daphne. I have no roots here – not one root, not of a people, not as a person, no empire....'

'Well,' she says, reluctantly, it seems. 'There is a motor.... Two lovely ladies, Zeynep and Sonay.... They will need to leave. But would they want you in the back? There'll be some kind of test....'

'You mean,' I say, 'there is a road?'

'Of course!' says Daphne. 'There always has been. Take rides on elephants, there is a road you leave behind! The soldiers too – it's just that bombs aren't fair, they can erase the differences, the colours too ... roads orientate, they are the target. It's just – in you, I saw you like things difficult, don't want to leave, and yet you have no skills to settle in. No hopes.'

'It's true, Daphne,' I say. 'Chris, Raoul and you – you're all a mystery. It's quite like tigers – you know the others are like you, but you don't bond, at most you screw and then run off. The elephants, though – they have a social sense....'

'They'll have to go,' says Daphne. 'They will eat us up, those hungry ladies. Now, we have tanks, but no one yet they can be used against. You think I'm quite unarmed? Effectively, it's so. I stay and stay, I bind the stones, the ruins. Much good does it do, but someone needs to do it, I suppose. You have to keep things going on, even if it's only fugitives that stay: every massacre requires its innocents....'

*

Sonay and Zeynep – two lovely ladies. They have quarelled, they don't speak together.

Zeynep tells me – she doesn't talk to Sonay, 'They killed all those people, over and over. They'd already lost everything, even Buddhism didn't make them breathe above a whisper – they even tried slaughtering each other. Everyone was killed, for sure, over and over. And there they are still, again. But it doesn't prove immortality.'

'I'm in good shape,' I say. 'My motor's hardly used. No former owner – and yet, you can't say I'm independent. I don't eat like the elephants, enough's enough.... I think like the jackals, I'm always frightened, but don't sting or lurk....'

'Oh,' says Zeynep, laughing and ogling, 'You're a pretty smart underhand kind of guy.'

'It's the test,' I say, 'Everyone goes through it, you too, Zeynep. It's like low-carbon steel, nothing fancy, but you're tested, tested for extinction – and you come through. Every morning I pass my test for normal, survive. It is essential, so it seems. You go on and on, until you can't.'

'Oh,' she says, laughing. 'Where we're coming from, they have a ways to go, they tumble and they rise – and so do we, true Turks. I won't ask you what you are, I don't want silly tales.'

'Well,' I say, 'I had to walk a long long way without the motor, when it broke up amid the grass. I must have had some ancestors, those legs....'

'Oh yes,' she says. 'Our fall. There's holes, designs that you can't see. Or else – you see, and down you go. It's how we're made.'

Sonay jumps in, 'Aren't you concerned,' she asks. 'End of the world? From all sides it comes! Our best people, urging it on.'

'No,' I say. 'I pass my test, nearly every day. I shall survive.'

'It's probable,' Sonay says. 'Repetition. People reminding you of people, places of other places, every Daphne, every old stick, the myths ubiquitous, reminding you of lying Greeks. Saying they'd been everywhere, bringing mathematics. A big lie.' She turns on me. 'Your politics – quite disgusting. You could have found out about it, more easily than the millions who suffered from the toadies and the exalted ones. "On with the revolution" – that was your shout, and yet you never broke a law, evaded tax....'

'I'm lazy,' I admit. 'My brain is sooty. But – I was enthusiastic.'

'You did suggest the short cut for us: over to Astana,' says Sonay. 'Then days and days of grasslands. That redeems you. That was clever. We could ignore the poor people, all those thousands that we saw, dressed like you and talking quite like us. That was repetition – you can't escape it, in a world that has no insects left, just people clinging on, wanting to die at home. A human touch, sort of. Buzz buzz. Bees without the sweetness, unable to find a flower.'

'I told Daphne she should ride with us,' I say. 'She said it would deflate. The cash she has, it stretches there, she has some hopes of backhanders....'

'What can you do here?' Zeynep asks.

'That's the blue mosque,' I say. 'I saw it first when shepherds coralled their flocks around the grounds ... those orange markings, how did they get them off the wool...?'

'We're in commerce,' says Zeynep. 'There's always something left to sell.'

'What there is, almost everywhere,' says Sonay, 'is people. You saw: Daphne moved the nomads in and out. Then ushered in the representatives from rich parts – showing off their songs. Sex and culture, their selling points. She's a fixed pin. She mustn't move, she throws no shadow, stands for nothing – if she had feet she would have run away. The people there – they don't yet move. Most people are not movable – they hope. They read about it, or they're told. Moving – a step before the last – where Daphne is, and where we've been, and where we are now – arrived. People – a mass, a horde of them. They're waiting for the word, the flood, the 'quake, the drought, the war – then they'll be up and on the track. Pack what you can, nothing heavy, nothing guys can steal too easily. Forget that you're a people, forget empire, frontiers – frontiers are not what you need. You'll need to jump them. You want shallow rivers, not a sea; cheap *passeurs* and sleepy border guards. People, my dear,' and she hits me on the back to liven up. 'Everywhere. They're not counted as if they are on sale, because they do some useless work that gives them food. Better that way than beg for crusts.

'There are the camps, of course: they're termite palaces. But there, the people are locked in. Supplies of folk you need – it isn't fluid. What you – we – need's not guys in flight to save their lives – it's guys who run to find a life. They're not serf souls that come in bundles, labelled, ready counted. The guys you want, they have diplomas and pretensions. What you seek is people pumped up, in crap jobs, subsistence pay. Waiting. Making do and getting by. They are the ones who do the humble work, or maybe none at all ... they suspect, but they don't really know, how they are dispensable. They're disorganised and vulnerable. Their new job – it has to have a title that resounds. You need invent a future, a career. Then, they'll do anything, for life. Won't marry, won't have kids. They're labour power, in fake shoes, lucifer tattooes, crap music in their ears....'

I'm fascinated. 'I thought you two would have a store,' I say. 'With taste, gew-gaws, down in the souk.... But no – it's soldiers, barefoot accountants, legislators – all that stuff.... That's what you recruit – the best! Moderns! And preachers. Choirs and missionaries. Scholars. Students ... the sturdy beggars who say they wouldn't clean the streets....'

'You colour it too fierce,' Zeynep says. 'But, yes, we do provide. They're the fall guys. Eyes on the prize, the wealth, the slick inventions that will make them unemployed. They love to be the vanguard, on with new lives, but of course, they're the reserve army, uncounted, numberless: ever re-created and re-born, tiny napoleons fresh and steaming from the womb....'

'Think of the farmers,' says Sonay, 'who loved their animals and made them fat and loving too, before they put them on the truck and sent them off. There's so few living things are left, we thought, we'd best be ready for the end, and pray and read the book and do the five.... But then we looked around and saw – if you like farming – people is your crop. The old agencies – a single sweeper, typist – and their work was done. They found an individual, took a fee. Now, we send off thousands. Plump and loved – some very plump and maybe not loved so much....' and she laughs. 'Farming. Someone else will plant your crop and wipe its orefices – you dress it up and pack it. Send it off. Wars and revolutions, slumps and crazes – they all need lots of people, walking up and down until the bosses take control....'

'Alas, Sonay,' I tell her. 'It sounds a fantasy....'

'Maybe,' says Zeynep. 'But it isn't so. States get paid to put a million guys in camps, two million kept from journeys that might take them into work. Your stock is colour-coded – browns not wanted here, blacks are out or only go with other blacks, and whites are rowdy, unreliable ... and then there's gods ... don't pick and mix the faiths....'

'You're not a state,' I tell Zeynep. 'Only they can handle quantities and print the manifest, have someone write the leaflet.... Hire cops and all the rest....'

'Don't be stupid, use your eyes,' says Sonay. 'There's an opening here for you.'

'I'm not so sure,' I say. 'It isn't really me. Not my world. Maybe the world is not my world.'

There's silence. The two seem indifferent.

'You see,' I say. 'You're bosses. I don't want to be a boss, nor take orders from you.'

'We aren't bosses,' Zeynep says and laughs. 'We're wholesalers.'

'There's demand,' I say. 'Someone must have a use for these guys. Even if they sit, do nothing ... no matter how hard they graft....'

'Oh,' says Sonay, 'I know where you're going. That book *The Peoples' Way* – repopulating, trekking east to west, now south to north. We'll be the Genghiz, if you like, giving another push. People not much loved – first, Saracens and Slavs, Albanians, Roumanians.... Turks. The book – it wasn't Proust, it was about people like us, easterners who infiltrate – to me, we're stimulating, our customs enviable.... Now we bring new stock, move it where there is a space.... They called us the barbarians...!'

'I don't know about that,' says Zeynep. 'I think there's no design. No pattern, just disposing of a mass: people – a quantity. A collective noun.'

'A penny, a cent, per head, for a million,' Sonay says. 'It's just enough for us to take a trip, to rent that motor, go see where people aren't yet on the move....'

'I feel your feet dragging,' says Zeynep, tugging at me, miming someone who hauls a leather sack. 'We're not intricate personalities. We prepare the ground for what you'd maybe like to try – in miniature; the human tragedy, the crooked path, the hard life.... Humans – always learning, always ignorant, never at peace, always at war.... It's a daunting tale.'

'Me? Try something? You mean movies?' I ask. 'Do a series of them, since I'm sensitive?'

'Yes,' says Sonay. 'There's a cinema near us. I could go with Zeynep....'

'It's good you think there is some big force protecting you – perhaps with some cash....' says Zeynep. 'Exposure? Denunciation? We expect it. It's been a constant since the Prince....'

'Oh, Italy....' I say, downplaying. 'Perfidious....'

'She means Kropotkin,' says Sonay. 'He's the Prince that she admires.'

'And yet,' I say, 'there is a flaw. People. No one wants people. Not really. They're a drag, a drug. You say you do, there's traffic, you'll trade in them, the new, the hopeful ones.... Millions here, no past, no future – naturally, it attracts a trade.... But – who would want them? All those brains...? Voices with an accent. Ticking aslant, like watches in a pawnshop....'

'You're right,' says Zeynep. 'That is the flaw. Where's the demand? Why do they want people, if indeed they do? It's not the people – this here's the regime of machinery. That's the next step, the coming thing. The stainless species.' She laughs. 'I can't explain it ... people. Maybe it's because they come so cheap?'

'Look,' I say. 'You may have something. You have the numbers. Dawn. A million eyes are opening. A tough day coming, most will make it through. Massacres – they're everywhere, if you've a past, there's massacres lodged in it. Lots survive. Now, there's the "Trek of the Peoples": once they were called barbarians. Then, they became us, and they will again. And after, we went out in all the world, and spread the word. It was remarkable. All over Asia, Africa, America, all pouring from one place to another, millions like us, nowhere particular to go, all the diplomas, books read, philosophies nutshelled, goals scored or assisted, pigs stuck.... Big empires tacked over other big empires.... I grant you all that,' I say. 'So now, somewhere there must be a place, someone must want people: there's not much else. The elephants – they're almost gone.... And there's the cinema – I don't know if I'd satisfy. I have a delicate, even a repellent, taste, and you need millions – dollars – to make a few metres of one....'

'That's all nonsense,' says Sonay. 'I never heard such racist rubbish. Have you ever seen the eye of God?'

'No,' I say, at a loss.

'I never met anyone who has, although a lot is talked about it,' she goes on. 'Someone, something, must be looking, though. Someone would say, if we had got things wrong. It must be so.'

'That's casuistry, Sonay,' I tell her. 'Self-justification. Not that anything bad's been done, of course, or that you've worsened things, exploited a misfortune....'

Staying with them – it would be difficult. They have those silences, they're caustic. They remind me, both of them, of Anna Karina. It makes it hard to choose between them, besides, no one now recalls dear, bold, Anna. She's become an ancient, doesn't resemble Zeynep, nor Sonay. Nor herself.

'Put them in stone,' I say. 'The old Khmer had it right: the rest goes up in smoke, but stone remains, is scattered everywhere, the jigsawed parts, turned into holy sculpture and shatterbanged into every capital's museum, just body parts, chainsawed up and all bled out, heroic dancers white as white.'

'You're bright,' Sonay says to me. 'Keep searching, but keep your questions limited to sheep. Nothing romantic, none of your aleatory tosh.'

*

'*Amor mio....no hay espansiòn como la que vivimos.*'

How I loved them, unsaid, unrecorded, Zeynep, Sonay ... my love... 'there's no expanse greater than where we live...' It's true, it doesn't last, it's a river losing itself in deserts. They say the founders were blind, to build Constantinople, this city, on the European shore.

I wait for them – they went to look for some people, there's people all around. They don't come back – maybe I moved, walked away, all kinds of people, fussed and displaced, in the hot streets. The sun up there – the eye of God. My movie.

There's immense life here – it makes you sad, to stand still and watch, contemplate ... all these stories going gone to waste.

The urge comes to see dead souls, now that I've a profession, and a skill. Chris will have left, the sounds bouncing off the esplanade, leaving no mark. Raoul – on the road, kind to people hitching.

Here's the esplanade again.

'Daphne Laurent', it says, on the screen – the bug screen: 'Inspector of the Ruins.'

'I'm making – or, better, I shall make, a movie,' I say. 'I recognise that it's my vocation.'

'You'll see the elephants have gone – there's just ghosts left – a trunk, a tail,' says Daphne. 'That's how I got my title – they give you one when there's no money in it: just an honorific.... Inspecting what isn't there. Ruins – they're afterlives, spectres.'

'Without the stone – here could be the centre of Brazil,' I say. 'Remember – ruins are what has been destroyed – but also what's survived.'

'There's bosses everywhere,' says Daphne. 'Alive and prospering. New or ruined – to them it's all the same. It is their gift. They'll have an installation made, put plaster replicas – much better than the ghosts....'

'Oh, I know about all that,' I say. 'What disappears ... the cash you need to find a specimen, coax it in a cage. They're not the same as us, Daphne, the bosses. They're omnivores, what they see becomes quite homogeneous. I know I'm different. It's like: I love women, Daphne: it's that I've never met one. They're all more or less like all the rest, like me and you.'

'There you have an obstacle, my dear,' she says, cracking her long fingers. 'You need some continuity, say things so they can cohere. We need long sentences – those will persist and multiply. Forget those movies, and Brazil. Forget the animals, the women – all that's in your sentimental head. Chris – or maybe Raoul – for sure they were responsible for carrying off the statuary. I have no evidence, of course – they were professionals, and you, compared to them – you are a booby, no project, no suspicion – only your imagination. Imagination's endless, without substance. If you can't be a boss – try a humble job....' And she pulls her inspector's cap down on my head, over my ears.

'Yes,' I say. 'You're right. I hear the trumpeters.'

They're like acufene.

The cap is limp with sweat. We laugh. There's silence here. 'They've gone!' I say. 'All those creatures, I didn't know their names, if they sting or you can eat them....'

'Yes,' she says. 'You're lucky. You wouldn't eat the caterpillars. All the same – they've gone.'

'I'm sorry for everyone,' I say. 'Not for them.'

'There's lots of politics here,' says Daphne. 'You may have noticed them....'

'Oh, I'll put it in the film,' I say. 'Really, it's all about that. Not just here – here's too complicated, but taking in a continental spread.'

'I'm sure it all links up,' says Daphne. 'Accumulation, disappearances and eking out. Now – I must do my rounds.'

'See if something's shown up?' I say, and laugh. 'They don't forget. They always come back to where they were born.'

'You'd take money for your movie?' Daphne asks. 'Lots. And give me some.'

'Of course,' I say, 'but it's mostly in my head – and there's lots who leach on you in films – insurers, box lunches, all that.'

'And if you'd no money, and couldn't eat the grubs?' she goes on.

'Yes,' I say. 'I'd do anything. I know no one, so – no inhibition, no shame. Grub would be grub – just avoid the plurals. Though even so – yes, I'd do anything, at least at the start when you have the strength.'

'Remember,' Daphne says. 'There's a road here. In the old days, they used to bomb the roads, and the streets – they were where the cops, the soldiers did their work.... Now, there's what they call "quiet wars" – they don't bomb the roads, or streets. They're like here – it's quiet. I guess it's war.... If you know that, you know everything, and you can go right on and make your movie.'

'I see what you mean,' I say. 'But if you look around – streets and roads. They're much the same.... Distinguishing, it's not as easy as you say.'

*

'You know,' says Daphne. 'Your movie – it really shoots itself. I mean, you know: it's easy.'

'I know,' I say. 'That's what I'm afraid of. It's what I think.'

It's all despoiled. Why did I come back? The site's been robbed but it's been made appetising, there's the grass cut, and stalls, tickets, it's real clean.

'You've got a TV, Daphne,' I say.

There's no need to answer. Ruins; bodies still and running.

'That's Alep,' I say. 'What a cameraman! I'd love to use him – I guess it is a him. Showing that movie – must be at the start, years ago – they must be careful now, keeping in with who is winning, no recriminations. Show, but don't tell, don't blame – just people helping, no one is responsible... They don't put on both sides – where's the resisters? I guess they can't be shown, it all looks wanton. Someone must have let them down....'

She turns the picture off.

'Those Turkish girls,' Daphne asks. 'What'll become of them?'

I don't explain. It's hard to give a summary and not have it sound bizarre, although theirs is a massive enterprise, though it's really the edge of something opening up, a crevasse, vent, volcano, crust thinning down ... a tilt, the peoples on a slide, melting like pistaccio ice-cream, *'Les invasions barbares'*... – they start to fall away, Sonay and Zeynep, although you think they must be rich with what they do, really it's the mark of something quite unstoppable, you're standing on the edge, the rest will crumble but you're firm, solid, the fixed figures giving size to the vanishing landscape, you can't expect to make your bucks and stroll away.... It's like you're on the beach – let's say Biarritz – you forget about the tide; that your cart, your stall, won't float ... people, our riches, under the ostrich-feather parasols ... sucking air into their wormy lungs....

'Hey,' Daphne shouts. 'Don't drift away! Another one-way voyager is sleeping here, he's just like you, it's quite a weight....'

It's Jean-Paul. He looks like me. 'He thinks like all of us,' says Daphne. 'Everyone who comes here – doubles up. You tramp – you meditate. You gawp at poverty – and count your cash. Where are the elephants, you think – and peer into the grass for snakes, you find a stick ... to kill, or keep you tottering upright.'

*

Jean-Paul, Daphne and I – we lie down on the sleeping mat. 'It's our tradition,' Daphne says. 'The rest have beds – but I don't care. I inspect the ruins that there were – and someone else inspects the people, as they come and go.'

Later, Jean-Paul kisses us, and says, 'Well, we slept together, and I don't know who you are....'

'It could be a puzzle all your life, if you let it be,' says Daphne. 'Live with it. I can't despatch you, I've made a step up now, all I do now is inspect.'

'I'm sure you've done your dreadful things,' Jean-Paul says to me. 'Mine are awaiting. My family – they killed Algerians – now, there's a thing you don't say now....'

'Oh,' I say. 'That was bad luck. I sent guys off to do the awful things. That's how it works – not many get to swing the axe or heft the club. If you finish school, or have some cash, it's normal that you send guys off ... in your name they go, when they die they won't remember you.'

It's rather lame; Jean-Paul doesn't mind. He says, 'I'm not here to start it up again – this was the edge of empire, an earlier one ... they felt it sharper here ... more soldiers, less water, new taxes too.... I'm here to see how it was done. The stones, the prayers, the sculptors, dancers, guys with axes – and the elephants ... how did they set it up and make it last....? Is this the best that people do...?'

Daphne puts on her cap: 'I'm off,' she says. 'There's music coming, the grass must be cut back, the snakeries ... you understand....'

Jean-Paul says to me, 'The nazis now. My take: it will offend, I know. If they had had a better guy on top, who'd read the book on making empires last, not starting with the neighbourhood – he might have made it go five hundred years. His guys – depraved and ignorant, they'd have marched for ever, killed whatever came in view, reached every shore, massacring the best.... Instead, the most ignorant rolled on till the gas ran out, obedient to a boss who longed for suicide....'

'It always ends.' I say. 'The boss is weak, the great chief dies – his kids, mouthy, improvident ... the water fails, there's floods, there's bugs.... It always ends, Jean-Paul. If making empires is the top – lots have been made, and none go on. The guys with saws cut off the dancers at the calf, behead, dis-arm – the esplanade sinks down.... It all becomes a play-park, an opera venue, a zoo for lemurs, spectres....'

'Oh no,' says Jean-Paul. 'Don't get me wrong. I'm pleased, that it all ends. My interest's keen but only hypothetical. Is there a way to make one empire last? If not, what is the other path? Are we capable of neither one – not hierarchy, not anarchy ... not order and not liberty....'

'You've a philosophy,' I say. 'But not much.'

'Much more,' he says. 'I travel to these sites. There's tours, of course.... Africa is full of them, huge empires, imperial peoples, India too.... Then there's the Americas....'

'You disappoint me, Jean-Paul. It's all a gawp for you,' I say. 'As if looking at some empty shells told you about the sea. You have the urge to spend and trade, like monkeys swap their gooseberries.... The dynasties, the pantheons, all's on a guided tour – nothing's discovered, everything's laid open, no secret recipes; just like it's always been.'

'I fear you're right,' Jean-Paul says. 'Maybe the empires aren't a key to anything except themselves. The countries that we have right now – they're the old empires with new lines around, cut up, jumbled, a stew, a salad.... For me, the

travelling's become my life's end – it justifies, you meet new
empire builders – like those Turks.... They're everywhere,
Zeynep, Sonay – there's great propensity to empire in the
Turk.... Just think – there's been the Skiing Türks and Ox-footed
Türks.... A sprawl.

'Then there is Chinggis – as if a wasp has wandered in the
pattern in your kaleidoscope.... But,' and he embraces me, holds
me too tight, in glee, 'I may find solutions yet....'

Zeynep and Solnay – they may ski, it's true. I noticed nothing
special in their feet.

'What do you seek? Another pattern?' I ask. 'An empire of
the empires, like they say we have, a world of different hordes.
or maybe....'

'I have a problem,' Jean-Paul says, still clinging on. 'Last
night – you may have heard the hootenanny. This travelling. I'm
full of bugs. I have been colonised – they buzz and maul, I'm
almost not myself and nearly them. Oh, what am I? A bag, a bag
of bugs? A swarm of swarms? Or just infested, the soft flesh in
a dying shell, taken over by a clawed and bristled beast, a crab
of crabs....'

'I heard a mustering,' I say. 'A flourish, even. I don't eat the
caterpillars, they can give you gripes and butterflies...'

'Well,' he says. 'It happens thus – not just with Turks. Where
there were peoples – in there comes a military hierarchy,
smoothes them all down, sex goes to work, promotions too, and
mercenaries of every stripe and spot.... Who whom? you ask....
My colleagues say – it all depends on language – what do they
speak ... and that defines who is the biggest cheese, the tallest
poppy.... It's too bad that often we don't know – to us descends
a silence, some have a language that has left no trace.... The
Jouan-Jouan – had their power, enjoyed it, hated it, and
disappeared, left not a word, no carving on a tree, no word-list
in a cave.... Is that our fate?' he asks me, and he steps away, I
see his belly wreathing, moiling with its wingèd life. 'Our words

– they'll fade, be piled in everests of junk, of messages unreadable, unread, the discs effaced becoming abalone, our intimate machines stripped down in Côte d'Ivoire, revocabularised, off to Lanzhou.... Empire of empires, that leaves a universe of universes made of indecipherable words and unused space....'

'The vision terrifies,' I say. 'And yet it is predictable, a legacy we didn't want to leave, a will of scumbled sentences, passing nothing to no sons, no daughters, all the wisdom packed into a single mussel shell placed – quietly, in what passes for our dark – upon the sand, to wait until the destined wave embraces, sucks it up, and carries it away, where six-armed octopusses.....'

'Yes, yes!' shouts Jean-Paul. 'It waits, it waits!'

'Oh no,' I say. 'You mean it's happened all before? Another empire of the empires, a thick lexicon reducing to a single page, a single word?'

'Of course,' he says. 'The Word. You must have heard. A single word – in the beginning ... the new one, naturally, maybe for the thousandth time. You start with only one. A flourish. What is it? Light? That's logical. Power? That's much the same. Help? A waste, but comprehensible.'

He is exalted. I say: 'This is musty stuff, Jean-Paul, a don's delight. It isn't so. The empires leave their statuary, even if only toes and ankles stand firm....'

'Yes,' he says. 'Mine is just fancy. No one gives a fuck about the messages they get, don't read, eliminate – the book is dead, and so's the word. You're right – scholars justify their trade in vocables, but life, real life, goes on regardless....'

'What then, Jean-Paul?' I ask, exhausted by our brilliance.

'A place, a country – empire,' Jean-Paul says, opening his brain to me, using his unique key, his bounding tongue. 'Of the dispossessed, the orphans of new empires.... People without countries, without a frontier, a mass ... unwanted, mere fingerprints, their kids tugged off, made into mince....'

We contemplate. I say,

'There's people there, here, already, Jean-Paul. Everywhere. You'll move the anti-empire folk around, they'll snowball up then melt away....'

'Maybe,' he says. 'Zeynep and Sonay – they have on their book some millions: strays and waifs.... Then there is Daphne – she patrols this space. She deals with all the chancers – Chris, Raoul, planning a theme park, for sure, and visualising towers. We all inhabit ruins, prize them ... all's been pristine, all is junk – the cliffs and mountains, the Rushmores, graffiti, eroding, rusting out, so familiar they are in our bones, our eyes.... Daphne has her cap and badge: official – she can pace out the spaces, the expanse of ruin that's available – to make fresh habitation....

'Come all ye! Come, people with no aspirations, a past to be forgot, a future that you hope will not attract events or taxes, conscription or the plague...!'

*

'What you need, Jean-Paul,' says Daphne, 'is a remedy extreme. Your bugs – there is a way....'

She takes off her cap, inside there is a coil, beige, eyes. 'You must consume this snake,' she says. 'She'll do the rest.'

'That's it!' Jean-Paul shouts. 'At last – ah, to be rid of them. But then, the snake...?'

'Yes, that's the catch,' says Daphne. 'Every culture's reached that point. Dear Doctor Propp, who took the fairies out of fairy tales for us – maybe you could have him extract your snake.... Structure, Jean-Paul: that is the snake. The bugs are just a circus. You must choose. Chinggis? Or Kropotkin? Authority or licence, the arbitrary – or the pondered and observed.... Even here, upon our mat, the names come round again.... Small male flies, gopakking round the light-bulb....'

'I'll think about it, Daphne,' says Jean-Paul. 'I really shall. A lot. For the moment, I'll be sticking with the bugs.'

*

'Suppose, Jean-Paul,' I say, as we three snuggle down again, 'This end of the world they talk so much about, how would it make a difference....'

'Oh, not at all,' he says, quite angrily. 'Naturally, oneself would feature in the general rubbing-out.... Annihilation. And so too all the other candidates.... But speaking scientifically, no, the absence of an object, a material, a guinea-pig, need be no barrier at all. It's typical, that theory precedes the demonstration by friend rat or fruitfly in the cage. Or with the bomb. Someone would take it up, my theory, that's for sure. Someone unseen, out there,' and he gestures. 'They watch us, even though they cannot feel us, tickle our brains, or other parts exposed.... If an idea is any good, the universe will take it up – although of course there's those who say that everything, the future too, is stored and lurking, already waiting for the off but not quite visible from here.... Nothing invented, nor discovered – just waiting for its moment, time plodding round, a warder with the poisoned gruel, from cell to cell....'

'Your vision, Jean-Paul,' I say, 'it's not encouraging.'

I'd not expected otherwise, but still –

'Listen,' he says, coming close, too close, again. 'Don't take up arms. It's never over, and one way or tother, you'll be dead. The best arms now – is music, doing tours for everyone; and plastic stuff – toys for the kids, and toys for you.... If you get guns, depending where you lived, you fight for peace, or victory. Peace – the soft choice, victory, the tough. But don't in either case be tender – those you can't kill, don't let them start up banks and stuff – they'll peel your shoes from off your feet....'

'This is tired stuff, Jean-Paul,' I say.

'You're right,' he says. 'That's why I'm seeking something new. Time is irreversible – it's the bourdon – we make the melody....'

'Lots of things are irreversible,' I say. 'The elephants – they ate the trees.... Now, they've gone as well.'

'I don't need a public,' Jean-Paul says. 'I don't propose a trip with you. My friend, Damien – is bringing music in. You don't need chairs, not now. We'll chivvy off the snakes, the fans will sit on grass.... As for you – do you have hope? Are you angry? Lazy? Who was it, told us how it would be for ever?'

'Pareto,' I say.

'Will it be so?' Jean-Paul asks. 'Eternity?'

'Probably,' I say.

'Who'll give you orders?' he asks.

'Not those Turks,' I say. 'Or whoever takes their place.'

'You know we'll break like eggs,' he says. 'Fallen from the clifftop nest?'

'Of course,' I say. 'And Daphne will inspect us.'

'Do you know people here?' he asks. 'The people? Are there many peoples?'

'I can't tell,' I say.

'So, when the music guys arrive – they are another people, peoples, taking over: like soldiers moving through?' he says.

'You've a good hand there, Jean-Paul,' I say. 'I fold.'

'They'll steal the recipes,' he says. 'Not only soldiers – they are priests, ladies-in-waiting, a curse on Trojans and on Rome, I say. We're Carthage – already been laid waste.'

We're silent, quite exhausted. 'You can't build!' shouts Daphne, shrilling. Has she been listening? It seems so – 'This is the moon. No gravity – it'll all fall down. Float up. Leave us, leave me! Plan magnificently, fail, and go away.'

*

'It's a magnificent event,' says Damien: 'Musicians are musicians, even if they can't play too well, the singers – their instrument's always left behind, partly, in transit somewhere else. The fans – I wonder why they're called that? Many of these groups we shall not see again – the poor ones disappear, the better cost too much....'

'That's everything said,' Jean-Paul says: 'Now – the news is that people here resent you guys.'

'That's good,' says Damien, 'Or, it isn't bad. Bombs? Fireworks? Demos? A manif? A good trambusto helps it all along.'

'That's trite,' says Jean-Paul. 'You make it sound like echo.... And you – you look as if you're wearing someone else's clothes....'

'You're the expert,' Damien says. 'Fashion – its seasons and their round. You may have noticed, dear Jean-Paul, that every movie, every play – the details may be different, but the theatre's just the same, the public too ... always the same, a play is almost live, a movie's not, so you don't need applaud or see the end.... And so, and so. Structure – without bones all you have's rump steak. What matters is the occupation of a space, that looks the same. It's like the mass, sometimes the priest has dressed up like a clown, who notices? What matters is the frame, and not the daub within. .... Soldiers, Jean-Paul. Be thankful they don't shoot, just stand around, some smoke, some drink, some want to copulate. Me? Wear funny clothes? People like me, they always say the same, because they do the same, they like it and it must repeat....'

'You're protofascists,' Jean-Paul says, laughing.

'Pre-fascists,' Damien says.

'You talk about theatres,' I say. 'What does that make you? If they're a mirror, how come they don't reflect but show us ghosts?'

'The esplanade,' says Daphne. 'Don't mess up the esplanade, Damien.'

'You're a great man, Damien,' Jean-Paul says. 'They'll get a movie out of you. But you are grounded, stuck in a duplicate. If you have a vision – it's a space, a desert, a forest, a motorway, that people can inhabit, – and they do! It's their panorama, their perspective. A space, but quite full up. Your spectacle – it's only smoke and when it blows away – there we all are, exactly where we were, the day, the night – they are indifferent....

'Knock down, build up – can we get out of that, and not by talking in the air? Not unread messages, and people running everywhere. Instead, an ordered space, commitment without substance.... Real emptiness, no monkey chattering....'

'Well,' says Damien. 'Your take on history, Jean-Paul – it's always been a mystery to me, to all of us, old friend. But I can tell you, the people here are lucky. They can protest, or they can come in free, to see the concert, sing along – international stars, like in the firmament! Here, it's a paradise. They could maybe hear the noise, but they didn't suffer from the bombing, nor go through the purifications. That was their ancestors! Lucky! I should say.'

'To expand a little more,' says Jean-Paul, thrusting onwards. 'The first big war, what was then world war, ended in Westphalia. Everybody to their place. Praying to what they liked. That was a good foundation. From then, it all went down and down. Science – gone global: deciding who is who, and new ways of getting rid of you. Or just fresh chivvying: taking your cash, who marries who, what country you can go to, how long for, what work, and "no you can't".'

'Liberty Hall!' says Damien, and laughs. 'That's where you'd live. It didn't last. That was a union place in Dublin. Nothing to do with anarchy, though.'

*

The stage is tall, the people and the music too: they show, they leave.

'Pay-off,' says Damien.

'All the flesh!' says Jean-Paul. 'Waving like plants. Like it was before.'

'More ruins,' says Damien, giving Daphne a brick-thick wad. 'Can anything be ruined twice?'

'Of course it can,' says Daphne. 'They go beneath the grass, beneath the seas, rectangles surmised, infinity of drowning states. New life accelerates the deaths. I'm a resister – but, some living things are gone for good.'

'The growth of any one is product of its eating others,' says Jean-Paul, holding his squirming belly. 'True in part.'

'Dealers, fixers,' Damien grumbles. 'Bosses and riggers. They sprout, they flower and fruit.'

'All these rightist states,' I say. 'They pay for arty stuff and ecstasy – so people think love and opinions are for free. They give you cash, Damien?'

'They're mean,' says Damien. 'They think they've won for ever. Maybe they have. No one is organised against them; the past – it frightens those old exalted ones, the few, the opposition.... As for the autocrats – the winning makes them cynical, they help themselves. They think short term, alas! hooray! – they're stupid. My heroes, possibly my comrades – they're coopted, isolated....'

'So,' I say, 'Damien, you were once a hard pure man....'

'Yes,' he says. 'I read the books, I knew the jacobins. There was a universe, it all blew up. Those who survived forgot the politics, went in for things you start off with, sex and passports, and can't change a thing....'

'They should begin a movement in a place, not found more sects....' I say. 'But where? It's all turned into gelatine or gelignite....'

'I think you need to seek a place where they believe in second lives and more,' says Damien. 'Not just believe, but live them too.'

'A primal nowhere,' I say. 'So, these songs your guys brought here.... Love, death – all rhetoric?'

'Oh,' he says. 'I told you. It's dross. Tailings. All the energy got used before the fascists won. Who listens to the words, if you could hear them anyway...? It spreads, the plague, spreads everywhere..... Jean-Paul is right – you must be insubstantial. It resists, the luminescence of the ghost. The rest, material conditions if you like, it's what we have, and the powerful make you clean their bloody boots...The rest is sects, it sounds like sex, it keeps your noses up, pointing to the sky, like hungry dogs....'

'So, you're a ghost too, Damien,' I say. 'A part of you. It's wonderful to have you sitting here, as if you breathe.... I knew that you were dead – the four of us asleep on Daphne's mat. You were the one who didn't groan and grind, absent, untroubled, while we squirmed and Daphne twined her knotty legs around our waists....'

'You boys!' says Daphne. 'Keep it down, your talk, your politics, your nursery tales. Be thankful for your life.You have arrived, Jean-Paul; here you can stay, and stand upon the esplanade, watch the sun go down and up....'

'And me?' I ask.

'You have a rover's eye,' she says, coldly. 'If it isn't Turks, it will be Arabs. You long to be enchanted – maybe to be dumped as well. And so – you are a militant?'

'No one ever asked me to be something else,' I say.

Not true.

'I can't imagine being otherwise,' I say.

Not so.

I say, 'I'm with the people, but I'm not a humanist, the people's changed, changed totally, I don't believe in them, we are at odds, I don't share confidences, I don't wave my arms, don't sing along....'

She interrupts, 'And did you ever think of doing all that here?'

'Not exactly, not thinking, just imagination, of living somewhere else, some other time,' I say.

'We all remember things we haven't done,' she says. 'It's punching a way out of our jute sack.'

'Let me, Daphne, have another night, even on the mat....' I ask.

'Oh,' she says. 'I'll get another mat, with all this cash from Damien. He'll be back – ghosts are lonely, you think they're somewhere else for centuries, then – there's the whistle....' She tilts my head against the light, though it can't hold a shadow any time. 'You could sleep outside, but then – there are the snakes ... the landmines too. Now, don't quiz me about those public things that you can't do a thing about: I am a bone, not one you gnaw. I am a shoulder-blade, so sharp I cut up other bones.'

*

Bedtime again. Time for thought.

'Zeynep and Sonay, I wonder, did they believe? Islam is the only one made for us. In all its clothes, the body is one, *the* one, though you may not look and comment if it's beautiful, or if it's just the one that wears the clothes, simple, colourless maybe. There's no vindictive God. Cynicism doesn't enter: there's no suicide – that's out; no death, no corpse, no end. God is a master with a tawse. We learn, there's no graduation, ever, the master understands us all, quite intimate, but, of course – not as a human would, not being vulnerable like us....'

No one interrupts: maybe they sleep. I go on:

'There's only one kind of death. It's ours. That isn't real, it's kitsch. There is no dance of death, no Shiva, no carpenter hammered on his plank. The world, with us sticking on it, of course – it's outside physics, it's a shimmering spot in space, our *umma*; a spot like on a pool ball – our earthy earth, now here, now cannoning, now sunk.

'There was astronomy, but no universe. Peace – it was for us. But now, we, the world, are not the same. In the universe, there is no now, there's past and future – and you'll never get to them, so wait, wait ... and you won't see, not ever, anything.'

'The great Friend, the Buddha they respect here,' says Daphne, 'has a message. Keep off the grass. If I were you – I'd heed that. Your disbelief – it does you proud, don't fiddle with it. You've seen them coming through – philosophers, gophers, tourists, impresarios. They don't gather moss. There's hillocks of it here – if they could gather, it'd all be gone, just rocks beneath – even water....'

'But,' I say, 'it all, matter, moves. It's just – I don't do removals, trucking people, not like Zeynep and Sonay.... Or seeking transparency through Jean-Paul ... the silence, illuminated, ether.'

'Oh,' Daphne says. 'I think you're there. You've reached transparency without his aid. It's useless following a metaphor – that's what those religions are. Forget it, forget meditation: are you so interested in what's within? You're not enough concerned with things external – you eat bad, wash seldom, cheat on your bills. Zeynep and Sonay – what they do is hard-edge, countable.... They're right: we all prefer slavery to the camps, though sometimes you get both, but that's bad luck.'

'Lives are a story,' I say. 'That means people, situations, should develop. They don't, they plod. So – what is it?'

'You don't listen to what I say,' says Daphne. 'Besides – I got promoted.' And she twirls her cap.

'If you've a question, you travel, roam everywhere,' I say.

'Oh,' Daphne says, 'I have questions, but I'm not a nomad. I don't have animals to feed.'

*

'I love people like you,' Daphne tells me. 'People who are always wrong. You keep on coming back – and don't stay long.'

'Damien, Jean-Paul?' I ask.

'That's who,' she says. 'Just as much.'

'Yes,' I say, as we go down the steps. 'This big hole near the esplanade – I'd wondered....'

'This is the ordnance hall,' she says.

There's bombs and rockets – bangs hanging, impending like in dreams, and mines – stacks – 'Some were accidental,' Daphne says. 'Besides, we couldn't set them off – they'd bring the ceiling down.'

'The ceiling, Daphne – goes on for almost ever, then it curves,' I say. 'And comes back on you. I once read the book....'

'Mind where you tread,' she says. 'If there was a revolution here, you wouldn't need go out in the streets, just set this off ... you'd have a plain where you could start again.'

'It's not like that,' I say. 'In the world, this world. There's no "again", just "on and on". I know – in the end, no doubt it all turns out farce, but meanwhile – it's a string of tragedies. The only hope is starting over, and you never do....'

'Best not to hope,' says Daphne, leading me towards another hole – 'Stick to the ruins – those were built with hope....'

'Vainglory too,' I say. 'Maybe, if there were elephants again.... They used to flock to empire....'

Down the second hole – there's a laboratory. A sign says, 'Believe in nothing – if you must believe, believe in the unattainable.'

*

'Don't linger,' Daphne says, pushing me ahead. 'It's just their joke – they're brains, they left their bodies far behind.'

'Tell him,' Daphne says to a guy – grown white and underground, tall as a root. 'What you do. And don't say why.'

This head guy says, 'Oh, here we do some capital work – we calculate how long before the world will end. All the scenarios, all the risks. Then we advise. For capital, for soldiers, builders of towers and shelters, people who wait for deaths and births, people who buy telescopes for looking up, or divers' masks for down, helmets for insurrections and for motorbikes ... we calculate the odds. Of course, we don't encourage bets, besides, there's no pay out. It's art, our estimates.... You frame it, wave goodbye, and off it goes. It's a galleon painted on the sea – seeking specie, braving whales. Wishing to go round and round the earth. The sea – it hides everything there's ever been and ever sunk. Daphne knows, nothing is ever left in view except for ruins....'

'Prophecies as well,' says Daphne. 'But – these guys here, they're optimists – they give you centuries to make your plans....'

There's rows of busy whitecoats: old men in gowns that look like shrouds, clicking on their abacus, young ones giving each other spinal taps, or could be rape, old women doing poker work on younger women's nails, and desks with suitcases that calculate the bets – a screen with one huge number, its digits trickling like sand.... 'That's our fake currency,' the head guy laughs. 'One day the whole world will come and ask us what it is, convert it, and we'll all be rich, richer than Golconda....'

I gawp, even Daphne gawps, although she knows it all, her job to see the ruins up above are still in place and tourists come and go without a pry, without a curiosity....

'Well,' the head guy says to me. 'What can you do, what do you want? We'll train you anyway, to do what is required, so what you say's irrelevant....'

Daphne smiles, encouraging: I say, 'Maybe something to do with animals.'

She frowns.

'We're all animals here,' the head guy, Sergei, says. 'Down the chain – I guess there's snakes. I see you more as of the foxy kind....'

'About the holidays....' I say. 'A key to the door, so's to leave....'

'You've done time, I guess,' he says. 'That's why you count free days, though there's no tattoo on you, no cobweb and no gang. There's no politicals left now – you must be clandestine. Or did you just evade?'

'Time?' I say. 'Done lots. I swim in it.'

'He maybe just got caught,' says Daphne, spreading her thin wings on my head, so's to protect. 'He has a nasty look. You can see he's thinking thoughts that you can't read, that haven't been revised for years.'

'All casuistry,' Sergei says. 'The only person over us, Daphne, is you. And your cap fits, I see. We make the rules here,' he says, pulling both my ears –

'Oh,' he laughs and says. 'No, you can't see the rules. The code? They're common sense. Anyone can understand the principle. The most important thing...?'

'Survival,' I say. 'What more could there be?'

'We'll all drink to that,' says Sergei, taking a bottle from a drawer.

'They call it Ghost,' says Daphne. 'White spirit. It will make you drunk in two-four time.'

It does. 'Of course,' says Sergei. 'We love, seduce, and waste our visions in requited and unrequited lusts. The question is, my dear,' and he embraces Daphne and me. 'Is survival thick or thin?'

'Thin,' Daphne says, and simultaneous, I say, 'It's thick.'

'Then,' Sergei says to me. 'You win the joust.'

On with the Ghost!

Our brains gain weight, they plod around, waving their arms like fat people do, the very fat – some places don't let you say they're fat, some that there's no fatness, no! So, we pinch in our mouths, Daphne farts through hers, it's pretty funny, but not to tell, not here....

'Don't stare at us as if we're freaks,' says Sergei. 'Some of us are very very old – it seems to happen when they work out there's millions of years to go, and they slow down, the old ones.... Others, when they calculate the time is short, how the seas are parched, and we are lying on the shore in Jonah's whale, waiting for the skin to crack, reveal the tiny pinkish wormy saint inside – there is new life! *Novaya zhizn'* – and we rise up, like angels! Angels, Daphne! – then we're young, reborn – we race! We have to love, to screw, to solve equations, colour in the maps, have kids, desert them, punch out our lovers, shoot up on a bench ... in breathtake time....

'I promise you,' he says, holding me tight. 'It's only life. You go through it, or you don't, you die, or else you don't.... But though it can be very very slow,' he says. 'I've never seen an individual here who doesn't die, or go upstairs; maybe the old kings were different....' and he laughs. 'Maybe a guy with many pairs of arms – he suffers when he goes to school, they make his life a hell, but possibly – he never dies, just fumbles on, his handicap makes him a juggler, a lover brilliant but not much tried, an oddity – and all the dancers, well, for sure, they die. You're left alone – over and over. Solitude. Those are the true freaks. None of that sort slaving here....'

'What can we say to that?' I whisper, and Daphne says. 'I told you. It is art. Until the gyring ends, not only here but everywhere – it's art. That's what they call – '*die ewige Kunst*'. A sketch, a scrawl of what's immortality. Don't see it as a likeness....'

'What they do here is strategic, sensitive, a universal,' Sergei goes on. 'The tall poppies – they would bomb us if they knew. But on the other hand – it doesn't matter, none of what we do. Not a fig. That's how work is. They pay you, it is hard and dull, and when you can't go on, they take away your key. And – that's it. You make your story as you want, and tell it to whoever has the time to hear.'

'Yes,' I say. 'It's time. You swim in it, until it all dries up, and then you're on the shore. They used to say the other shore was communist. You don't hear that often now....'

Sergei sings loudly, 'Here come the clowns!' – I didn't know there were words to it....

'Back to our desks,' he shouts.

'Sergei was a vagabond,' Daphne whispers. 'Now he runs all these scientists, their experiments. Some vagabonds are wonderfully prescient.... I don't mean you, of course – you aren't!' she says to me. 'He calls the people upstairs "The Chinese". Sometimes he says they were bombed by the Americans, sometimes, he thinks – the Russians. In any case, it's clear they won. Or didn't lose.'

GHOST

The great white spirit. We drink a lot of it. Economics is important too. We do the sums. I do the work, I'm not paid, there's nothing to spend it on.

Rich people, lots of them, just carrying on, or a few poor people, loving animals and eating them, then not having animals at all?

It's a simple way of thinking, because it's not like Paris, here there is everything, there's no hiding, no ambiguities, no one talking you out of something, pressing your knee, touching your tit.... No, it's straightforward, and we speak every language in the world, and Sergei has to call in a guy when the snakes start coming down the airvents.... A delicate job, that costs.

Ours is hard, complicated, work. We have lovers, naturally, and here age doesn't matter: – and there's nowhere you can go with them. The work, of course, is futile, but it's a relief not to have, each of us, different houses, a different size of everything, different pictures on the walls, our different lovers to take back into them.

'I'll have Sergei give you time off,' Daphne says. 'There's someone coming through. We can all sleep on the mat.'

*

Here's Mélisande. 'What is it that you do, sweet Mélisande?' asks Daphne.

'I examine people,' she says.

To me, she says, 'We'd have bombed you if we could. My bosses are elected, the people aren't, but they believe in better, flatter, worlds. It's strategic work you do, it upsets all the prophecies.... If you decide a date when all will end, it's economics that's involved.... The problem is: above you, there's the ordnance. It'd bring the floor down, accelerate the end if we should rocket you.

'Listen – I'm not used to mats. I'm a Malinowski type: fieldwork in the morning, afternoons I plan to rest in the hotel....'

*

Later, I ask Daphne, 'Why her? Why Mélisande? She wants to shake the world above, down to the toes and ankles, the torsos chainsawed off and crated on to Paris.... All, everybody, photoed, pictured in a book. Voices of silence, you can bet ... the quick, the dead. It seems we're dangerous – they don't know why. Never forego a paradox, it carries like a barn owl's hoot. Why, Daphne? Why host a spy?'

'Oh,' she says, 'I fancied her, I longed for her – her beauty, seen on a screen down in your snakepit there below....'

'They all look beautiful on screens and scrolls,' I say. 'When you get close to them, the flesh – they transform into different lengths of snake.'

*

'Young Sergei,' Mélisande asks me. 'Is he really young, like his profile says?'

'Oh Mélisande,' I say. 'His tattoos! He's cobwebs everywhere – elbows and kness and buttocks too ... he's done time from Vladimir to Kharkiv, he's led so many gangs the new ones' logos were stencilled on a leg that you don't see. He had it taken off, just like the statuary ... sent to the museum imaginary where all his family waits and reminisces on their plinths....'

'He is redeemed,' says Mélisande, fiercely, with conviction. 'I'm certain. He has made a sacrifice, suffered the confinement, the exclusion, the paradox of being contained, secured:

preserved and yet unfree.... He gave his leg,' she says, rolling
her eyes, up, down and roundabout. 'What greater destiny can
any person have, than looking down the road, to see.... when,
where, how, it ends. He is not the destroyer, but, even more
precarious and bold – calculates where his, our, life, the life of
everything we've spied on, ends.'

 'I hadn't seen it that way, Mélisande,' I say: 'It's not sex, then,
that you seek? It's not a life of piracy you see in Sergei – but the
mystery, the last things.....'

 Daphne is entranced. She says,

 'And is it true, Mélisande, that you could call the bombers
down, but it's from love of all the people roundabout you
pause.....'

 'Oh,' says Mélisande, 'I'm not political. But politicians – they
need scholars to inform them, identify their enemies, where to
point the stick.... Otherwise they wouldn't know which country
they should bomb, what cluster they should target, what motor
in the desert.... My work is humble, but it orientates....It's not
the people, Daphne: I don't advise a bombing because the rest,
the other bombs, would go off in their sympathy...'

 'If we're not going anywhere,' says Daphne, 'If, sooner, later, it
will end quite inconclusive, then tradition, things as they are,
'relax, don't fuss' – they're as good a choice as anything.'

 'That wasn't what was said,' I say. 'We're going towards
somewhere, that's for sure – extinction. That's our work, that's
what I do.'

 'Well, then,' says Daphne, continuing to stare at Mélisande.
'We shall amuse ourselves. With our long lives, the prostheses
invisible, our duff parts replaced, our friends and neighbours
cannibalised – our limbs and brains are interchanged – a
dancing leg stuck on a missing arm, the extra heads stuck on our
shoulders for when we need – second, third opinions....'

 Mélisande strokes Daphne's lined and knotty face – she
giggles, 'Even the skin!' she says, 'the nose, the mouth, the

cheeks – why wait for corruption – graft on new parts – inside, we are the same ourself, it's vanity to think the outer shell is personal. It's packing, that is all....'

'Bombs, Mélisande,' I say. 'Let me go back to those. You'd think of hitting us because of strategy, because we poke deep into secrets that the old gods knew, kept to themselves.... Why they had us pray and sacrifice our best.... Just for that? No wickedness, nothing aggressive that we've done....'

'Ah,' says Mélisande. 'The species! Of course, it is aggressive. And perfidious. But what falls on your head, in any case – that's fortune, a spasm, tic of the universe. Think of the dinosaurs, the molten rock....'

'We do, we do,' I say. 'Think of it all the time.'

'My word, Mélisande,' says Daphne, admiringly. 'You are strong meat!'

'I understand,' I say. 'You'd bomb us because our calculations might be right.... But if you did, you'd blow the ordnance high – stuff left from other wars forgot and terminated....'

'That's childish,' says Mélisande. 'Put like that. But yes, you're right. Now, there's the matter of my passion for Sergei – if that is concrete, it gives another reason to desist, at least until desire is slaked....'

'And my ruins,' Daphne says, waking from her dream. 'If there's a blow-up, they would disappear.'

*

There's no hotel for Mélisande. The locals' huts are full of bugs, she says. We three lie on the mat – she paddles with her feet. She snorts. Daphne and I can't settle – I even put my hand in Daphne's, and she presses it, and thrusts it off.

*

Mélisande has written, *'The local people hold in high esteem and dread, and rightly so, the Judge, the lord of hell, Yama, who stood upon the esplanade and watched them all file past. First came the elephants....'*

She's seized the wrong religion, but she's right – we dread the ever-present Judge, who punishes, rewards, and never asks for evidence....

Sergei is told about all this.

'You're right,' he says: 'Mélisande – she is the judge, she's loyal, her state ... those guys, who can't find us on the atlas page, they follow her....Of course, the people here resent her, and her state.... I've been through it, and the first times I survived....'

I say, 'It took the fear and hubris of some dull guys, picayune they were, wavering and gaseous – with banal visions that you swap in dodgy bars – to kill their millions, and in return they left not a saying you'd remember, not a joke. No paradox, no regret, no rhetoric. Then there arrived still duller, blunt and mediocre guys. And at once, they got the briefcase marked The End.... They had the power, the ordnance, to end the world – and we don't even calculate for that, dear Sergei. It's a probability, extinction in a week – yet we sit before our screens and meditate on centuries, millennia, that may or may not come....'

'Yes, yes,' says Sergei. 'Don't tell Mélisande what we don't do. We choose to close our eyes to war – we're tired of contemplating it, so we have concentrated on the hot, the cold, the water and the bugs – these guys that we elect, to strut and threaten ... how can we predict the scene they bring? It is our species' essence – sneaky, suicidal, unforeseeable....

'It's trite – but it is also true. It works for lovers as for bombs – I know. I have been everywhere, betrayed and been set up ... victim for lifetimes, it seems, of tiny cells....

'The key, my friend! Give me the key!'

'Everyone who comes here,' I say. 'Curious – they come from rich or powerful states. Raoul, Damien, they're all a threat like Mèlisande. They think about the elephants, they know we all may – will – follow them; it's ritual – a huge pyre, a little corpse atop.

'The cadaver's just a composite: some offhand thoughts, Jean-Paul's philosophy: and the locals standing round, entranced. It will make a blaze, then all's gone, all of us, some with regret and some with faith. So, after that, there won't be other kings, each holding on the tail of one in front ... just a great fire of bones.'

'I'll bet my leg's in there among them,' Sergei says, and laughs.

*

'Then,' says Mélisande, 'there were the killings here. People will come to see that all's been cleared away. They're attracted, afterwards, to where it has occurred.'

'No, no, it wasn't here,' says Daphne, brusque. 'All that was over there, and over too's the killing and the rest.... No one has plans. No projects, no scores to settle, no futures to construct. Here, all is normal, except for the people, people like you, Mélisande, passing in and out ... to see the ruins. Those are a mystery, of course, sawn up, decapitated, then overgrown.'

'Don't fool with me, Daphne,' says Mélisande. 'I know all about the past.'

'If that is so, my dear, then you must know – it's swung away, beyond our grasp,' says Daphne. 'Irretrievably.'

'I love stories,' I say. 'I'd love to know about the past. But Mélisande – you are as you are, and that makes me ... dislike what you say, all of it.'

'You don't like me for my honesty,' she says, kicking at the dusty mat.

'You seem to have honesty,' I say. 'That's all. But look at what it does.'

'I'd settle for honesty,' says Sergei. 'If no one goes to jail. The way the world ends – it's of interest to almost everyone, depending when.... Ours is a tilt point, I suppose, that's why the laboratory was set up here. Once, the place seemed crucial, portentous. Now – no one remembers why it's here. Knowing or not, it wouldn't make a difference. Would our reason, knowledge – would it change a thing?'

'Oh, that's deep stuff,' says Daphne. 'The evidence is there. Too much, facing every which way. Sergei's just adding more confusion to it all.'

'Think about the power,' I say. 'We've all been bad, but Mélisande's the lady with the stick.'

*

I can do, predict, no more. It's all set up here, a firework display. The past is laid out like a carpet, figured with grasses, covering the dead, a turf heaving with zombies. Countries laid waste as if they were a cancer; blood-red Khmer, vengeful, cutting to their bone, and deeper still.

Sergei – redeemed from his awful past, organising the prophecies of an awful future.

Mélisande – what will she bring? Assassinations, bombing? 'Find your enemy, eliminate her and him, claim victory and leave.' That's what the manual says, the Americans used that, they still try, but they didn't write the book....

If you're a vassal, it doesn't matter much who is the lord; French, Swedish, Croatian; Ghorids and Ghaznavids.... Kambujas, Thais....

Daphne. I'm sure she has a plan to build a city there.

There is no shining outcome. All co-exists, rats in a sack. The whole, quickly described – is this: all I do, and don't accomplish. All Jean-Paul says and one day we'll read back to him and laugh. How I'll live my real life before everything ends, and even after.

*

I have my ticket, one way, this time the plane – it doesn't crash. I land somewhere quite different and huge. The art's for sale, and export too – you don't need chainsaw it off. There are no dancers and no gods, there's figures just like us, no Sergei, no Jean-Paul. No Daphne, and no me.

*

The crates say 'Made in China'.

'Stack and unpack,' says Philomène.

'Unpack and stack,' I say.

All life is contained, in the boxes, communism, capitalism – all co-exists – 'It's all political in there,' I say to Philomène, my boss.

'You were over there,' she says. 'You must have scented something. You're cheap – you may be nasty too – that's why I'm paying you. These artefacts – these arty facts ... we'll plug them in and make them tick around the walls ... don't ask me if art snuggles down the best with money or with protest, our customers have made the calculation. They want the feisty statements, but it's an investment too....'

It's a fine crop – Zhu, Zhang, Way, Liu and Guo, Yue and He – and there's a Cang – some of them are huge, and none is small....

'I told you, Philomène,' I say. 'I wasn't really there, where I was – was quite different.... I left, it was all poised and imminent, but then again – anything can happen anywhere, that's why for all of us it's worth the wait and look....'

'I'm quite indifferent,' says Philomène. 'We don't wait philosophically, we wait because our lucky number may come up. Your job's to sell this stuff, no more. When you've made millions – then you can invest. Till then – you're used to sleeping on a mat....'

The crates are solid, they could be exhibits too.

'It's hard, Philomène,' I say. 'Coming here. For me, without this job, it was sleep in the street, or in the Foreign Legion.'

'This *is* the Foreign Legion, dear,' she says. 'I'll make my name with puffing these odd distant guys – I'll go far out, and maybe have a son with you. This city's full of daughters – study, study, and can't sew. Now,' she pulls out a thin skin from a crate – 'Is this a picture or a paper? There's thousands of dumb heads looking the same way. Do you think it's satire?' she asks me, hammering in some nails.

'I know nothing, Philomène,' I say. 'I want money to spend on good things, that is all. Some of these guys have problems over there, their country, enormous people, places, all on a slide, a ramp ... but the prices we ask here – they are universal, and so's the people making them.... Critics who please rich guys, a paradox.... Do they hate it, having things both ways? The cops? It's all a buzz, a plan: onward! I told you, Philomène, I've Daphne back there, she must have had a plan ... she was so calm, her green cap – who gave her that, I ask – and no one tells....?'

'Oh, I have plans,' says Philomène, handing me the hammer. 'First – progeny. assorted children, loving me. It's the best symbol of the lot. Sex has none, no symbolism, law, or language. Language is symbols, but it doesn't move, it procreates, over and over, sterile multiples. Stasis. Where's our real life? Back in the ruins?'

She is unanswerable, exasperating – a true boss.

The pics, the effigies – all cliffs of people, abundant, many grinning.... I scrutinise each one, each face inscrutable, but Philomène's impatient, rummages, makes a confusion....

'Idiot!' shouts Philomène. 'See! – the world, it doesn't spin, not any more. Spin meant every insignificant place, each stretch of sea, had its moment on the leading edge, momentarily stood out whirling in the light, then disappeared, back in the dark. Now – the earth flies onward, there's no revolving, and we are the two alpha dogs – we are the first in to the light, and there we stay, our noses sharp: what do we scent? What's in the wind...?'

'Grub stew?' I say, at a loss. 'Some people love it,' – I don't mention dog – people love that too, and maybe in return are loved, best friends, all that.... 'Steam boat....' I suggest....

'Forget it,' Philmène cries out. 'We'll open up a gallery in Lanzhou: it's always fascinated me.... We are the top, my dear, the leaders. See – the dialectic's finished, it's been overcome. That was the goal of those old guys, centuries ago, they didn't understand what was to do, but – that was their implicit aim. An end to contradiction. No motion, no progression, no push and pull, no up and down. I told you – stasis. Opposing principles entwined – the tophats with the caps. Topkapi?' and she laughs, thrusts on. 'A single principle, becalmed, that makes big bucks – critique and profit ... red capital ... China, in short – before we open up our store. And here ... right here, you see it, the.two of us, resisting ... embattled, conflicted, two against Thebes, the Bir Hakeim – challenge and success....'

Philomène is revving up – hanging up and pulling down....

Daphne too – said she was resisting. She meant that everything around's inimical, threatening, to be shooed away.

'Philomène,' I say. 'Out here, upon the edge – the wind is strong, it blows the words away, they're just palmettes of artificial flames, programmed to flicker twice to left and thrice to right.... That's what your stasis is – banality. Greengrocery. Ugli fruit, dark gooseberries.'

'Our feet are firm,' she says, my! the storm shrieks, the wind whips our manes into our ears, our eyes, our long brindled tails stream back, as stiff as sticks – 'On!' she cries. 'On, on!'

The speed's immense – the distances are huge, and yet – distance requires an 'in-between', something to cover, a feature you must overleap. We're travelling ... and yet it's black, all black, there's nothing over, under; it's like standing still, this space race.... Travel is between two spots – here, there is nothing, no place, no spot, no tundra, no ocean and no ice....

'Yes,' she says. 'But if you think of it as time, not galloping through space – we shall grow old and white, no one will see our colour change, we'll stand here till we're bones, then dust and nothing, nothing, not a smidgen, not a smirk, is left... Not distance, we don't move, there's no here, no there. It's time. Best not think of it as speed and space, as if we saw a landscape, maybe a steppe, a greenland, a featureless enormity.... Remember, we age, but we have no past. There's no before and after. Forget all that; no dinners on the grass. In quick space, the past does not exist.... Quite irretrievable.'

'But, Philomène,' I say. 'It's in the void we just ran through, we're all there, our young vigorous selves, looking up and seeing us, ageing, fleeting like thunderclaps, our mouths agape, like witches tripping....'

'You plod,' she says, much disappointed. She pulls from a crate some plastic shapes, wrapped in white crepe, hands them to me, and says, 'Snail brain – hang these bodies up on hooks.'

*

'About our son,' I say to Philomène. 'I warn you – this selling stuff, it isn't my career. And – I don't fancy you – maybe as a boss, but not down there, down on the mat....'

'I wouldn't suggest it,' says Philomène. 'If you and I were not asexual. If you prefer, both wholly sexual. It's similar for both of us, for you and me.'

'Forget the children, Philomène,' I say. 'Boost me, float me, promote me – but don't bet on duplicates in miniature.'

*

'Those bodies look real good,' says Philomène. She makes them swing. 'Maybe some detail, some protuberance has been rubbed off. Maybe there should be a mechanism, a wind ... to waft them to and fro.'

'I've not thrown anything away,' I say. 'The packing's over there ... they don't come clothed, the manikins, you know. I've done my task, meticulous. This stuff – it's new to me. I wasn't there, I told you. Indochine – that's where I was, what it was called.'

'I know,' she says. 'I saw it. Catherine Deneuve. Love, sex, interracial stuff. La France-Asie! Like in Debussy. I should love to go.'

'I know,' I say. 'It wasn't China. It may seem precarious still, but tourists come and go, the dead have disappeared. They've had their massacres. Others await, or start – just think of that huge extent: the Uighurs, Kazaks, Turkmen ... the Turks ... the Kurds. Not mentioning the Syrians, and then you hang a left, and you're in Africa.... All on a brink, the horrors yet to come, undescribable or by the book ... and everybody just like you and me, and bits of here, this city, Paris, copies, variations, follies and towers all around. Awful, terrible, Philomène,' I say.

'That's not the point,' she says. 'I know all that, and so does everyone – we're there, they're here, the world is not Swann's Way: no more, if ever you could say it was.... It's not the point.'

'I love those places, Philomène,' I say. The guys ... Astana on to Istanbul, Sonay and Zeynep, we three in precious places....'

'Go on,' she says. 'Unpack. Some live, lots die, they all must work.... The guys, they speak, we hear, we're on our way, they on theirs.... The pictures – they communicate, that is their job, they have the means, they're not competing in a suffering. They don't have lives, existences, they're not like guys. If you want to see the paintings twitch, there's books to read....'

'Will this stuff endure?' I ask. 'Or should we press on to sell them quick? Touch up, where they have scuffed?'

'Wrong again,' says Philomène. 'People collect. They need to switch their stack of cash – from abstract into concrete, there and back, from bank to installation – and what's more, people like contemplating pain. Pain in a frame, the sufferings. Pain: from work, from power, conscription, glory – there is pain there,' she repeats. 'These boxes were all full of it, and now you see it all wired up.... Close to! First person....'

My! she's strong – she comes behind me, half-garottes, 'You're in luck,' she shouts. 'I don't have a padlock handy for your stupid lips,' and up she lifts me – up, up to the ceiling: there's a hook – 'Learn about it: pain!' she shouts. 'Scream while you can! Thief, terrorist, false preacher – dangle there! Reflect the pain that swings and pirouettes up among the lights on every continent...scream, and they'll send the Légion, maybe they'll have cutters and will snip you down....'

I gasp out, 'This is old chapeau, dear Philomène,' but after all, she dominates, and there is no one else to intercede. She must work out with weights. She's hooked me up, lit in the window of the gallery, a crowd of guys peeks in – street-sleepers, druggies, enlightened social-democrats, who knows? No one has cash. I'm crazy, desperate, I would confess to save the family I haven't got.... Or wait for some rich connoisseur to load me up and take me home.

'Have you forsaken me, dear Philomène?' I cry, as she goes foraging in the crates, she's made a pile of wood and chips, maybe she plans to burn them underneath my feet....

'Now,' she screams. 'You nothing! Now you feel the pain, you know the suffering, and that it never ends, the market will go on, but I don't care: the real, the agony – that is with us always and it makes us twist and weep.... Now maybe you can understand what those Chinese guys had in mind, as peaceful in their studios they thought of tanks and blood and crating up their stuff and sending it to me....'

*

The crowd outside – it laughs and points, they wonder, and a guy taps on the glass – I shout, 'No, no – I'm not an artist, I'm a victim,' but it seems that they don't hear, and Philomène goes out among them and she shouts, 'I am the artist! the guy hung up is just a doll,' and quick she cuts me down, and says to me, 'Put these traditionals back there – they co-exist as well....'

There is calligraphy and scrolls and screens, and water-buffaloes and guys in boats beneath the crags, and certainly that goes on too, together with the pain, it makes you cry, there's pain there too, and maybe deeper and more subtle too, because the painted image fixes in you as the real does not, and tells you that the beauty will persist and you will not, the fish fished out, the crags destroyed, but still we have these fabulous brains that let us conjure up what isn't there, and it's laid down in memory, though it has never been....

'Don't dream,' says Philomène. 'And don't mistake. I'm not responsible, your wounds are superficial, it is all a show, a lesson – a hand, a brush, waving towards the tangle of events and motives, wayward effects.... This gallery was a workshop – imagine the pain that laboured here, the early deaths, the wages skimped – ah, it makes you grind your teeth in helpless rage....'

*

'We've had our fun,' says Philomène. 'Now, it's time to be the boss again,' and we sit across her desk.

'I talk,' she says. 'And you unpack. I hang. I'm all symbols. You want your life – but it's beneath the dead, you see them all around, they don't make sense, they oppress, they quote, they wave their books.... It pins you to the floor ... the babble, and the press of other lives, all failed, all like your own....'

'Yes, Philomène,' I say. 'What can be done with me?'

'The world will end long before we find an answer,' says Philomène.

'That sounds like a quote,' I say: 'Not finely shaped.'

'Oh, books,' she says, 'You've never heard of. The new novel, *nouveau roman* – it didn't lead to anything.'

The show is on. We say what we think to many people never seen again.

'Well, you know about Indochine,' says Philomène. 'As much as our friend Deneuve, I bet. So, you could know about China too – you know about me, in just a day. You'd need to learn to do it quicker in Lanzhou, finding out everything, parsing everyone....'

'Places are always different, never like they've been described,' I say. 'Or no one would bother travelling.'

'That's plausible,' she says. 'But no way true.'

People buy the art – they love it.

Philomène's dissatisfied. 'You think I'm superficial. Of course, China is full of people. I'm just one, not even living there ... I think I'm from the southwest, the most interesting part....'

It's true; no argument. I say, 'I know things, saw mysteries that people don't. It keeps you concentrated, far from the local guys.... My friends, we were all travellers.... The big pic – that's where we were.'

Sergei and Mélisande, I think – they ought to go together, it would solve the problems they both have ... problems that can drop down on our heads.

*

'You know,' says Philomène, 'listening to you, I wonder where you've been. Where were you then, in Indochine? Slavery, poverty, shootings – all in the movie. It is frightening.'

She doesn't look frightened, not at all.

'I don't do history,' I say. 'Not even of the future. I respect everything – people, chance and destiny, in equal measure.... You think you've gone through something, you hear the money train coming down the track to you – and then it turns out quite quite different. That's my observation.'

It's not so strange – that everything explodes. And, that we know it may.

'I don't believe in Sergei,' says Philomène. 'Though no one's making me.'

'He's more plausible than you,' I say. 'But believing and seeing – that's old hat too. You'd be foolish going through your life, doing that: believing, seeing ... seeing, believing. Miracles? Stupid.'

'Yes,' she says. 'It does sound odd. It doesn't work. Someone must be doing all the things you say they do out there, parading, watching from the esplanade. Doing, not believing anything particular. Of course, the end of the world – that's unusual stuff. Seeing it's inevitable; and then you're gone – no time left to believe.'

*

'Who are you, Philomène?' I ask. 'What are you waiting for? They don't make pictures here, in Paris, any more. They lost their colonies, lost the refinement, the culture we're told to respect. Now, it's humdrum fascism, the commonplace, homespun....'

'Who are *you*?' asks Philomène. 'What right have you to feel nostalgic – for any place, or any time? What protest can you make, for what? Against? Do you have some recipe, some remedy, not tried before, you urged it, and were cast aside? Would that have led us to a different place? Your line – maybe not doing anything at all? You skate across the atlas. Yama – is always there, but then it's there for everyone, has always been.... Down in the hole – there's ordnance, and beneath – there's guys that's reasoning out why, and when, and how – it'll all blow. You must believe it all – the poison and the antidote – what matters isn't you, your belief, your disbelief: it always is the snake ... unseen.

'If not the end, then something else. We've now sold all the pictures. They're out there – in the vaults and in the vestibule. Our mission's done.

'You, my dear, are fired ... re-hired – and fired. I don't solve anything for you.'

'That's *my* argument, Philomène.' I say. 'And as for pictures – we can't buy them, we're the lucky ones who see them first, hang them, then see them go. It's better than a plot, a plan, that makes the great ship, circling the world, circle the same, but change its route....'

*

Philomène insists. The new, it tugs.

We're off to see the esplanade.

They're all there, still – some visiting, some stuck, deep-rooted.

'Aha!' shouts Sergei, seeing us. 'Here's my legs, walked back! One limping, but one – ah! Philomène! We read about you – splendid, ever ready for a race! Now I'm complete, with three of them ... a lucky triskeles.... I'll have them ink you on my heel....'

'My!' Daphne tells me. 'You look terminal! You know, the pictures, the parades, the chronicles – they're not the keys to anything, they don't inform us, make us smart. They just confirm you: that is what you are. You are where you are, where you go, have gone. France this and that, Napoleon, Françinde, Françafrique and all the rest – it doesn't matter where they come from – gobble, gobble too much cake, it makes you sick and kills the appetite. No one regrets; no Americans, no French – who remembers a vomit, quite long ago? Maybe....' And she pulls her green cap down on my sweating head – 'It's me you sought? And that's too bad. I know now all I need to know, and you aren't part.... Mine, all mine, until it's not. No lesson here – you don't learn sense, you learn the rote, and cram it in your memory until it overflows....'

'And Mélisande?' I ask.

'She's worst of all,' says Daphne. 'You have too many bosses – Sergei, now Philomène: but Mélisande, she has an infinity. Some say "do it with spies", and some with drones, and some with bombs or dollar bills. She'd make it end, that is for sure. But, she's not alone, she can't decide a thing, and then there's all the other guys.... More flags waving than carried in parades....'

'Sergei,' I ask. 'Did you find when and how it ends?'

'Oh yes,' he says. 'That's definite. But – we can't tell. We must keep mum and schtum. It's delicate, then there's the risk of spilling beans, even the magic ones, and the morale of our hands to watch as well. We know how the earth goes down and when. The ending's incontrovertible. But then, there is the wild card, stipulated from the beginning of the game: a saviour. Not quite a friend, and not with fingers on a hand that you could hold.

"*Veni, creator spiritus*".... What'll he, she, look like? I'm betting on transgender, or maybe,' he sings,

'"*Das Ewig-Weibliche
Zieht uns hinan.*"'

'I could be that spirit,' Daphne says. 'That is for sure – "the womanly eternal pulls us upward...."'

'I know,' I say, 'Philomène did it to me in the gallery window.'

'A saviour that doesn't save?' says Sergei. 'Just cuts your rope? That's no big deal.'

*

I am alone with Philomène.

'Is this the crew?' asks Philomène, much disappointed. 'I can bring in the elephants. No prob. Just sounds. But it would be a show, ephemeral – there must be sales, material production! Exchange. What we eat. What we wear.'

It's hot. She takes off her wraps, unpacks herself. She's golden. Naked.

'Are you the saviour, dear Philomène?' I ask. It comes out quite involuntary. She laughs:

'We're all like this, in Yunnan,' she says.

I'm overwhelmed. I think – so, this is art and history, what it's all about – and she is right, that in the end there's nothing, nothing material that we can take away. No sale, no red star. Just a gaze, a traveller's gaze upon a golden nude, ending there, no conclusion, no postlude. It's not a quiz with answers and a prize – just good to see; why you came all that way.

*

'There's no revolutionary spirit left,' says Mélisande. 'There's ordnance and prophecies. We're used to those, there's nothing new: anyone with power can handle the familiar stuff. The strange new thing is – what has died, is not replaced. Not with a double, a repeat, and not a variant. A project? There always used to be a plan that was to throw all things around, and promised there would be new lands, new roads. Shake it, turn it upside-down – what came out would be more reasonable, more from the root, more exalted and more down to earth.... There is no more of that.'

*

The Ghost goes passing round.

'I'll take Mélisande outside,' Jean-Paul says. 'She's right. I've nothing more to say. I'll explain to her – that you, the powerless ones, are trying to understand. We know about the march, the famine, all the revolutions renewed, the persecution and the purification. The building: starting from the soil, the purging, the corruption and the rest. It needs to be explained: the empires, and the graves.'

Mélisande objects. 'Sergei is powerful, Philomène is strong. Daphne's an employee of the state....'

'Sergei knows the answer to his question, so he has no secret and no power,' Jean-Paul says. 'Philomène – she could be the eye of God – that sees, and sees, and can do no more.'

'I'll go outside,' says Mélisande. 'I can't follow drifting mist and steam: you guys that's left, lounging here upon the mat – you're empty cylinders, without a taper to a spout.... No use to me – I'll go outside, sit with Jean-Paul, poor guy. Philosophy? That died along with all the rest – the brains, the empathy....'

*

After a while, Mélisande returns. 'Jean-Paul will sleep outside – he says he doesn't feel the bugs. You guys – are you wiser? Do you know more now than if you'd read a book?'

'We'd drunk the Ghost,' says Sergei. 'The bottle's empty, so the genie has escaped, I guess.'

'I do believe you're drunk,' says Mélisande, laughing. 'I thought you'd gone to meditation – the wheel, perhaps, the syllable. The rumble of time, the hum of ecstasy? Instead – just to get rid of me? Jean-Paul too, not wanted on your trip?'

'Philomène,' says Sergei, poking me with his thumb. 'She's wasted on you.'

He doesn't say it in a friendly way.

'There's been lots of projects here,' says Daphne. 'I brought some in myself. The more magnificence, the more catastrophe – but they needed to be done. Besides – some things – they can be foretold, but other things, they happen too.... And everything is changed....'

'Even by being drunk,' I say. 'Though there's not much insight there.'

'You won't get me to spill my bean,' says Sergei. 'That info's worth a lot.'

We know what is to be known, and what each one could do if there were many many more of them.

*

'Philomène,' I ask. 'What's to become of us?'

'I told you. Lanzhou,' she says. 'Then somewhere else. Not with you.'

*

'I'll keep an eye on Mélisande,' says Sergei. 'That way I can begin my work again, and everything will simmer on, and she will wait. No drastic moves. Nothing military, no noise.'

'The last parade,' says Daphne. 'Then you will all be gone – except perhaps Jean-Paul: but he can stay, no trouble comes from him, he needs no tools, not even paper and a brush....'

'I'll do the audio,' says Philomène; she's much enthused. 'Exactly as it's always been. Elephants. And ancient instruments.'

'And who'll be Yama, on the esplanade, and who the king? Should it be each of us, in turn?' asks Mélisande.

'Oh, count me out,' I say. 'I'll be the crowd. Watch and applaud – that's me.'

About the author

John Fraser has lived in Rome since 1980. Previously, he worked in England and Canada.

www.ingramcontent.com/pod-product-compliance
Lightning Source LLC
Chambersburg PA
CBHW020414180626
46812CB00003B/977